… plague killed them all except one man – Tu'an … and God fashioned him in many forms, and that man survived alone from the time of Partholon …

Lebor Gabala Erenn
(*The Book of Invasions*)

TU'AN

BOOK TWO

D. KRAUSS

INDIES UNITED PUBLISHING HOUSE, LLC

The madman lived just south of the lines. Soldiers manning those lines would have killed him long before now, but lingering superstitions regarding the mad stayed their hands. Not that he wasn't abused. The soldiers often kicked in his door and rifled his goods and slapped him around until he was bloodied and crumpled. After they'd gone, he'd get up, rehang the door, and move the remaining cans of stuff the soldiers didn't want – beets, pumpkin, dog food – from a no-longer-secret stash to one that was, leaving a couple out to placate the next group of soldiers. It was a good arrangement.

He wasn't really a madman; he was just playing a role. But, played too long, reality blurs, and he went about mad chores – dusting, sweeping, arranging – even when rounds from the enemy across the creek whistled through his attic and manufactured more rubble from the whole pieces of his house. He even raked his yard, every day, in rain, snow, in summer, when there was nothing at all to rake. This convinced the soldiers he was mad. It convinced him he wasn't. No one could see the clean and ordered interior of his house because no one visited anymore, except the soldiers, and they made short work of it. But the yard was on display, and by ensuring every square inch of it looked good, he let the enemy across the creek, and the officers and the sergeants and the looters on this side, know that civilization continued.

Besides, raking made him feel good. If he stood in the yard just so, and leaned on the rake just so, while a cool breeze evaporated the sweat from his brow, then narrowed his eyes to block out the wreckage and the empty yards and the shattered houses … at that moment, his old life came back. Even if passing soldiers jeered or sergeants yelled at him to get inside or officers frowned mightily, even when he could not avoid seeing the columns of distant smoke, the moment existed.

It made him happy.

1

Chirp.

Collier immediately keyed the radio twice, acknowledging the incoming signal. Jonesy was about to start some crap. He took in a deep breath and held it, getting his jitters under control. Again. Got them every time, no matter how routine the ops.

He snapped on the night-vision goggles for a quick look-see. Ghost-green pine trees and tangled underbrush loomed, a hint of the New Lisbon Road just beyond. He frowned. That road ... he didn't like it. Right at the moment Jonesy comes whooping across with Reds in hot pursuit, some other group of Reds would be tooling around the corner and there Collier'd be, flanked and taking fire from two directions. Again.

He'd made his objections to this spot quite clear but Major Arce gave him the icy stare and said, "Sergeant Rashkil, just do it." Salute, holler, "Yes, Ma'am!" go off and get yourself killed.

Major Arce. Rosa Arce. Rosa ...

There, on the breeze, her perfume, a natural mix of cold air and clean skin and desire, close, so close. Holding each other, gasping the last of the passion, returning to earth.

My God, Rosa. Rosa ... Knock it off. Hard-ons make running away difficult.

Collier grinned but still drifted, savoring their rendezvous three nights before in that little cemetery hidden behind the wreckage of some old Methodist church in what was once Pemberton, New Jersey. Midnight, the dark and their passion a blanket, exchanging breath for breath until they were the same air, the same life, the same person ...

Dude. Seriously. Stop it.

He snapped off the goggles, raised them and shut his eyes for a moment to readjust, turned his head slowly (just in case some Red IRing noticed the motion), and stared hard towards the rear, where he'd posted the two privates. Both of their helmets were clearly silhouetted against the trees, heads bobbing, obviously chatting.

Idiots.

How many times had he warned them? Keep your helmets, your backs, your butts down! And don't freakin' move! Even crappy Vietnam-era night vision will spot you, and, with a little diligence on the spotter's part, lead to the spotting of one Sergeant Collier Rashkil skulking near the road while grinding his teeth in rage.

Just can't get good help these days.

Ain't that the truth? When everything went TU about five or six years ago, the population of idiots grew geometrically to the point they were now ninety percent of all survivors, which meant they were ninety-five percent of all new recruits, so ... how many idiots were in the ranks right now? Let's see, if the Blues had lost about seventy-five percent of those recruits during last month's nightmare slogging fight across Pennsylvania, then seventy percent of the idiots (but, wait, is there a true proportion between ninety-five percent and seventy-five percent?) were now gone, but half had been replaced, which would be forty percent idiot enrichment so …

Man, was he getting punchy.

Collier bit down hard on his inner cheek, trying to raise some pain adrenaline. So freakin' tired. What he'd give for eight hours, even six hours, of straight, uninterrupted sleep. Or six hours of straight, uninterrupted Rosa …

… Rosa, my life. I see you standing in a glade sheltering a creek, that winds slow and soft across the front of our log cabin, deep in eternal woods enveloped by mountains, the creek waters singing to us, the music in the waters …

Wake up!

Collier shook himself. Damn! Had he just drifted off? Collier peered towards the road, all senses screaming but things were quiet, thank God. The stream, though, was still singing. Collier furrowed his brow. What the hell?

Oh, yeah, that's right, there's water in the small dam a few yards off, and it tinkles rather nicely. Just a country dam, nothing spectacular, maybe five, six feet deep in the spillway, enough to cover him if he needed to jump in and hide. Probably die of hypothermia and leeches before the Reds found him there, but he'd rather do that than be shot or, worse, captured. Doubtful the Reds were any more sparing of prisoners than he was. Chew him up for all they can get and then shoot him in the back of the head, just like Collier had done dozens (hundreds?) of times.

He gave the water an appreciative glance, then peered back towards the road, tempted to snap on the night vision again and check things, and then check what further mischief the two privates were up to but, no, keep your night eyes, bud. He wondered if the privates saw his head nod from sleep. That would be embarrassing. Probably both asleep themselves. Or, one asleep while the other watched. No way. That'd be too smart.

About as smart as sitting here freezing his ass off next to a country dam, while waiting to be shot.

He chuckled. Yeah, if he had a smidgen of smart, he'd be hiding out somewhere in deep woods enveloped by mountains, instead of here. But a lot of smart people – Rosa, Jonesy, Captain Palmer (although his country-boy shuckiness made Collier wonder how smart he truly was) – were here, because the smartest of them all, Colonel Caldwell, had chosen the flat, open farmlands of south Jersey, with the only natural barrier an easily fordable Rancocas Creek, as the place to make a stand. So much for smart. Even a dumb boot like Collier knew they were better off in Pennsylvania, hiding out in the low mountains behind the Delaware and the Schuykyll rivers until help came.

Like that was going to happen.

Collier smiled grimly and listened to the water and worked out its rhythm. He wondered if he could pick it out on a guitar, maybe throw in some counter-rhythms and call it the Water Song. Or, better, the Dam(n) Water Song. His hand itched for a guitar and he stroked the rifle in compensation. When this was done, when someone won and they all drifted away, he'd have to see about a guitar. If he ever got back to the Valley, he'd try his hand at making them, good ones, all sweet pine and resin. The world cannot have enough guitars. Rosa and he and their five or six kids would all share a little stone house up on some ridge near Staunton or down towards Lexington, away from wars and politics, and turn out guitars. They'd load them up on carts or burros and bring them down to the market towns and barter for food and ammunition and clothes. In the evening, he'd play songs he'd written, like the Dam(n) Water Song, and old ones he remembered: Metallica's *Never Land* or Incubus's *Wish You Were*

Here. And those Dad had liked, Springsteen and Floyd …

Shots ripped out somewhere across the road, followed immediately by shouts and someone tearing off a long burst of M-16. Collier's jitters came roaring back but he gulped them down and smiled. Here we go. Looking back, he raised his hand and motioned and watched the privates break laterally. At least they were doing that right. Sometime in the next, say, four or five seconds, Jonesy would barrel through the flanking privates and form the back, then Collier would collapse on the pursuing Reds and they'd have 'em. All a matter of lovely timing.

Collier took out the small flashlight and stared across the road. Movement, frantic and fast: two shadows swooped to the corners of a ruined house opposite, stopped, then fired short bursts at the woods behind them. Two … where's the rest of 'em?

Damn.

Feet pounding and shouts from the woods, followed by someone opening up on the backyard and the two survivors shooting back. Collier crawled to the edge of the tree line where he could get a better view. The two shadows hauled ass down the ruined driveway of the caved-in house, whipping across the road. They were breaking too far left and Collier looked frantically down both sides, expecting the unwanted Red patrol to suddenly appear.

Nothing, so he flashed once and saw both shadows alter their course in mid-stride. Please let one of those shadows be—

Jonesy, thank God, burst through the tree screen and dropped beside him, panting hard; the tall, skinny shadow blurring past them both and towards the back, obviously Private Swift (more thanking of God). Jonesy gasped, "Lost two. Six coming!" slapped Collier hard on the shoulder and bolted after Swift.

Collier had to grin. Jonesy and he were gettin' pretty good at this. Must be all the practice. They went out almost every night during the run through Pennsylvania, grabbed any Red they could and handed 'em over to Major Arce for her tender ministrations. The resulting intel let them avoid Red ambushes and slip into New Jersey, depleted and hurt and desperate, but still formidable and largely intact. The 1st Combined Arms Division. The Ghosts.

Oo-rah.

Self-consciously, Collier slapped the tattoo on his right bicep – a ghost with fierce black eyes, bayonet in its "O" shaped ghosty mouth, an M-16 hugged to its chest. Jonesy had come up with the design and one night, somewhere near Bristol, they'd cut it into each other's arms. It caught on among the good soldiers and became a sign of who you could trust. Rosa had one; didn't even whimper when he cut it into her. Caldwell did not.

Hmm.

Running feet and shouts snapped Collier's head back towards the road. Yes, there, three or four, no, six shadows, all gathered at the front of the house. Idiots, bunching up like that. Collier could take all of them with one burst. Maybe the Reds' discipline was collapsing, too.

Not bloody likely. A victorious force had lots of élan and high morale and, especially, discipline.

Most likely, they'd paused to get bearings. C'mon over, you Red bastards, or this carefully contrived and quite sophisticated ambush would quickly go to shit. Maybe he should encourage them—

A round blasted from somewhere behind Collier, momentarily startling him, but then he grinned again. Good ole Jonesy …

Four of the Reds came screaming across the yard

while the other two loosed long bursts at Collier's position. He scrunched into the pine needles as tracers sprayed the trees and couldn't help admiring the effort. Good fire discipline, good tactics. These Reds were no slouches.

Well, of course not; they were Americans, too.

The four flashed past him into the box, but Collier stayed down. He had other worries. Gunfire erupted as the back of the box engaged the Reds. General firefight hell now, tracers flying and branches crashing and people screaming. Collier watched the two across the road hesitate. No doubt, the extra gunfire had rattled them. Instead of chasing what they thought were two desperate fugitives, they'd stumbled into a trap. Precisely, guys, and now it's decision time: do you invoke patrol discipline, lay down cover fire and provide an avenue of escape for your buddies while calling for help (or, if you don't have a radio, one of you running back to get help)? Or, do you say, "Fuck it," and go charging in to help your buddies, er, comrades? C'mon. Choose. We don't have all night.

"Fuck it" won.

Collier watched the two shadows come together in an obviously quick conference and then bolt right for him. Good, closer, closer, keep up your momentum. The Reds cleared the tree line and ran past Collier's right, heading for the tracers.

Collier rolled and stood, whipping the 16 up to his left while pulling out the Taser with his right hand. Now was the time when night eyes paid off: the two Reds were clearly silhouetted against the tracers, hesitant, trying to figure out who was who.

Big mistake, fellahs.

Collier fired, stitching the Red on the left up the spine, blowing his innards across the woods. Not bad for one-handed shooting, left-handed at that. The other guy whirled, going to his knees. Collier was impressed. Good reaction, Red, probably thinking Collier would overshoot, but no chance of that, Mao. Collier canted the Taser down and fired the clips into him. The Red did the chicken dance as Collier squeezed more juice into him. Shut down, amigo, shut down. The Red danced a bit more, stiffened, and toppled over. Collier hoped he hadn't fried him too much. These jury-rigged Tasers were a bit unreliable.

The shooting became sporadic, a sign that it was over. Now was the time to use night vision and Collier flipped his down and clicked it on. Okay, no one standing, good; that meant his patrol was still in cover and, either the Reds were all in cover, too, which was bad, or were all dead, which was good. Collier looked at the three or four smoking lumps in the underbrush. Seemed dead enough. He watched for movement, ready to cut loose with the 16 or fry the captured Red a little more, if need be. Nope. Nothing.

"Clear front," Collier called and got four answering "Yo's" in quick succession. He squatted next to the quivering Red and detached the clips, then checked the pulse. Thready, but what do you expect after a few thousand volts? Just don't die on me, you little Stalinist fuckhead.

Jonesy crawled up next to him, "He okay?"

"He'll live. You?"

"We're good. Swift got grazed but he's all right. Your two privates are all right, too."

"That's a surprise," Collier paused. "What happened?"

Jonesy shook his head, "Damndest thing, Coll. We worked back to that Browns Mills access road and saw the bastards up near some trashy house, so we stepped out and they just opened up on us."

Collier pulled a knife, a lighter, some cigarettes, and some gaggy crackers out of the Red's pockets and pitched all of it into the woods. Not worth keeping. He stuffed all the papers he found into his own pockets. Probably just letters and pictures of no intel value, but they made good reading. Proof of life beyond war. "They just opened up?"

"Yep. Got DeFelice and Scrothers in the first burst."

"Hmm." Collier frowned. "That's odd."

"Telling me."

Everybody on both sides wore basically the same half-assed fatigues, Pre- and Post-Event stock issued years ago and, subsequently, stripped from the dead, both ally and enemy, as needed. Couldn't tell who was who anymore, except for a red or blue bandana tied around an arm, and how many times had he taken his blue one off as subterfuge? So it was a bad idea to start shooting without first confirming identity. Might be friends.

"Maybe they're getting antsy over there. Maybe we're winning," Collier said, and then wrinkled his nose as an odor washed over him. "Or maybe they smelled you guys."

"Fuck you, Sarge. There was a leaking septic behind that house."

"No shit. Or should I say, lots of shit?"

Jonesy snorted in reply and Collier chuckled as he rolled the Red over, plasticuffed him and pulled the Red's pants down to his knees. If Lenin woke up, little chance he'd get far. Jonesy retrieved the rest of the patrol and then all of them searched the dead Reds, pulling out equipment, discarding the useless and pocketing what they wanted. "Any cigars?" Collier asked.

"Nothing, man," Jonesy said.

"Wouldn't tell me if you found any, would you?"

"Get you own, white boy."

"Thieving bastard."

"Your momma." Both of them snickered and slapped each other's shoulders somewhat helplessly. The privates stared at them like they were crazy while Swift toned, "Jesus," and watched the road for movement. Couldn't help it; both of them got giddy towards the end of these things. Of course, this Slappy White routine would get them killed one day. Who exactly was Slappy White? Dad had always used that phrase, and now Collier owned it. Things stuck with you.

"Let's go," Collier said and pointed at the unconscious Red.

The two privates muttered but one hoisted the Red across the other's shoulders, fireman style, while Jonesy and Swift flanked and checked across the road. Collier took point, heading north towards Eliot's position. The others fell in, Jonesy taking drag. Silent, they picked their way along the berm, staying deep in the tree line but within eyesight of the road. Probably had about twenty minutes before the Reds came looking for their lost buddies. Should be in Eliot's perimeter by then; that is, if that freakin' idiot had actually put out a perimeter.

It's what, about 0400? Collier took a covert glance at his watch. Yep. Okay, at this pace, about thirty minutes to reach Eliot's perimeter, another thirty or so to get with Deavers' patrol down the Creek, then deliver the prisoner, yadda yadda ... so, in the hammock by 0600-ish. Sleep for two hours (at best), smack some recruits around, write the report, go see the Major, get the take, make a date, and by this time tomorrow night, Rosa in the cemetery.

Sweet.

Collier walked, lost in her smell and her touch and her eyes, those eyes, so black, so luminous, dark crystals sparkling with heat and want and life. Internal sun.

Walk and walk and lost and lost and—

Wake up. You're there.

2

Collier blinked fully awake and held up a closed fist to halt the others. He peered through the trees. Eliot was positioned in the buildings across the road, some kind of old government center paired with a mental hospital – Button Wood Hall, according to the maps. Crazy people and bureaucrats sharing the same complex; for once, someone had planned well. A water tower had collapsed across the intersection and there was a lot of wreckage and crap all over the place, making it an ideal spot to infiltrate the Reds. Not anymore. After tonight's festivities, even the dullest Red will know this is a staging area.

Collier stared hard – looking for the oddity, something out of line, something that just didn't seem right – and listened hard, filtering out the sounds of night birds and rubble settling and rats stirring … God, was there ever a world without so many rats? Yes, there was: back Before, back when you were a kid playing Nintendo in an intact house with an intact Dad and Mom and even a dog and you went to school and had lots of friends and ran from house to house and played Pogs in third grade and guitar in seventh and fought with Dad and the education system and got sent to boarding school and was there when the Event happened so you survived ...

A familiar tremor creased his heart: his old pal, Grief, here to remind him of people he once knew, the life he once had, the world so recently with us, all now a ruin, a wreck, broken walls sunk in swamp and bog; avert the eyes as you pass and make a warding sign. Grief for this present life, bound in death and murder, always fighting, always running, and wondering why.

Why?

All right, all right, snap out of it.

Collier dropped the goggles and flipped the switch and examined the wreckage once more. Still nothing. Okay. He pulled out the radio and keyed it twice. Hello, Eliot, we're here, itching to go home. Can you pull your head outta yer ass and get us there?

What the hell's Eliot doing on this mission anyway?

The Major had told Coll to button it when he and Jonesy yelped, "What? Eliot! No way, Major!" "Orders," she said.

The Colonel's fair-haired boy needed some medals, Collier guessed. Funny, that. Most fair-haired boys usually got safe, fat assignments guarding prisoners or ruined supplies at out-of-the-way depots. Yet, here Eliot was.

Yet here he *wasn't* because there was no response. Collier clicked twice again, wrath rising. More moments passed and still nothing. Collier looked back at Jonesy, whose green-lit face showed alarm. Two more clicks. Zip.

Jonesy crawled up. "What the fuck, man?" he whispered.

"That fucking Eliot, that worthless rat bastard shitbag."

"Creative, man, but what do you want to do?"

"I want to shoot the sonofabitch."

"I'll load while you do it. But, we gotta get out of here." Jonesy glanced down the road. By now, it was crawling with some real pissed-off Reds.

Collier considered. "All right. You and Swift take the right, over by the big yellow house. Me and the privates will slide around this side and cut through the looney bin yard, meet you at those storage sheds behind. We'll try the password there, see what's up. Then I'm going to shoot Eliot."

"Cool, but hey, man, his radio might be out."

"My ass."

"That it is. See ya." And Jonesy grinned and crawled towards Swift. A few words and they were gone.

Collier smiled. Good ole Jonesy.

He gestured at the two privates, who dragged the Red over with them. "There's a problem," Collier said, "We're not getting a response, so we gotta quarter over to the inner post and see what's up. I'll lead, you two stagger, and for Chrissake, don't shoot unless I do. Follow?"

One of the privates … Zoll? Who knew? There was no more point in learning a private's name than an LT's … waved an arm at the Red. "With him?"

"Yes, with him! What'd you think we did all this for?"

"He's gettin' awful heavy, Sarge," the other one, Akin, or something like that, whined.

"Suck it up." Collier's tone was murderous. He'd shoot these two right now and drag the Red himself, if necessary. He looked at the Red, who hadn't stirred. Well, crap, the privates may have a point: deadweight was tough to move.

"All right, both of you carry him together, then. I'll cover," He cut off the ensuing protest with a curt, "Let's go!" and rolled to the right, sliding through a little tunnel running under the wreckage. He checked the road and then sprinted across it to a set of big pecan trees offering lovely cover. He turned and watched the two privates emerge, both hoisting the Red, and running in tandem towards him. Pretty smart. Maybe these guys weren't total idiots, after all.

They flopped next to him, panting, and Collier tore to his right, bee-lining fast and hard for the corner of the first big building. He slid down the wall, rifle ready, and peeked around the corner. Jonesy and Swift, crouched behind an outbuilding next to it; Jonesy gave him the "All clear" sign. Okay. Collier waved the two privates up and raced for the next building, Jonesy and Swift covering. He dropped by the corner, got a thumbs-up from Jonesy, and then frantically waved in the two privates, who were just taking their sweet-ass time getting over here, weren't they? Both of them fell hard and heavy next to him, wheezing like a couple of worn-out greyhounds. The Red rolled over and groaned. Collier quieted him with a kick to the chin.

"Jesus, you two sound like a couple of goddamn trains. Shut it!" he whispered savagely.

"Sarge, he's so fucking heavy!" Zoll.

"I don't care, you're loud enough for artillery to zero in. Get control. Now."

"Shoulda just left the fucker." Zoll, again.

Collier whirled and leveled the rifle on him, "Say one more word."

Zoll paled, obvious even in the green light, and clapped his mouth shut, pulling in air through his nose. Akin stared, jaw dropped, but smart enough to say nothing because Sergeant Rashkil had a fearsome temper.

Sergeant Rashkil had killed privates before; hell, he'd killed corporals and other sergeants and even officers who said and did something to piss him off. He'd been busted and promoted a thousand times but never executed because he was just too damn good.

Sergeant Rashkil had survived eight, no, nine promotion moves, and was still in charge of 1st Squad. Wounded sixteen times, three of them serious, a fanatic, an iron man, a crazy old-timey vet who'd fought the Richmond Campaign and went ten miles into the Zone during the Test and didn't get sick and fought with the rear guard during the Big Run and was here, right now, confused and grieving and heartsick, but loved Major Arce and what he remembered about America and wanted, like most of the Blue Army, to restore it and would not, by God and all his angels, allow the Reds to impose some half-assed Marxist regime, instead.

So, say one word more, you whining baby-ass shithead.

Zoll didn't. Collier glared at him for a moment more, then broke position and turned back to the corner of the building. He'd have to kill Zoll later, of course, because the guy had a grudge and would, eventually, work up the nerve to drop a grenade in Collier's locker or knife him through the hammock while asleep. Pure spite was worse than a promotion move; with that, at least, you had a good idea of when it was coming. Collier couldn't be lucky all the time, so, had to off Zoll soonest. But not right now; he still needed the stupid bastard.

Eliot's perimeter was behind some giant storage shed for trucks or snowplows or whatnot; that is, if the freakin' fool had actually posted one. If not, they'd have to run about a thousand yards farther north to find Eliot's center, and then find Eliot himself so Collier could shoot him. He waved at Jonesy and clicked the radio twice again, and then again, and surprise, surprise, nothing. Jonesy cupped his hands around his mouth, and Collier nodded. Time for voice contact.

"Panther!" he spoke in a loud whisper. No need to

shout. A human voice carried well in this silence, even if the word itself was lost. Should wake someone.

Jonesy waited a moment. "Panther!" a little louder and more insistent this time.

Dammit, where the hell was Eliot?

"Raider," a whisper drifted from the direction of the shed and Collier felt genuine relief. God, it was like hearing you got an 'A' on a tough final exam, back in the days when final exams and grades meant something. He glanced at Jonesy, who stood with a half-raised fist. So, he heard it, too. Collier nodded and pumped his own fist twice, then turned towards the privates. "All right, we're breaking cover. I'm going first, Jones and Swift will take drag. You two carry the prisoner up behind me, but don't move until I signal you. And don't waste time. We'll be having company in about ten minutes and I don't want to be anywhere near here then."

The two privates exchanged looks and nodded. Collier waved at Jonesy and watched as he and Swift moved to the corner, Swift taking high, and leveled their weapons towards the shed. Collier counted down then called, "Out!" to let Eliot know they were coming. He better damn well have a broken radio, Collier thought, as he slipped low and sprinted for the shed wall.

Collier dropped into cover about ten feet short of the corner, leaving an open space where the privates could leap-frog. He turned back and pointed. The privates dragged the Red to the gap, Jones and Swift covering. Okay, do a snap-look around the corner, locate the pass-through team, get acknowledgment, move Jonesy and Swift, and then run past the shed for one big happy reunion. Then shoot Eliot.

The privates were at his back and he spotted Jonesy's upraised fist and raised his own and nudged his goggled eye past the corner ...

And froze.

There were several low buildings half-mooning around the shed's back, overlapping it. Must have been a marshaling yard, where the trucks all gathered to load or something, back when road maintenance was an actual job. It was like an amphitheater, no cover from the back of the shed to the first buildings and the woods behind them. But that's not what stopped him.

The beams did.

Lines, bright red ones, crisscrossed Collier's green-lit world in a semicircle around the yard, in the perfect configuration of an ambush box.

IR illuminators. Which only Reds used.

Collier savagely flipped his fist to an open palm and pumped it twice in Jonesy's direction. He felt the privates startled response behind him, but Collier's motion conveyed enough urgency that they remained still. He looked back and found Jonesy and gave him a "Trouble" motion, and then scrutinized the wavering beams.

What the hell?

Maybe Eliot was just being Eliot. Where he got IR illuminators, Collier couldn't figure, but it would be just like that dumbass to use them, and also like that dumbass to set up in ambush configuration instead of pass-on: one guy at point to wave them in, two guys behind to cover and then the next three to escort them into the perimeter. Allows everyone to simply fade away if something goes wrong. Gotta be it; Eliot was just being his usual moronic self. Or …

… this is exactly what it looked like: a Red ambush.

Collier swore under his breath. How's that possible? A whole crapload of things would have to have gone wrong in a ridiculously short period to (a) move Eliot off the position far enough that (b) Reds could steal in and set up an ambush … on a team the Reds had no earthly idea was actually coming this way. Even a fuck-up like Eliot couldn't manage that.

Could he?

Let's find out.

"Raider!" Collier called out the secondary, no longer worried if his voice carried back to the road. If the Reds were that close, they were screwed, anyway.

Silence.

Shitdamnandallhellfire. "Raider!" Collier insisted.

Nothing.

"Jonesy! Abort!" he called out and lowered his rifle.

All hell broke loose.

Tracers and gunfire exploded from the yard and woods and slammed into the corner of the shed. Collier flattened and then fired off a long burst while screaming at the privates to drop. Jonesy and Swift low-crawled at sixty miles per hour back to the corner of the opposite building as tracers sought them. Collier loaded a grenade and shot a 40 towards the yard, followed quickly by four more, and then sent three bursts to either side. Jonesy and Swift flopped around the corner of the building and stood, Jonesy giving him a thumbs-up.

Collier shook his head. Amazing how much flying lead you could run through without getting a scratch. Even more amazing was how a single shot from a hundred yards away could get you right between the eyes.

Jonesy engaged around the corner as Swift launched grenades. The two privates were firing hard and fast. Okay, that should slow the Reds down. So, Eliot, you craven little bastard, just before the Reds slit your throat, you blubbered out the countersign, huh? Good thing the Reds weren't smart enough to ask for the fall-back counter or you'd have given that, too, you sonofabitch.

Collier heard the radio squawking the alert tone and he looked over to see Jonesy holding it up. Collier fired off another burst and then put the radio to his ear. "Go, man, go!" Jonesy yelled, "We'll cover you. Get the Red back to Battalion, man!" and Jonesy clicked off. Collier gave a thumbs-up as Jonesy fired a savage series of bursts towards the yard. No John Wayne bullshit here; the Red had to be delivered. Only Collier could do that now, and only Jonesy could cover them. That's just the way it was.

The return fire intensified and Collier saw it shifting towards their left. Trying to flank them. The privates were shooting hard in that direction, the forgotten Red in a lump behind them. Collier fired his last 40 and then dropped to the Red and hoisted him into a fireman's carry. The two privates turned towards him, bewilderment on both their faces.

"We're going to get out of here," Collier said. "Follow me. Jonesy and Swift will cover us. You'll owe them your lives." He paused, reading their uncertainty and fear. No time, just no time. "Let's go," and he ran straight back towards the intersection, the Red and his weapon and equipment slapping in rhythm. He didn't look to see if the privates followed.

3

Nightmare.

Collier gasped through each agonizing step, lungs seared, muscles numb from the sheer torture of the Red's weight across his neck and shoulders. God, a drink of water, a thirty-second rest, please, but to stop for any reason would be suicide. Shots and explosions and yells seemed to come from everywhere at once but he knew that was just acoustics; the fight was mostly behind them. Mostly. Some noise was coming from the flanks, but those were outliers and not a problem if he could just stay ahead for another quarter mile or so of ankle-grabbing, face-tearing, foot-snaring trees and brush. Another ten minutes and they'd be clear. Please God.

He gulped air and switched focus to someone more inspiring: Rosa, I'm coming Rosa, I'm not going to let them get me, Rosa, at least not without one more look into your forever eyes. Keep me alive, Rosa, keep me running because each step is agony and I am on fire and broken and I simply cannot go on …

And went on. Another step. And another.

When he and the privates cleared the tower wreckage, they ran smack into the Reds deploying up the New

Lisbon Road and turned tail and hauled ass with what sounded like a whole Division in pursuit. Pounding out a hard uphill mile or so until they reached an old electrical station, they slipped onto a small trail that led behind the ruins of some big community college. Straight from there to the conspicuous pine tree looming over the trail and then hard right for the Creek bank, Collier fervently praying the NVG batteries didn't die, the firing from Jonesy's position fading with the distance, but the yells and shooting from the pursuit remaining steady. A horribly sharp stitch had quickly expanded across Collier's stomach about the time they reached the pine tree and locked his lungs but he had to keep going, just keep going, because it's either the Creek or death and he was intent on the Creek because …

Because he had too much left to do.

The Red had to be interrogated. Based on what Rosa extracted, the Ghosts would slip away. Again. The Reds would get frustrated and call a cease-fire. The war would end. He and Rosa would find a life …

So he would be damned if some crazy Marxists or his own failing breath would prevent that. Press on.

Collier wondered if this was how history's extraordinary feats of endurance happened, simply because some schlub had stuff left to do. Xenophon in Persia, Napoleon in Russia, Puller at Chosin … a hoplite or a grenadier in the ranks intent on a peaceful life.

Whatever keeps you going.

The shooting was now a little more distant. So, the Reds have slowed down. Good. And smart. These were close woods and the Reds had no idea if Collier was still running or in ambush. Keep being wary, Reds, gives me a much-needed break.

He stopped beside a giant oak and dropped the Red hard to the ground. What's one more broken bone?

Collier fell to all fours, his rifle caroming off his shoulder and wheezed great gulps of sweet, cold April air. His body went into re-circulation agony, the pins and needles across his shoulders and back making him gasp but welcome, just the same. Proof of life.

The two privates danced over him, anxious. "A minute," Collier whispered, "Just give me a minute." C'mon, recharge, get your air. The creek was just yards away; call the signal, wade across, fall into Deavers' lines and blessed safety. Hope Jonesy and Swift were there, too.

"Sarge, they're coming!" Panic laced Zoll's voice.

"We got time," Collier breathed.

"They're right behind us, Sarge! We gotta go now!"

One upside of anger was its ability to overcome exhaustion. Collier hoisted himself up, settling his weapon and equipment into place, "We got time, Private." His voice carried all the warning necessary.

Zoll hesitated, turning with an almost helpless appeal to Akins, who stared back at him, pale. Collier frowned. Infectious terror can run through a patrol – hell, an entire Division – in micro-seconds, putting everyone to flight. Akins had caught it big time from Zoll and both were body-languaging towards the water somewhere over there past the last clump of trees. Zoll's rifle barrel kept crossing Collier's body, so he moved his own up. "Take it easy," he snarled.

At that moment, the Red groaned, long and hard and much too loud. Collier spun and socked him hard across the face, but it was too late.

Zoll and Akins took off, racing towards the creek. "Sonofabitch!" Collier cursed and grabbed the Red by the collar, dragging him along after the privates. It took him about a minute to reach the overgrown edge and he heard the two privates splashing through, no doubt already up to their hips in the freezing, racing water. "Bolter, bolter, bolter!" Collier screamed out the emergency password, security be damned; if Deavers didn't hear it then, by God, they'd open up on those two idiots ...

The opposite bank exploded. Collier threw himself flat as bullets flew overhead, bringing branches and bark and pine cones down on him. "Bolter! Bolter!" he screamed again, but who could hear that above the firestorm? He parted some weeds blocking his vision and saw the two privates in the middle of the Creek, tracer fire and muzzle flash silhouetting them as body parts flew and green night-vision blood sprayed ...

... and the red beams of IR illuminators converged on their dancing forms.

Son. Of. A. Bitch.

Collier watched. Both privates were held upright by the lead wind raking them from hip to head and ripping up the trees around Collier. About two more seconds and they'd just be bloody pieces floating away. Ten seconds after that, Collier would be a bloody spot here on the bank. He hugged the ground as metal and death whipsawed the night and thought furiously and simultaneously along two lines: how the hell do I get out of here, and how the hell did this happen? He had no answer for the first, but did for the second:

Betrayal.

Someone among the Ghosts had sold them out. There was no other way the Reds could know Eliot's position, the password, AND this crossing point. Even if the Reds had got all that information from blabbermouth Eliot, there was no way they'd had enough time to set up two separate ambushes, especially one right here, so close to Deavers ... which must mean Deavers has been wiped out, too. Which was impossible without some kind of huge firefight that would have brought the rest of the

Ghosts running, so what in the holy fuck is going on here? Rage coursed through him: when I find the bastard who did this ...

If he lived long enough.

In the two or three seconds it took for the ambush to finish cutting the privates into small deli-sized slices, Collier realized that living long enough to choke the life out of the traitor rat bastard wasn't a guarantee.

Because the Reds couldn't let him get away.

Their little Ghost traitor was far too valuable to let US Army Sergeant Collier Rashkil emerge from the night and level accusations leading to a very thorough and ruthless investigation and subsequent identification of the asset, closely followed by US Army Sergeant Rashkil skinning the shitbrain alive. Which meant the Reds hunting him in the woods and the ones across the Creek would be very motivated to find US Army Sergeant Rashkil, and skin *him* alive, instead.

As if on cue, the sounds of a large group maneuvering somewhere behind him grew louder and a burly voice from there called out, "Ortega, Ortega, Ortega!"

"Daniel!" immediately came from the opposite bank and the last bit of firing dropped off.

Ambush over. Search starting.

Collier grasped the Red's collar, choking off any sounds he could make. "You're coming with me, asshole," Collier whispered fiercely at the still unconscious form, "You've got a lot to say." He crawled hard and fast up the bank towards Pemberton, dragging the Red while staying in the tree line, adrenaline and rage making him powerful. He stopped about thirty yards above the ambush point and took in a silent, huge breath. He pulled the Red across his raw shoulders and leveraged up a tree to a full stand, then stared back along his route. There, movement. They were looking for him.

He settled the Red and walked further into the woods, getting out of the search line, then headed back towards Pemberton, trying to keep as many trees between him and the searchers as possible. He got about another hundred yards before he stopped, gasping from the effort, and leaned against a tree to take the pressure off his back. He looked. Damnation, they were still on him. Relentless bastards.

Yes, relentless bastards. Which means, no use. It was no use. He wasn't going to get away, at least not with the Red in tow.

He half-ran to the trees bordering the Creek, the Red causing him further agonies. The water flowed dark and fast towards Pemberton, something that worked in his favor. He dropped the Red and then his backpack, reached in and grasped the waterproof cloth, pulling out Dad's book and its marked map of the American University campus. He slipped the cloth into a pocket, tight fit but secure, then rummaged through the backpack to see if there was something else important in there. Can't be too careful these days. Nothing, except for an old Snickers bar he was saving for a special occasion. He left it.

The search was getting closer. Too bad. He pulled out his Ranger knife, the good one, and stared at the Red. "Fortunes of war, fucker," he whispered, then slashed the Red's throat, deep and hard, the gurgling and the spasms starting almost immediately. Collier slid quickly down the bank, opened his pack and let the water fill it. He dropped the rifle into the water and, after one more good look at the movement in the woods, pulled off the night-vision goggles and dropped them in the current, watching them sink after the rifle.

He slid into the current. Cold, God, so cold, the shock tearing his mouth open, but he stayed silent. He squirmed along, digging into the mud and pulling on overhanging branches and protruding roots when the current did not carry him. He was making good progress, but this was silly. If the Reds didn't get him, the cold would. Already his thinking was muddled. Face it, Sarge, your number's up. Dad, I'll be there soon. Mom, set a plate at the table.

Rosa, goodbye.

4

"What happened?"

Rosa used her interrogation voice, the one of steel and threat. Coupled with hot metals and simple pliers, tongues loosened. She wasn't allowed to use those things on their own people (at least, not right off), but her tone implied their future employment.

Eliot shrugged, and Rosa's eyes narrowed. You don't break attention in my presence, troop, especially when you have a disaster to explain, one involving my lover, my *amante*, my cherished one ...

Collier. Oh my God, Collier.

She was falling: the pit opening and she was going, going ... and this bastard shrugs? "Stand at attention when reporting to me, Sergeant!" Pure snarl and she watched with satisfaction as Eliot blanched and pulled himself up, a look of terror crossing his face. Even Rosa's escort, two of her loyal soldiers, jumped. Had a fearsome reputation, didn't she?

The glow in the sky promised sunrise in about a half hour, a cloud-shrouded one. Mornings came earlier now as spring advanced. It was still too cold; ice and snow lay in patches across the dark open field where she stood with

Eliot and his patrol, scattered behind him like a sullen group of schoolboys ... appropriate, because they were behind what was left of the Pemberton Elementary School. Did Collier's Dad go here? She didn't know. But his ghost stood behind her, gibbering, accusing: how could she let this happen?

How could she?

"Well?" Her voice dangerous, coiled; she needed to kill someone. Eliot would do.

"I don't know what happened, Major," God, such a petulant voice. "We were exactly where we were supposed to be but Rashkil and his group never showed. It kept getting later and later and we even reached the abort time but we decided to stay because, well," he hesitated, glancing at his corporal, "it was Rashkil and we figured they were just running a bit late." He stopped.

You're quite the hero, Eliot, she thought, but said nothing, staring hard at him. She let the silence grow. Excellent interview technique, that. As was skinning.

"Well, anyways," and he started to shrug again and she tensed to smash him but he must have seen it because he was rigid with fear again. "Anyways, Ma'am, we were discussing what to do when a Red patrol slammed into us and we got into a fight and had to hightail it out of there."

She blinked. Slammed? "How many did you lose?"

Eliot paused, "Well, none, Ma'am."

None?

She peered at the patrol members, some standing, some sitting, a couple racked out. No bandages, no stretchers, no torn clothing that she could make out in the dim light. "No one wounded, either?"

"No, Ma'am," Eliot suddenly sounded uncomfortable.

Hmm.

"Let me see your weapon, Sergeant."

"My weapon?" Puzzled and wary at the same time.

She held out a hand and, after a moment's hesitation, Eliot unslung and passed over the rifle. She sniffed the barrel and then dropped the clip. Full. "Did you fire your weapon, Sergeant?"

"Uh ..."

"Really no need to answer, Sergeant, you obviously did not. I'm betting neither did the rest of your patrol." She handed the rifle back, keeping the clip. "So when you said you got into a fight, that wasn't entirely accurate, was it?"

Eliot said nothing and she felt something odd and dangerous shift across his patrol. They were suddenly attentive. Maybe it was the implied accusation of cowardice, but that should elicit hot denials and anger, not this studied scrutiny. Obviously, they didn't like the track she was taking, but for some reason other than personal honor.

What's going on here?

Don't know, and won't know unless she pressed this. "How did it happen?"

"Ma'am?"

"How did a Red patrol 'slam' into you? From what direction?"

"Umm," Eliot hesitated again and Rosa frowned. Trying to come up with a story, huh, Eliot? There was no firefight. You lied about that, and now I'm asking about things you haven't considered. Devil's in the details, you pathetic excuse for a US Army sergeant. "Well, from the east," he offered, after a moment.

"East." The mental map of the area popped into her head. "Where from the east?"

She could almost see his brows furrow in the dark. "Ma'am?"

"From the road, from the woods, from beneath your feet, where exactly did this patrol come from?"

"Road?" Uttered in true puzzlement.

"Yes, Sergeant Eliot, the road, the east-west road that crosses the north-south one at the entry point, where the tower came down." Exasperation. The Pemberton-Browns Mills Road was the main feature of the area. The Reds used it while traversing the Blue's front and Sergeant, you better by God have had some kind of security on that road while you were waiting for Collier

(*where are you?*)

to return, you shovelhead.

Eliot glanced at his corporal, who returned a warning look, and the alarms in Rosa's head crescendoed and she knew, immediately, Eliot had made some kind of mistake: a terrible one, a costly one, something that meant a firing squad for him and the corporal and maybe the rest of the patrol because it ruined a vital mission and worse, much worse, killed valuable personnel: Jonesy and Swift and the privates and, oh, Eliot, you fool, you stupid, stupid, fool, you killed Collier ... she mentally smacked her forehead. Good God, of course!

Eliot was out of position.

She stepped forward. "Give me your GPS," she barked.

Eliot took a step back and gestured at the corporal, "He has it."

She turned her fierce gaze on the corporal and pointed a warning finger at him. "Don't think, don't say anything, Corporal, just give it to me." He hesitated, his body turning away as if he wanted to run and the alarms screamed at her now and her other hand was on her pistol. If this little ferret-faced corporal (what the hell was his name, anyway? Buckner?) so much as blinked, she would shoot him.

That must have been apparent from her stance because he stopped, moved his hand to one of his pouches, took out the GPS, and placed it in her hand. She stepped back, keeping an eye on them both and noting how the rest of the patrol had bunched behind Eliot. There was something threatening in their position and her escorts stepped up, wariness in their eyes, hands fingering triggers. Okay.

She turned on the GPS, read the waypoint, and frowned: it was right. "Who entered the coordinates?" She looked up, her features lit in soft green, making her look like the angel of death, she was certain.

"I did," Eliot spoke right up. "Based on the mission brief."

"And I verified it," Buckner piped in, unasked.

Unasked.

She looked back down at the screen, looking for anything, an erased image, some kind of anomaly; but, no, it was the right location.

So why didn't Eliot know there was a road?

She quickly reviewed the briefing she gave last night

(a thousand years ago)

and, yes, she had clearly explained positions and movement and wait times and clear-words and signals, several times, in fact, because it was Eliot and he was a shovelhead and she didn't even want him on the mission.

No, she didn't, did she?

Colonel Caldwell, sclerotic and morbid and arbitrary and tactically brilliant, coming into her office that morning, "You're doing a grab tonight, is that correct, Major? Put Eliot on it."

In surprise, she'd said, "Eliot? For a grab? Are you sure, sir?" Caldwell rarely asked her to include personnel on a mission, just the occasional LT in need of experience. Never a grunt. And Eliot's shovelheadedness was generally acknowledged throughout the command; even Caldwell knew about it. Yet …

"Put him on," Caldwell had said curtly as he walked

out.

And Eliot did not know there was a road across the site.

Something skittered across her mind, chitinous and ugly, and she shivered at its touch. She'd long ago learned to trust her instincts. Those nights hiding in the ruins of Manhattan, odd noises or wrong shadows and her alarms rang and she ducked and was unfound or got in the first shot or knife slash and fought her way free, most of the time.

Most of the time.

She blinked away the images and stared at Eliot and the corporal and wondered what her instincts were trying to tell her. The GPS said they were in the right place and even Eliot couldn't screw that up. Unless, as they all feared, their one good satellite had finally gone silent, making all their precious GPSs obsolete, or …

… or Eliot had deliberately set up in the wrong position.

The thought shocked her. There wasn't much that could shock her anymore, but this one did. She stood still, not even blinking, overwhelmed. Why, for God's sake why? Was Eliot mad at Collier? Probably. Idiots were jealous of their betters. But to the point of ruining an entire mission? Seemed … excessive. Maybe this was some kind of half-baked promotion move. No, not that, either. Captain Palmer would never promote Eliot, which Eliot certainly knew. So, why do this?

Feet suddenly pounded around the corner of the school and straight for them, and she spun. Everyone else ducked and went for weapons. Running feet meant anything these days, from a suicide Red to a promotion move to simple chow call. She watched a figure careen through the mud, get bearings, and then settle on them. "Major Arce," gasped the figure, whom she recognized from one of the other platoons.

"Here, Private," she replied and he turned towards her, dropping hands on knees to catch his breath. No saluting out here; that attracted snipers.

"I got sent from the compound to find you," he gasped out again. Compound? No wonder the private was winded, running that whole distance. "Jones and Swift are back."

God! "Where are they?"

"Medical." As the private choked out the last word, she caught, out of the corner of her eye, Eliot and Buckner exchanging startled glances. She turned and stared at them. So, you didn't expect survivors, huh? Two very competent survivors, at that. And if Jonesy and Swift made it …

"Sergeant Eliot," she snapped, "get your patrol off this field before the Reds see us and start shelling. I'll expect your full, written report by noon." She left the many threats against his failure to do so unspoken.

She turned quickly, almost bowling over her escort, and strode towards the school. The escort fell in behind, keeping pace but also keeping watch on Eliot and his boys. She didn't worry; they knew their business. She had a far more urgent concern now – getting to Jonesy before Eliot did.

5

A few weeks, maybe a month, previously ...

Lieutenant Colonel Kant stood on the banks of the Ohio, watching the muddy water rush past. Snow melt and rains pushed it and he wondered how quickly a boat could reach Cincinnati, going one way, or the city of Wheeling, going the other. He imagined an endless stream of his soldiers, red banners flapping in the breeze, faces grim and heroic, heading to both.

Close with the last of the enemy, rend them, and free this corrupt and decadent land.

Soon. Very soon.

A twig snapped on the bank above him. Kant did not turn. "You're late."

"I am sorry, Comrade, it was difficult to get away." Captain Quesnell said, far too loudly.

"Do not call me that. You do not know who is about." Kant's voice was still and calm, but rage boiled within him and he had to fight down an urge to rip out the idiot's throat. He needed him. For now.

"I am sorry, Colonel."

That was better. Kant forced calm. Remember, only the gifted can lead; the rest must be guided, taught, reproved constantly. "Innocent sheep need the shepherd," his father's voice echoed down the years. Yes, Pai. So never pass up a chance to teach. "You are still late."

The man was contrite. "I am sorry, again, Colonel, but the staff meeting ran longer than usual, and the President levied us with new requirements."

"Captain, to explain is to excuse. Do you understand that, in our work, there are no excuses?"

Quesnell hesitated and Kant waited, his hand drifting down to his pistol. The Captain's next words determined if he lived or not.

"You are right, Colonel, I have failed. I am unworthy of this task and you would do better with someone of more capability."

Benevolence warmed Kant and he turned and smiled at the stricken Captain, head bowed, eyes properly averted, awaiting the judgment of his superior. "No, Captain, you are worthy because you learn. Now, tell me."

Like a puppy narrowly avoiding the rolled-up paper, Quesnell eagerly took a step forward. Kant frowned and leaned back. Maintain your distance, Pai had said, or the masses will corrupt you.

"He has agreed." Quesnell's voice bridled with enthusiasm.

Kant nodded, keeping his face wooden, unmoved, although his heart leapt with joy at the coming together of so many plans over so many years. If he were a believer, he would have thanked God. Instead, he thanked the hidden spirit of man, always yearning and cooperative.

"When?" Kant asked, keeping the emotion out of his voice.

"Two or three weeks, we figure."

Kant turned back to the river, watching it, "That actually means a month or more." He paused, considering. "Fine."

"Sir." The Captain moved closer, as if he wished to touch Kant, and Kant hoped he wouldn't be so foolish. "This means so much. It means ..." Quesnell struggled with the words.

"What, Captain?"

"That the war will end," he finished, triumphant.

Kant eyed him coolly, "Is that what you and the others believe, Captain?"

Quesnell blinked in surprise, "Well, yes, sir, of course, sir. How can the war continue?"

So young, Kant thought, so naïve. He looked at the Captain's unlined face, his severe military haircut, the shining blue eyes, youth incongruous with his rank and responsibility. "On the contrary, Captain, the war will just begin."

Quesnell's brow furrowed and Kant took a breath. "Your vision is short, Captain. The end of fighting does not mean the end of war. Enemies remain and must be eliminated. The people still cling to their bourgeois ideas of freedom and independence, even when such ideas destroyed them. We will not have peace until those ideas are gone and man's mind is turned fully to his brothers."

"But, surely, sir, this will put us in the right position!"

Kant sighed. "It will merely end this phase, this civil war. The land must still be freed. Do not be mistaken, the freeing will be bloody, long, and painful."

"But, sir ..."

Kant froze, and the Captain blanched, sudden panic rising to his face. Kant's discipline was legendary among the cadre, his judgment swift and cruel and the puppy knew he'd overstepped a line. Kant could kill him now or he could show mercy; either would enhance his reputation. He decided on mercy.

He left the Captain hanging for a moment, then

allowed a tiny smile. "It's all right, Captain. I, too, sometimes wish this would all stop. But wishing will not do it. We must *make* it stop, and that will be hard work."

"Yes, sir, of course, sir, I am guilty of rushing things, I know. I do not wish to offend."

The Captain's relief was almost comic and Kant was again amazed how easy it was to manipulate the weak. Pai took it as a given but Kant saw every instance as a small miracle. The sheep.

"Guard against impatience, Captain. This is the work of generations." He let the reproof stand.

The Captain bowed his head in gratitude. "Orders, sir?"

"Arrange things. Tell the others to get ready. And convey my warmest regards to the asset, tell him he'll be rewarded."

Confusion clouded the Captain's face. Kant looked at him grimly. Yes, Captain, I said rewarded. With a shallow grave, of course.

Quesnell lingered a few moments longer than he should have, then turned and glided through the trees. Kant watched him go. No doubt, Quesnell would turn this conversation into self-praise, convinced he was vital. Keep thinking that, Captain, because your own shallow grave awaits. When the history of this moment is re-written, there cannot be any contrary witnesses.

Pai's grizzled face suddenly swam into his vision. "The favelas," it lectured, "that is what 'free will' leads to, the murderous streets of the River January, the fat tourists and decadent whores on the beaches, starving children slaughtered by the police. You are called to end it, *filho*, it is your destiny, and you must be ruthless."

Be ruthless.

Kant's eyes drifted over the hillside houses rising above him. Marietta, Ohio. The French and the English placed their forts here, where the Ohio and the Muskingum met. The hubris of a people who thought God's Hand was on their shoulder. He looked at the Victorian row houses, grand and preening once but now empty, their privileged and arrogant dwellers dust and bone. Zealots brought them low. You didn't see that coming, did you? And you did not see me, raised in your midst. Now comes the New Man, the one you thought you'd beaten.

He glanced only once at the granite statue next to him. Franklin Roosevelt. The American who tried to have it both ways, Four Freedoms and a social state. Ludicrous. The state *is* freedom. Roosevelt's had been a lie.

His wouldn't be.

6

After the soldiers had settled into trenches and the patrols had tramped down the creek to see what the Red enemy was doing, the madman stole from the back of his house and slipped towards the water. At that glorious moment when dawn's light shot from the woods and the creek glowed with gold and rose, he stepped gingerly into the park, wary of the trenched soldiers who looked at him with mild surprise. Crazy old coot, they said, maybe we should shoot him. Sometimes he prayed they would but was glad when they didn't. The memory of this place should last a little bit longer. A little bit.

He loved that memory enough to risk murder. It was another chance to pretend ... the park was empty and quiet because cold drove out the mothers and their toddlers, and traffic had momentarily subsided, leaving only the sounds of birds and the creek rushing over the little dam just above the bridge. That is, if he ignored the far-off shooting and shouts and the occasional explosion.

The Blue soldiers lost interest in him, settling back in the works they'd built along Mary Street to watch the creek. Waste of time – the creek was too wide here for the Red soldiers to cross. The Blues probably knew that, but an abundance of caution kept them here enduring shells the Reds threw at them. Not that they were safe anywhere else; those Red People shelled pretty much everything in Pemberton, probably hoping for a supply house or headquarters, but usually just hitting an unwary soldier or two. Why weren't they more accurate? In Vietnam, he could call a strike within feet of his intended target. Today's armies had the artillery instincts of the Civil War. Lost capabilities.

He knew those Red People. They came to see him, too, just like the Blues, hurting and stealing just as much but wanting something more: information. He'd tell them anything so they'd stop hurting him, some of it actually true, but that was due more to coincidence than anything because he simply wasn't paying attention to the war; indeed, was actively trying not to see it. He only saw Before, a world of no plague and no fighting. Like, right now it was a spring morning of ten years ago, before the Towers and the Event, when it was cold and early and silent and he was the only person walking along the flowering, leafing Creek, half the sun giving half the light. Let this moment last forever, let the war stay hidden.

So when he saw the body floating about five yards out, his instincts were all pre-war. If they hadn't been, if he'd been aware of the fighting and the misery and the horror of these times, he would have just watched the body disappear under the bridge. Instead, he chased it up the bank, splashing in and grasping a handful of soaked blouse, hauling the body out before it got caught in the dam's undertow. A soldier. What was he doing here? Ft. Dix was twenty miles away. He was surprised when the soldier shuddered and coughed and then groaned. Should be dead.

The soldier opened his eyes and stared full at him, then began shaking violently and, just like that, it wasn't ten years ago, the park was not peaceful because war is on my doorstep. Oh, Lord, please, make the war go away. Again. He stared at the soldier, who had slipped back into unconsciousness. Maybe he should put him back.

But, no, not this one. He knew the soldier's father.

That wasn't odd. War created coincidence. He remembered getting on a bus in Kunsan, Korea, between his Vietnam tours, and finding one of his best Pemberton friends sitting in the back. War brought several paths together.

"John Rashkil," the madman said aloud. The sergeant stirred a bit and opened his eyes again then shut them.

"Hey! Old man! Watcha doin' down there?" someone shouted from the trenches and he heard scuffling and they were coming. They'd think he'd done something to the soldier, and would beat him. Or worse. He ran under the bridge and found the path up the other side and through the very thick woods to the old house everyone thought was haunted when he was a kid and which they all broke into at some point to prove their courage. He dropped under the porch to hide for a while. It was safe here. There was no war here.

7

"Yes, I received it last night."

Price drifted, half-listening to Colonel Leideig's end of the phone conversation. Bright spring day outside the window, golden and warm. There was a dogwood-covered ridge near Farmville and on a day like this, wow, all color and cool breezes. One of Pap's favorite rendezvous and, after Price took over, one of his. Wish he was there right now.

"You'll have it soon," Leideig hung up. Price idly wondered who that was. Phone calls were rare in this post-Breakout world. Couriers, like Price, were the normal means of communication. Only very special events prompted radio and phone calls, and only to very special people. Like Leideig.

The Colonel rested his grey and mottled chin on tented fingers, filmy grey eyes looking off. Plans and counterplans raced through that devious little mind right now – how much for this piece, who gets a cut, who gets a knife? Then off Price goes to some out-of-the-way road in some dead town where he'd meet equally grim and suspicious couriers and they'd exchange packages and, maybe, gunfire and Price would bring whatever to whomever and then drop a few more gold pieces (a couple more than Leideig knew about) into his stash. Escape money.

"Henry," the Colonel smiled, absolutely no mirth in it, the one-color eyes impassive and calculating. "Just how long have you been couriering for me?"

Couriering? Was that a word? Granny'd shudder at such butchery. He could just hear her, "Now, Henry boy, you speak rightly, the way the Lord intended." Once, he'd pointed out that English was not the Savior's idiom. That got him a lecture about blasphemy and a switching from Pap and he'd learned to humor the old people. "About five years, sir." Leideig already knew that, but humor the old people.

Leideig's smile broadened a bit as he coughed into the ever-present tissue. Breakout had not been kind to the Colonel's lungs. "And have you benefited from this position?"

Price's shields went up. Did the old bird know about the skimming? "I've done well, sir, and I'm appreciative."

Leideig laughed and smacked the table with an arthritic hand. "That you have, boy, that you have! So have I. So have we all. I can't complain and I certainly hope you don't." Leideig's laugh turned into a wheeze and he spat more lung into the tissue. Price eyed it uncomfortably. Might still be contagious. "Because," Leideig wiped, "we've got another situation and, to tell you the truth, this one could set us up for life."

Henry's eyes widened. Gawd, Colonel, could you be more indiscreet? He glanced meaningfully at the open door and then gave Leideig a warning look.

Leideig missed it, of course. "Damn shame for the 1st, damn shame," the Colonel muttered. Price blinked and almost laughed out loud. Shame? Those guys were sitting pretty way up there in New Jersey, almost as pretty as the

4th here in the Valley. Got the Reds stymied, they do. Hadn't he, just a few weeks ago, waltzed right into the 1st's center, delivering and picking up packages? Hardly saw a Red the whole trip.

"I have another job for you." The Colonel spoke softly and Henry was full attention. "Not as bad as the last one, not so far away. Are you interested?"

Formality. The Colonel could testify at court-martial that Price wasn't ordered, he volunteered. Like there'd ever be a court-martial. "Always interested, Colonel." Like he'd have any problem volunteering. The Colonel's business was so much like Pap's that Henry felt at home. And, with just two or three more runs, Henry could actually go home. See those dogwoods.

"Good." The Colonel opened a desk drawer and filled out a set of blank orders with a gold pen Henry had picked up from a Richmond run about three and half years ago, just after the Campaign. Henry watched, bemused. Handwritten orders. Quaint a mere six years ago, now standard, with the dearth of power and disks and motherboards and qualified technicians to keep them running. Good thing, really. Computer-generated orders meant a lot of unnecessary eyes. Only the necessary saw handwritten ones and the Colonel's signature stopped their queries.

"You are," the Colonel said while finishing off the last page, "going back to the Fairfax Court House."

Henry frowned. Fairfax Court House in the old Zone. He didn't like going there. Sure, sure, the Event was long past and the Test had shown it to be relatively clear; less than half of the patrols meandering up to the District line even got sick anymore, and only half of those died but, still. Death was in the very dust there, and Henry wasn't one to tempt fate.

"You're going to see Colonel Ostroff again. He's just

been put in charge of what's left of the 3rd."

Henry blinked in surprise. There were still elements of the 3rd? He thought they'd pretty much evaporated after Richmond.

"You'll need a truck and I'm giving you two privates to help." Leideig said that last matter-of-factly but Henry jumped right in. "Colonel, I don't need them."

Leideig looked up. "You will for this one. It's a bulky, heavy load and you might get some undue interest."

"Colonel, you know I work best alone."

"Yes, Henry, you are rather talented. But this is more delicate than usual and I anticipate … difficulties." The Colonel's sickly grey eyes turned owlish and Henry frowned. He never knew all the nuances of any particular shipment, who fetched and who stored and who got paid and who got killed; preferred not to know, actually, because it gave him deniability at that mythical court-martial. But simplicity was his motto, and additional people were a complication, and complications tended to cause breakdowns that tended to cause questions and shootings and raised his risk. And made skimming harder. He'd handled bulky shipments and "undue interest" before. What's different here?

The Colonel read his mind, "There are some negotiations with this one, Henry, that are a little more troublesome than I prefer. Like I said, you're talented but everyone needs assistance from time to time and this is one of those occasions." He waved a hand. "It's all right. I know these two and they are trustworthy. You'll be in charge, of course, and you have the option of shooting them if they become difficult." Leideig smirked. "But they won't." He handed the orders to Henry, who took them without a glance.

"The privates will pick you up at the usual place at

noon." Leideig said that matter-of-factly, too, and Henry raised eyebrows. A daytime run?

Leideig paused, uncannily knowing Henry's question. "We're in a hurry on this one. Ostroff is taking the 3rd to the New Mexican Territories." Leideig then looked down at some papers. Dismissal.

Henry left, keeping his head down so no clerks or administrators would really remember him and stepped outside; a quick recon but no one checking him out so he walked towards his platoon area to throw off any suspicion and then abruptly turned behind a steel building about fifty yards past the Colonel's. He whirled, ready to deal with anyone following but, nothing, so he relaxed and walked quietly down to the end, ducking into shadows. There was a mess of larch and mimosa pressing against a rusty fence still standing at this part of the old industrial park. The trees were budding but he could still see quite a way into the wooded tangle beyond, a multitude of brown limbs scratching and twisting their way skyward with ivy and creeper and lobelia carpeting their roots.

Henry took in a deep breath. Undertones of winter with an overlay of warmth, oh man, the best of both seasons. He pulled out the cigar Sergeant Rashkil had given him. It was now in almost pristine condition, after two weeks in Leideig's humidor. He'd slipped it in and out of there without the Colonel knowing (or caring).

The Colonel.

"Trust your partner about as far as you can throw him," Pap always said. Pap practiced that religiously, checking quarts and jars and kilos at least once a day, eyeing Henry the whole time like he knew the boy held back. Henry never did with Pap, respected him too much. Leideig was another story.

Henry regarded the cigar. He'd been saving it for a

special occasion, but there really was no such thing anymore. He shrugged, then lit it up. The first puff was almost orgasmic and Henry curled the smoke in twice, savoring. He watched it drift up and away in the breeze.

For the millionth time in the last six months, Henry wondered if it was time to go. The war was in stalemate; the Reds couldn't win and neither could the Army. Things were falling apart. Rumors flew about conveys abandoned, half the drivers shooting the other half to get away, officers packing up their loot and disappearing in the middle of the night. A general sense of hysteria was building in this joke of an Army. The only ones still fighting were the True Believers (suckers, all), the ones who hadn't quite made their fortune yet (Henry), and the too greedy (Leideig). His partnership with Leideig had been quite lucrative but all things come to an end, and spidey sense told him something was turning: that odd phone conversation a few moments ago, f'rinstance, this hurried-up run replete with a couple of unwanted oafs, for another. He had that Pap-developed sense of a double-cross in the making. If not during this very suspicious run, then the next one, or the one after.

He pulled in one more luxuriant puff. Yeah, definitely time to go. Once he figured out how.

8

Jonesy grimaced as the tech swabbed at his exposed and bloody knee with an even bloodier gauze pad. "Take it easy, man!" he yelped.

The tech grinned. "Big baby," and wiped a little harder.

"I'll 'big baby' you!" Jonesy waved a half-hearted fist at the tech, who made his grin bigger and wiped harder. Rosa could see the wound clearly, a skittering tear along the base of the knee and up the middle of the leg. "Doesn't look like a bullet," she said.

"It ain't," chimed Swift, sitting next to the stretcher with his hand in a bowl, "Klutz here tripped on a tree root."

"I'll klutz you!"

"Yeah, yeah." Swift pulled his hand out of the bowl and flapped it at Jonesy.

Rosa saw torn flesh and exposed bone and figured at least thirty stitches. "Now that's a bullet."

"Grenade," was Swift's laconic response as he dropped the hand back into the solution. Another tech wheeled a chair over, laying out instruments, then pulled Swift's hand over and studied it. "Hmm," the tech said, "you won't play the piano again, but should heal up okay." Swift said nothing, merely watched as the tech probed and cleaned. No lidocaine, not even a swig of homebrew, and not one flinch. Hard core.

Rosa pulled a stool up to Jonesy. "Okay."

"Fucked up, Major, completely fucked up." Jonesy winced as the tech sewed his knee back together.

"I know that, Sergeant. By the way, did you step in dog crap or something?"

Swift chuckled and Jonesy shot him a murderous look, "No, Major, a ruptured septic tank."

"Oh." She raised an eyebrow at the tech.

"Should be okay, Major, the wound's pretty clean. The smell's mostly in his clothes."

She nodded. Dirty wounds were certain death out here. No antibiotics. "You need a new set of fatigues."

Jonesy pulled at his blouse, "Damn shame, Major, these were Pre-Event."

She sympathized. New issues were rotten quality, hardly up to the grueling pace of the last six months, and the harder six to come. She wasn't even sure if they had *any* fatigues left, Pre or Post-Event, but no one would tolerate that smell. "Burn them, Sergeant."

"Yes, Ma'am."

"Continue."

"Well, Ma'am, I made first contact up near Browns Mills, but it was like the Reds were onto us quicker than usual and I lost two right away, but it still went well. We pulled 'em in and Coll – I mean Sergeant Rashkil ..." Catch and pause. It sounded for her benefit. She blinked. Did Jonesy know?

"... Rashkil tased 'em and we had it all bagged. It was good, real good, and we moved out quick and made it to the point and, well, Ma'am, they were waiting for us."

"Who was?"

"The Reds."

"Where?"

"At the point, Ma'am."

She frowned and had Jonesy give details, with Swift adding a comment or two. So, Eliot was definitely out of position. Reds had been there instead.

But that wasn't the worst part. "And you're certain they used the counter?" she asked.

"Absolutely, Ma'am. I heard it, Rashkil heard it ..."

"... and so did I," finished Swift.

She absently picked up a pencil from one of the trays near her and tapped it against the rim. The only other sounds were the techs fussing and Jonesy's occasional yelps of pain. She'd made up the passwords that day, basically pulled them out of thin air, not from any listings or approved usages. Couldn't be a lucky guess. Couldn't.

Which meant someone had given the password to the Reds. That someone was Eliot.

She stopped tapping the pencil and saw it clearly: Eliot meets with the Reds shortly after sending Collier and Jonesy through the entry point, gives up the password, then moves off. He and his patrol play grabass while Collier and Jonesy come back to an ambush. Both are killed, Eliot hangs out a bit for effect, rehearses a half-baked story about a Red patrol, then strolls back to camp, woe, woe, they never showed. Sorry 'bout that, shit happens, damned unbelievable those guys lasted this long, doncha think, Major? Salute and press on. Eliot looks innocent because the GPS, his corporal, and the rest of the patrol claim he's in position. No witnesses, no proof, just her suspicions. She loses Collier, Eliot loses a rival.

Smart. Damned smart.

Too damned smart for a shovelhead.

The ugly, chitinous thing skittered across her mind again. A plan too good for Eliot to come up with, but well within his range of execution.

Hmm.

"I'd like the techs to leave the room, please." She spoke low, no-nonsense in her voice.

Both techs looked up, startled, but her eyes weren't kidding, so they tidied a bit then slipped out through the partition door. Jonesy and Swift looked almost comical with their half-finished dressings and big, frightened eyes. She wasn't much in a laughing mood, though.

"You saw no signs of Eliot's platoon." It wasn't a question.

"No, Ma'am, and if he was nearby he'd have heard the fighting and come running. We figured he was dead," Jonesy peered down at the incomplete stitches.

"He's not."

Jonesy blinked at her, "What?"

"He and his patrol made it back fine. Said they were in position. GPS and the platoon members confirm it. You never showed, they waited past rendezvous, got hit by a patrol, ran for it."

Swift shook his head. "There's no way."

Jonesy's eyes went medieval. "That lying sack of shit. We were well on time, Ma'am, well on, and he was nowhere near there. What the hell's going on?" and, remembering himself, he added, "Ma'am?"

"Good question, Sergeant. Who else knows you're back?"

"Well, probably everyone by now," Jonesy said. "We came in through Collin's people. I sent the private when Swift was helping me into the tent here."

"Collin's people? You crossed that far east?"

"Yes, Ma'am. No choice, we had to clear the area and swing way out to escape."

"You didn't try to get back with Deavers?"

"No, Ma'am. Rashkil and the privates went that way,

hightailing it back to the road, but we got hit from that direction, too, so we took off the other way. It took everything we had just to save ourselves." There was an apology in his voice, sincere, and she wondered, again, how much he knew.

Collier.

She let the silence go on too long. "All right," she broke it. She walked to the door and gestured the techs back in. She looked at Jonesy and Swift. "Watch your backs," she whispered, and then stepped out of the partition and into the large open area that was surgery and recovery and emergency room, all in one. She glanced around. Ten to twenty people milling around, mixture of techs and the usual goldbricks and some genuinely hurt people, as well as a couple of staffers. Good.

She turned back to the partition and announced in a voice loud enough to carry through the bay, "That was good info, Sergeant Jones. When you're done, get some rest and report back to your platoon." Then she marched straight out of the door and into the compound area. Now everyone would know that she knew, which meant no sudden accidents should befall Jonesy and Swift. That would be too suspicious, and Eliot and whoever came up with this plan knew she was suspicious enough. Jonesy and Swift should be all right.

Even if she wasn't.

Because, she was already dead. Someone walking up right now and putting a bullet through her head would be a redundancy. She'd been poised to die since she heard Collier was missing and now, well, there it was. She looked, to any passerby, as stoic and hard as ever, but that was an illusion. She was the walking dead, and wondered if this falling grief, this forever plunge down a black hole of agony and ice, was the origin of vampires.

Because she really wanted to rip someone's throat

open right now. Eliot's, definitely. And whoever had put him up to this.

Find that person. Now.

9

It was past sunrise when she reached Deavers' position down towards Magnolia Road. The creek was wide and fast here, all the way to the Lisbon dam. Strong position, but dangerous, because their lines curved back towards Ft. Dix from this point, creating a gap between the creek and a small run on their left flank, which was Collin's sector. Deavers held the gap from the creek to the college, including the Browns Mills Road. The road was no man's land; the creek wasn't. It was Blue territory, and their safety depended on it remaining so.

There were about five or six places on the creek shallow enough to get a team across, even though the water was fast and cold, and she'd picked this one as randomly as she'd picked the passwords.

Didn't hurt that Deavers knew his business. So why didn't he contact her when the team failed to show?

"The Reds just opened up, just out of nowhere, Ma'am," Deavers responded to the question while trying to light a soggy cigarette. He looked suitably haggard after a suitably bad night, but he wasn't meeting her eye and that bothered her. Two of his privates slouching nearby looked haggard, too, and sullen. But that was normal for recruits, so she ignored them.

"How many did you lose?"

Deavers shook his head. "They didn't open on us, Ma'am."

"Pardon?"

Deavers gave up on the cigarette and eyed it forlornly. "They didn't shoot at us. They were on something across the water."

"The firing was away from your position?"

"Yes, Ma'am, in the woods." He pulled out his map, a civilian one lifted from a gas station. Resources were getting thin. "Here," he tapped the creek juncture, surprisingly displayed. Good ole Exxon. "We had faded about fifty yards back on this side after we got Eliot and Rashkil across the Creek and settled in to wait for them. I heard shooting, so I ran up to see what it was, and something was happening in the woods over there."

"Go on."

"Well," Deavers shifted uneasily, "I thought they were launching on us so I called up the platoon and we set formation but, no, they stayed across the creek."

"So what did you think was going on, Sergeant?"

Deavers eyes slid right and left, like he was looking for a place to run. Her guard went up and she glanced back at her escort. "I figured something must have happened with Rashkil's grab and he or Eliot was trying to make it across at the entry point, although it seemed a bit early and I hadn't heard a call on the radio but, hell, Ma'am, these radios go out all the time so I just figured someone over there needed our help."

She nodded. "All right, Sergeant, that was good thinking. So what did you do?"

Deavers gave her a surprised look at the compliment, but quickly turned away. Like he didn't deserve it. "I lined up the platoon for a run across the Creek but knew it would be tough because, even though you can wade it there, it's still hip-deep and fast and, well, then, we got hit."

"Hit?"

"Yes, Ma'am," Deavers was looking at the ground, "Hard, on the flank."

She blinked at him, "You were attacked on our side of the Creek?"

He nodded.

"How'd they get over without you seeing?" An accusation, and she narrowed her eyes to see how he took it.

Deavers shook his head. "Ma'am, they couldn't have, they just couldn't. We had the Creek covered halfway to the road and they didn't cross when I pulled up the platoon because I would have seen it."

"Are you telling me, Sergeant, that they were already across before you got there?"

"That's what I figure, Ma'am."

She pulled back, the enormity of it taking her breath away. Reds hiding on the Blue side, right at the place Deavers needed to be if he was to render any assistance to the returning grab mission. The firing across the creek must have been the Reds pursuing Collier, so he made it at least this far. She angrily suppressed the sudden surge of hope because the ugly, chitinous thing was screaming at her, gnawing its way out of her brain.

Eliot and his mentor were intent on this mission failing.

Why?

Better question: how?

As in, how in the bloody hell could they pull this off? How could Eliot have coordinated with the Reds to not only get the passwords and move off position after Collier and Rashkil went across the Lisbon Road but have them infiltrate the Blue side of the creek without Deavers seeing?

Simple. Eliot couldn't.

Unless Deavers helped him.

Her eyes narrowed. "I got no reports of an attack last night, Sergeant." Keep the voice glacial.

Deavers stared at his shoes, "I couldn't raise anyone on the radio, Ma'am. We had to bug out, run like hell, there were so many of them," he swallowed dryly. "Ma'am, we got lost."

"Excuse me?"

Deavers flapped the map helplessly, "We just couldn't tell where we were. We had to cut more north than east and we lost the creek and we think we were somewhere east of that Sunbury Village place but we just couldn't see, no moon, clouds over the stars, no night vision, and this thing" he slapped the map, "was worthless."

She stared at him. All that was likely true. No GPS or night vision for the line platoons because there simply weren't enough to go around. No topo map for the same reason. Deavers could well have gotten lost and unable to report. His position was far enough away from Pemberton no one would have heard the attack.

Sounded plausible.

No, sounded clever.

She turned to iron. "But somehow, despite being hopelessly lost, you managed to find your way back because here you are. And then settled in as if nothing had happened. Did it occur to you to send a runner?"

Deavers shook his head, curiously calm and unbothered by her tone. "When it got lighter, we figured out where we were and ran back to see if the Reds were still here, but they weren't. I was going to send the runner, but you showed up, Ma'am, before I could."

Also plausible … or well-rehearsed.

She switched tack. "How many did you lose?"

Deavers still wouldn't look at her. "Ma'am?"

"When the Reds attacked you, how many?"

"Uh …"

"You should be able to answer that question, Sergeant." She stated it flat and hard, her blood boiling as her hand drifted down to her pistol. She had enough information to start shooting people and was mad enough to do so but no, not yet; she needed details, like which of them, Deavers or Eliot, came up with this unbelievably stupid plan and convinced the other to participate. So, interrogation, blades and pliers and pulled-off thumbs. Starting with you, Deavers. You're going to be more than happy to tell me how you and your good buddy, Eliot, pulled this off—

Good buddy?

No, they weren't.

Eliot was a weasel, a Draft Gang recruit with a natural sense of cunning who'd moved his way up through a series of promotion moves and continuous ass-kissing. The Colonel was fond of the little creep, as a result. Deavers was a vet, in the Army before the Event and fought in the second Korean War, embittered when Breakout killed his whole family in Massachusetts. Draft Gang slugs and vets hate each other. But, then again, Deavers was an opportunist, quick to bend with whatever wind was blowing. So what could Eliot offer Deavers that would make him agree to kill Collier?

But, Rosa, they didn't. You did.

The thought stunned her. She went still, considering it.

Collier was the best: fearless, ferocious, more importantly, competent. They were so much alike. He was thrilled by her creative missions and she by his success. They thought on the same lines, had the same dreams, were fired by each other's touch, lived in each other's souls. He was her first choice for most missions, from grab to recon, because he was the most likely to pull it off, so all Eliot and Deavers had to do was wait for her to send him out. And they didn't have to wait long, did they?

It's your fault. Yours.

She teetered over that black pit. Just let go, just fall, long and dark and drifting, but she shook herself out of it. No time for that. Her eyes lasered Deavers. I have time for you, though.

"Major Arce?" a voice crackled on her radio. Wordlessly, she pulled it out of the holster: a Motorola "liberated" from Radio Shack or someplace like that. Not military spec'd but, hey, it worked. Most of the time. She keyed, "Go." Keep comms short. Everybody had each other's frequencies and the mishmash of models and encodings meant talk was in the clear.

"Major, Rashkil's been found," the voice, one of the compound guys, said.

She pushed off the pit's edge, paralyzed, holding the radio, saying nothing. So, a patrol had just stumbled across the body. Her hopes, bare as they were, collapsed.

"Major, did you copy?"

She shook herself, glared at Deavers and silently promised him three days of sheer agony before she killed him, then said, "Acknowledged." Pause. "Where?"

"Right by the dam."

Dam? "The New Lisbon one?"

"No, Ma'am," the voice crackled, "Pemberton."

She blinked. That made no sense. The Creek was too full of crap for a body to drift that far down. "What condition?" In pieces, she supposed.

"Cold, mostly, but he'll be all right."

Her only visible reaction was a slightly raised eyebrow. Inside, it was the Fourth of July and Christmas all in one. "Roger. On my way."

10

Collier stood naked in the middle of Fishburne's breezeway, a blizzard howling through the funnel at 90 miles an hour, blasting him with ice and snow while the whole Corps, arrayed on the stoops, laughed and jeered and pointed and he was freezing, just freezing …

Wake up.

Collier stirred. His back didn't feel right. A moment ago, it was a sheet of ice but now it was itchy and burning and uncomfortable because, whaddayaknow, he was lying on a blanket. Judging by the scratchiness, an Army wool blanket. So, someone had rescued him from the breezeway. Must be Davis, good ole Davis who wouldn't let a roommate die in cold and humiliation and had tucked him into the bunk with the steam pipes going full blast and soon it'll be May and school ends and Dad'll pull up and make some smart-alec remark but who cares, he was going home for the summer …

Can't be. That was five years ago. Six, maybe.

Wake *all* the way up.

Collier opened his eyes. Super-bright sun blasted through various windows and cut-outs. Groans and screams and mutterings and bustlings and sharp calls for

"Medic!" assailed his ears. Must be in Battalion's hospital. A shadow moved. Someone was sitting next to him.

Focus. The lights evened out and details formed and there, there, leaning forward, all luminous eyes and worry lines and dark, silky skin …

… Rosa.

He stirred, turning towards her, emotions jump-starting warmth in areas still iced, like his heart, oh Lord, his heart. "Dar—"

"Sergeant!"

Warning flared in her eyes and he bit off the word in mid-syllable. "Dark, it's dark," almost stumbling on the change but thought he'd pulled it off.

"That's expected," a male voice said and Collier turned towards it. White coat, fatigues underneath, youngish face. Doc Pretty Boy, er Voss, Captain Voss. Damn, must be really hurt to rate a doctor instead of a tech.

Or someone, probably a gorgeous major, had ordered it.

"Your senses will kick in one at a time, so don't worry too much about the darkness, it'll go." Voss grinned. Collier scowled. Was already gone, jerkwad. "You had a good case of hypothermia going there, Sergeant, but you'll be okay."

"When?" Collier asked.

Doc Pretty Boy shrugged and turned admiring glances at Rosa and Collier could have reached up and throttled him but, hey, if he did that to every man who slobbered her way, there'd be no Ghosts left. "Couple of hours, I think. No frostbite. The air temp was up so there'll be no permanent damage." Said without even looking at Collier so, yep, throttle time.

He stirred into action but Rosa stopped everything

with, "Thank you, Doctor, that will be all." Crestfallen, Voss hesitated, but Rosa's dangerous eyes flashed warnings. He slunk off.

Well done, Collier blinked.

Her eyes remained hard and murderous but there was a twinkle in them. "We found you under the Pemberton bridge. You were partway up the bank, but if a private hadn't gone down there to check on some noise, we wouldn't have found you until it was too late."

Collier frowned. Memory flash, someone leaning over him, but not in uniform.

"No," he said.

"Excuse me, Sergeant?"

"The private didn't find me. The old man did."

"Old man?"

"That crazy bastard still living over there on the edge of town. The one who's always raking."

"I know him. He found you?"

"Pulled me out. Said something …" Collier's brow furrowed. Words, distant, out of synch with the old man's moving mouth.

"What?"

He shook his head, "Can't quite remember, but it was odd." He paused. "Sorry, Major, it'll take me a few days, I think, to get it back."

"The private didn't say anything about the old man."

"Probably ran off before the private got there. He's skittish."

"I'll speak to the private."

He waved a hand weakly. "I don't think it's important, Major."

She nodded, keeping her official face no-nonsense now, but her gaze lingered a few seconds past appropriate, like a caress. There was a hurt in her eyes, though, remnants of some grief. What could that be?

Hit him like a mortar shell. Idiot! She thought he'd been killed! And then he shows back up? He closed his eyes, mortified. "Sorry," he whispered, "so sorry."

Silence. He opened his eyes. She nodded imperceptibly, volumes in that, and was back to business. "What happened, Sergeant?"

"We were ambushed, Major," he shook his head deeper into the pillow. "They were waiting for us, not only at rendezvous but at extraction. We had to split up. Jonesy and Swift stayed to cover while me and the privates ran with the grab back to the Creek." He paused. Jonesy and Swift. Damn, damn, damn. No way they got through. It was a freakin' miracle *he* had, and miracles were pretty stingy. Jonesy. Oh, man. After all the pals he'd lost these past five years, one more shouldn't make any difference. But it did.

She read it. "Jones and Swift are back, Sergeant."

He stared at her. "No way."

She just blinked. Relief flooded through him. "Are they okay?"

"They'll live."

Which meant superficial wounds, at best. "Thank you, God," he muttered. Or Great Spirit, Jahweh, Big Tortoise, whatever the hell you are. But don't think this squares us. One half-assed good deed after ten million evil ones hardly balances. Hell, bet you exact painful compensation for this little boon.

"When did they get back?" he asked.

"Early, about sunrise. It's past noon now. They've been released already."

He couldn't help a big smile. "Good ole Jonesy."

"Please continue, Sergeant," but there was a shared smile in her tone.

Okay. "When we got to the creek, the privates panicked and ran out and they got it from across the water." He looked to see if she caught the significance. She did. "I was trapped, so I slipped into the creek and drifted down. Guess I lost consciousness at some point …" he said, then pulled up the sheets and looked. Yep, naked. He swore.

"What is it, Sergeant?" she frowned.

"My clothes."

"They're being dried."

He swore even more, all protocol forgotten because the orderlies had, no doubt, rifled his pockets and that meant …

She reached below the cot and gently laid the waterproof cover, still damp, on his chest. Dad's book. He clasped it hard, and looked at her, gratitude clear on his face. "Thank you," he whispered.

Her expression didn't change, still hard and military, but the eyes were alight. "You are welcome, Sergeant. Did you see Eliot?"

"No, Major. Reds had his position, so I figured he bought it. But not before jackass gave them the password."

Long pause. "He didn't buy it, Sergeant. He made it back, he and his entire patrol. Unscathed."

"What?" He blinked. "Did he say what happened?"

"Yes, Sergeant, he did," her tone flat. "He said he was at rendezvous well past abort and you never showed and he was attacked and had to run."

Collier felt a slow burn rise in his chest, quite welcome, actually, because it helped his thawing. "That's crap. Pardon me, Major, but that's crap. He was not there. Not anywhere close."

"His GPS is accurate and his corporal, even his entire squad, confirms it."

"It's still crap, Major, I don't care how many of his people say it. They weren't there. The Reds were. And the

Reds had the countersign."

"I know," she spoke it quietly.

They looked at each other and Collier saw as much bewilderment and anger on her face as he felt. "What the hell is going on?"

She shook her head and pitched her voice as low as possible, "I don't know, but I'm working on it."

"Major, the countersign's bad enough, but they were waiting for us at the Creek, too."

She nodded. "Deavers said he was hit on our side, driven off the point."

"How's that possible?"

She paused, waiting for some clerk to push past the cots. "I really can't answer that right now, Sergeant." He took warning from her tone and shut up because she was damn sure going to find out. With bloody vengeance. He grinned inwardly. Her mind was a razor, seeing all possible paths, discarding the unlikely, leaving truth bare and clear. It'd kept them alive and actually thriving these past months. Caldwell got the credit, but she was the reason. And he had no doubts she would figure out what rat bastard had ruined this mission and almost got him and Jonesy killed.

She looked at him. "I wish I had the time to debrief you further, Sergeant," this she said loud enough to carry a few cots away, "but I have to get the 9-reports out. As soon as you can, write up everything and submit it. By tonight." She left without a backward glance.

He, and everybody else, watched her go. Eat your hearts out, boys, she's mine. And will be again at 2100. He drifted through one glorious image after another, the two of them embraced, locked, her eyes so deep and forever, pulling out his soul and whirling it into hers, dancing, just dancing across the night. God. He was warm now, hell, beyond warm. He lifted the sheets and took a look. Full recovery.

A warm bed, clean clothes, no wounds, a rare chance to catch a few hours of precious rack time, and a date when he woke up.

As Dad would say, "Groovy."

11

All the quarter-moon and starlight did was deepen the shadows, so Collier moved carefully across the giant brick pile that was once a Methodist church. One misstep and he'd go tumbling, break a few things while rousing the night patrols – what are you doing out here, Sergeant? Oh, just meeting my lover, you know, Major Arce? Our gorgeous intel officer? They'd shoot him right there. So, watch it, boy.

A few stumbles later, he quietly slid down the other side of the pile and onto cemetery moss. The starlight gathered here, silhouetting a geometric mess of canted gravestones, looming tombs, and even a column or two. Collier wondered how many of them marked long forgotten, long dissolved relatives. Odd: of all the places in all of shattered America where he and this last gasp of an Army could have ended up, it was Dad's old stomping grounds. There was portent in that, but he was damned if he could figure out what.

He got his bearings and headed towards a grouping of tombs forming a three-quarter amphitheater just off the center yard. He reached it and paused. A shadow detached from one side, alarming him until the shadow became

Rosa and they clutched each other, kissing hard and long and frantically. Restoration.

Desire was the guide and he opened her blouse and covered her smallish, hard breasts with his mouth and tongue, savoring their firmness and her response. She held him to her, barely restraining her gasps as he unbuttoned her trousers then slid down her stomach and found her, tasting her essence and gently, so gently, her center. Sound carried at night and she stifled her cries as much as she could but the pleasure was too much, far too much, and she inspired him to recklessness. Standing, he undid his fly and, holding her against the tomb, entered.

Their rhythm was ancient, impulse and response, that matched the whirling of the earth and dance of the stars. Something vital among the dead, and generations stirred from ghostly sleep and watched and remembered.

Matching his motion, supplementing it, her mouth buried against his shoulder, he felt her climax not only in the grasp, but in the satisfying tear of her painfully biting teeth and he simultaneously released, astonished as always by the power of it, the entire universe reduced to that one surge of overriding pleasure. There was nothing else but the pleasure.

"*Tu*," she whispered, "*quieres tu, mi amiguito, mi pasion, mi vida.*"

He didn't answer, didn't need to, only kissed her. He peaked and tilted and slowly spun to earth, a drifting feather of spent passion. They came apart naturally, quietly, but stood close, keeping the contact.

"Rosa," he finally breathed.

She shifted her hands behind his head and pushed him down to her neck, where he kissed the juncture at her shoulder. She sighed and rested her cheek in his hair. Collier wondered if a compassionate God would now move a bare Finger and freeze the universe, capturing them here in love and entwined. That would be all the Heaven he needed. But there was no Heaven, no compassionate God, either. Just His murderous world.

"Collier," she breathed, "Eliot tried to kill you."

"Not just that bastard," he said, rage quickening his voice. "Someone else, too. How else would the Reds have the counter AND the extraction point?"

She paused. "Deavers."

"Deavers?" He blinked against her neck. "What'd I ever do to him?"

"Nothing, as far as I know, so I'm trying to figure out why he'd go along. You think they're friends?"

He shook his head. "No. Eliot is pretty much hated by everyone, except fellow suck-ups. And something like this isn't Deavers' style. He'll stab you in the back, but in a nice way. Besides ..." He hesitated.

"Go on."

"Isn't this a bit beyond their collective capacity?"

She sighed. "It is. And that's what bothers me the most. Even with Deavers helping, Eliot's too stupid to pull off something this elaborate."

"Both of them together couldn't pull off a circle jerk. I think we have a traitor."

"A traitor?"

"Yes," he said, grimly. "The Reds were real intent on me not making it."

"What do you mean?"

Collier gave her the details of his nightmare escape through the woods and down the creek. "Pretty well-planned, doncha think?" he concluded.

"Yes," her voice was deadly. "Well beyond Eliot's ability. And Deavers. And just about everyone else here. Including me."

They fell into mutual thought. Collier broke it. "Why'd you put Eliot on this mission to begin with?"

"The Colonel told me to."

"Thought so. Why would he do that?"

Her next sigh was one of exasperation. "I don't know, and I think that's the key. I'm guessing someone pushed the Colonel to do it. Who's mad at you?"

"Who isn't?"

She wasn't amused. "Get serious. It has to be someone with the Colonel's ear. Palmer?"

He shook his head. "No. He and I are buds."

"One of your L-Ts?"

He snorted. "Who listens to L-Ts?"

"All right." She paused, thinking. "How 'bout Colonel Hoffman?"

He almost laughed out loud. "The exec? Phantom of the Opera."

"What?"

"Because you never see him."

She chuckled softly. "Have to remember that one. Problem is, all those guys are the best candidates. If it's none of them, then we're back to square one." She fell silent. Collier almost saw her brain glowing with the effort. He rested his ear against her skull to listen.

And almost lost the ear when she suddenly started, "Oh, God!"

"Take it easy," he said, rubbing the side of his head. "You've got it?" He warmed. He knew she would.

She hesitated before whispering, "The Colonel."

He was confused. "Well, yeah. He put Eliot on the mission."

"Because it was his plan."

Like hitting him with a baseball bat. "What?"

She let out a long breath. "The Colonel knows Eliot is a disaster, so it made no sense. But, now, it does."

"Why?"

She paused a moment before saying, "Because … I

think he knows about us, about this," she ran her hands down his sides. "He's jealous."

"How do you know?"

She snorted, "I know. He flat-out asked me to move into his tent once."

Collier felt a slow burn in his chest, "That sonofabitch. I'll drop a grenade on him."

"No, you won't. He's a man, it's normal. But thanks for *your* jealousy."

He grinned. "Look at you. I'm in a perpetual state of jealousy."

"Good, it keeps you on your toes."

"Actually, shorty, I think it's the other way around."

"That's Major Shorty to you," and they both giggled into each other's necks. "Shh, shh," she whispered, "don't get silly."

"Okay, okay, I'll behave. But, just because he's horny doesn't mean he knows."

"We have to assume he does."

Collier frowned. He hated assumptions. True, hard facts were his bread and butter. "I don't know, Rosa. Lot easier hiring a private to knife me."

"Yes, but then he has to deal with the private."

"That's easy, too." Collier paused. "No, this was way too complicated. Think about the arrangements, the contacts with the Reds."

"I know. But who else could it be?"

Now it was his turn to be silent. Yes, who else had the genius and resources to pull this off? Caldwell was about the only one who came immediately to mind but, c'mon, this was sure a long hard way to take care of what should be a small problem …

And then it was clear. "Two birds with one stone," he said.

"What do you mean?"

"He's baiting the Reds. And he's using me as the bait."

"What?"

"Do you remember a few weeks ago, that corporal who gave me Dad's book?"

"Yes, so?"

"He was from the 98th."

She paused. "I don't get it."

"The 98th's in touch with the 4th."

"And? Wait …" she thought about it. "A coordinated attack?"

"Maybe. It makes sense."

"But why kill you?"

"Two birds. Make the Reds think we're blind while getting rid of a rival."

She paused, considering, and the more Collier thought about it, the more sense it made, which was good on the one hand because the 4th could break their impasse, but bad on the other because the Colonel knew about them. "Hold on," she cut into his thoughts. "Something's not right."

"Tell me."

"It doesn't explain Eliot being out of position."

He mused. "You're right. It doesn't. If anything, it would look better if Eliot was caught in the same ambush. And the Reds knew way too much."

"So something else is going on."

"Yes. No. Maybe. I don't know." He frowned hard into the dark. "All right, then let's assume" – God, he hated that word – "the 4th isn't coming, isn't even in the picture. Do you think the Colonel might be brewing up one of his patented miracles, instead?"

"I … can't say."

"Can't, or won't?"

She let out a long breath and refused to speak. "So,

won't," Collier concluded. "Okay, respect that it's close-hold-burn-before-reading Top Secret mofo, but you know I don't talk, and the situation means lives. Or one life. Mine, for example."

He felt anger course through her. "Look, Sergeant, you know better than to try that crap with me."

"Yes." His voice was soothing, to parry the frenzied Aztec warrior she could easily become. "And I do not want details, but, if there's something you've seen that gives weight, at least confirm it."

She was still, pulsing, the warrior finding her level, then she said, "I've noticed some things."

"Okay."

"He's ... distracted. And he's using off-channel communications."

"Huh?" Collier was surprised. "What are those?"

"Couriers."

"Everyone uses couriers."

"But they're not the usual ones, from HQ."

"Like Price?"

"Who?"

"The corporal who brought me Dad's book. Him?"

"Yes." Worry in her voice.

"Price met with the Colonel?"

She nodded in the dark and Collier clucked his disapproval. "I didn't know that."

"You're not *supposed* to know that, so now I'm up for court-martial," she said with resignation, then gently kissed his neck. "As if this wasn't enough."

"Your secret's safe with me." He patted her shoulder. "So, what do you think that means?"

"That it's more likely we are coordinating with the 4th than doing something on our own."

"Okay," Collier said, "I'll buy that. A strike south, with help from the 4th. Still doesn't explain Eliot being out of position."

"No ... no, it doesn't. Nor does it explain the passwords and Deavers. Which makes me think the Colonel tried to kill you, but a traitor is involved, too."

He blinked. "Explain."

"The Colonel didn't need all these elaborate measures to ensure the grab failed. Assigning Eliot to the mission was enough. The rest of it ensured you didn't get that captured Red to me."

"Which means ..." Collier picked up her thought, "... that Red knew some real important shit."

"Vulgarism aside," she replied, "yes. And the only thing a low-level grunt would know that would be extremely valuable to us is troop movements."

He started. "Troop movements? Like, the Reds are moving on our flanks or something?"

"Yes."

Collier whistled softly. "Holy shit. Vulgarity intended."

They both stood face to face, the dark unable to conceal the sudden worry on both their faces. "Do you remember that old movie, *A Perfect Storm*?" she whispered.

"Uh." Boy, right out of left field. "Yeah. Vaguely. Why?"

"It was about two storm systems coming together at the worst possible time."

"Okay. Not getting it."

"If the Colonel is engineering another one of his patented miracles, as you say, at the same time the Reds are making moves on our flanks, then the result will be awful."

He frowned. "Are you calling this a coincidence, then?"

"No," she said, "I'm calling it a disaster in the

making. Whoever this traitor is, he knows the Colonel is up to something."

"But … how can he know? The Colonel never tells anyone what he's doing. Not even you." Collier added that last with emphasis because it was true: the man took no counsel, just brooded in his tent or commandeered house, issuing odd orders for baffling movements until they all looked at each other like the guy was crazy, dancing them on the edge of disaster and then, *boom*! They were smashing through the Reds' lines in a way no one expected. Guy was freakin' Napoleon or Patton, whoever.

She raised imploring hands. "But he's *always* planning something. The Reds know that. So, they take it into account and strike first."

Collier considered. If the Reds got on their flanks without them knowing, then any brilliant plan would go very wrong very fast. Collier had a sudden vision: long lines of ragged, starved soldiers herded down harsh country roads to hastily dug ditches. One rank after another gunned down, falling in formation, almost perfectly in unison. Rosa falls with them. He went cold.

"So, after last night's goat rope, we're blind. Whether the Colonel intended that or not, the traitor did. The Colonel thinks he's pulling a fast one, getting rid of me in the process, and the Reds are laughing. Good God." He paused. "Who is this guy?"

"The traitor?" Her turn to pause. "I don't know, but it has to be someone very close to us."

"Me, f'rinstance?" He said it flippantly.

"Or me." Not flippant, and Collier chilled. Yes, that close.

"I think we need more info," he whispered.

"We do."

"I'll see what I can get from Eliot."

"Don't kill him."

"Why not?"

"Because … he's just a shovelhead."

He chuckled, "All the more reason." She said nothing. "All right," he replied, "I won't, but I'll make him think I'm going to."

"Good. Thank you." She listened to the breeze for a moment and stared at the sinking moon. "There is one more thing I need before we go." She kneeled and kissed him and took him in, slow at first then more frenzied and he gasped, losing himself.

God, budge a Finger. Freeze this night. Please.

12

No time like the present. Collier loitered in the shadows of Battalion's main building, the glowing tip of a crappy issue-cigarette the only giveaway. He looked at it and grimaced. Ugh, dry and harsh and offensive to his trained palate. Remember all that anti-smoking hoo-haw back when you were a kid? This is the reason why.

He chuckled and took a half-hearted puff, fighting an urge to fling the cig away. Needed an excuse for standing here. While inside-smoking-bans had pretty much disappeared, a lot of grunts still chose the yard because it was a handy way to get out of a detail, get off by yourself, get a rare moment to think, reflect, plan. Desert or stay, cut and run, hold and fight, which? Everybody was thinking about it; each day, a lot more were acting on it – went out for a quiet smoke and a quiet walk to a carefully hidden stash and away, running the gauntlet of Blue and Red patrols, 50-50 chance of getting through and finally, maybe, home. Or what used to be home.

Can't blame them. Defeat loomed. The Ghosts had swerved out of the Red's grasp for months, but fingers were now twining about their collar. Endless patrolling and shelling and snipers, and the relentless, fanatical, sureness of an enemy exuding a confidence that, no matter how much we dodged, they'd have us, was beating them all down, and no one wanted to end up in those ragged lines on the edge of a long, long ditch. Best take your chances with the night.

So why not go with them?

He took another sorry puff. Good question. Instead of waiting for deserters at the obvious escape points and unceremoniously blowing their brains out as they stumbled up – oh crap, let me explain, Sarge, *pow*! – why not just turn a blind eye? Hell, should lead them. Better chance of getting away. But he wouldn't.

Because Rosa wouldn't. And, because of the memories.

Image: Dad, standing at the spot on Little Round Top where Chamberlain braced for Oates' screaming Alabamians, saying, "Coll, here, right here, a lowly little nothing officer, out of his element, a school teacher, for God's sake, saved America. History turns on such people." Collier'd spent most of that trip jonesing for a Playstation, but that particular moment stayed with him. Some months later, Collier asked Dad if he had ever saved America and the old man just laughed and said, "About a dozen times a day." Made no sense then but it did now: Dad proudly slipping his badge into his pocket, Mom packing Collier's lunch and nagging about homework, both of them driving three hours one way to watch him play Fishburne football, bringing homemade cookies and the latest CD – all that was America. Dad and Mom and coaches and teachers and friends and lovers looked down the years at him with expectation. Save it. Save America, Collier.

He was damn sure going to try.

The door to his left opened quietly, the blackout curtain dark upon dark and Collier eyed the two or three privates who walked out and off the porch, heading towards the latrines. They glanced at his barely visible shadow and sidled out of reach as they sullenly passed, eyes turned down. Collier watched them safely out of range.

The door spilled out more privates. Excellent, he'd timed this just right. Lights-out fast approached and everyone was making their head calls now because Taps violations meant instant execution. So, any moment now … yes, there. Eliot.

Didn't even glance around. What an idiot. In this Army, you constantly checked six.

Collier moved behind Eliot's right shoulder and palm-heeled him viciously behind the ear. "Fuck!" Eliot yelped as he stumbled forward. Collier grabbed his collar and kicked him hard behind the right knee, slamming Eliot down. "*Auch!*" Eliot fumbled at a bayonet. Collier kicked it across the yard and, in the same motion, ground Eliot's fingers under his boot. "Talk, you piece of shit."

"*Oww!* What the fuck, Rashkil?" Eliot scrambled at Collier's boot but Collier leaned forward, increasing the pressure. Eliot yelled louder, clutching at Collier's leg. A good shuto to the side of Eliot's pointy little head knocked him back against the porch. "Talk."

"Sonofabitch! Sonofabitch! What the hell you doin', Rashkil, what the hell? I'll get the fuckin' Provost on you, you bastard!"

"So, yell for 'em. Let's see what's left of you by the time they get here."

Eliot paled. He sobbed and drew in air, "I didn't do anything wrong."

"You didn't do anything *right*. You didn't do anything *at all*, fucker! You got two of my people killed and damn near me, Jonesy, and Swift, too. Was that the plan? You fucked up, then, 'cause we're back and I've got your ass now. So talk!"

Eliot tried to pull his hand out but Collier bore down and Eliot screamed, "Motherfucker! I was there! You never showed! I didn't do anything wrong!"

"You *weren't* there, cocksucker! I *did* show and you left us, man!" Collier leaned into it.

"What the hell is going on here?"

Collier looked up while maintaining boot pressure, his hand falling to the .45. A couple of MPs stood off the porch. One of them flipped a flashlight beam into Collier's eyes. "Turn that off!" Collier snarled. The two MPs started as they recognized him, then looked at each other. "Sorry, Sergeant, sorry," they mumbled and backed away, melting into the compound.

Collier cleared his dazzled eyes and stared down at Eliot, "No help coming, motherfucker. Talk."

Eliot groaned, "I did what I was supposed to do. You were in the wrong place."

Collier grabbed Eliot's crushed hand out from under his boot and savagely twisted Eliot's thumb until he heard a satisfying *snap*! Eliot screamed. There was some commotion by the door and a couple of heads peered out. They quickly disappeared.

Collier jogged Eliot's useless thumb, grinding the broken bits together, and then twisted his wrist up and over, holding it tight. "This goes next."

Eliot was crying, "You cocksucker, you asshole, you broke my fucking thumb. I didn't do anything wrong. I was where I was told to be."

"The fuck you were," Collier wrenched Eliot's wrist to the breaking point. "You were nowhere near Major Arce's staging point." Collier stared hard at him. "I'm going to enjoy snapping your knees."

"I didn't go where Arce told me to!"

Collier blinked. "Why?"

"My orders got changed. Please, Rashkil, my hand …"

Collier tweaked the wrist, making Eliot yelp, "Who changed them? Tell me, you bastard, or you'll be whacking off with your left hand the rest of your life."

Eliot choked, hesitating, and Collier increased the pressure, "Okay, okay, fuck! It was the Colonel! The Colonel changed them."

"What are you talking about?"

"After the Major's brief," Eliot was openly crying now, "the Colonel came up to me and cancelled the orders. Gave me a new location."

"Where?"

"About a quarter mile farther north."

"And you didn't question it? You didn't tell Arce? Me? No one?" Eliot said nothing. "And keeping the old GPS coordinates, was that the Colonel's idea, too? Was it?"

Eliot looked off, tears streaming down his eyes. Collier's rage flared, a volcano in his stomach roaring hot and white up his chest and throat. He flung Eliot's hand down hard, the thumb leading and Eliot went fetal from the pain, a small breath escaping from his lips. Collier pulled out the .45 and flipped the safety off, leveling the barrel at Eliot's head. Eliot stared, horror paralyzing his features, as Collier snarled, "You gave them the countersign, you bastard."

Eliot's brow furrowed and genuine puzzlement crossed his face, "What?"

Collier stopped the trigger about halfway. Eliot was an asshole, a craven wretch deserving of an old-fashioned *coup de grâce*, but he didn't know about the countersign.

Which meant someone else disclosed it. And, in a half-second, Collier knew who.

He re-holstered, took a step away, and then skipped

across the porch boards, kicking Eliot hard in the chin. Eliot's head bounced twice and he went limp. "Bastard," Collier spat and walked away.

13

"Colonel," Rosa stood at ramrod attention, *"here're the reports from last night's grab."*

He didn't even look up. She laid the papers on the edge of others scattered about his desk and watched him closely, looking for anything – a tic, a twitch, some sign of nervousness – but he was unruffled. Either he was the world's greatest actor or nothing was going on with him.

Let's see. "Colonel, we have a security breach."

That got his attention. He looked up, genuine surprise on his face, and actually laughed. "What do you base that on?"

She turned her radars on full blast, searching his face, "The Reds were waiting at the staging point, sir. They were deployed right across the intersection. Even worse, sir, they were across the Creek. We lost two privates and almost the non-comms." That, in itself, should give him concerns, given the rarity of trained sergeants.

Even if one of them was her lover, you jealous bastard.

He blinked once and shrugged, "Reds patrol, too, Major, just like we do. There are only so many places to look for us and the Reds can read maps as well as we can.

Coincidence, very unfortunate coincidence." He dropped back to his papers.

Her brows rose. Wow, Colonel, that's it? Need to throw some gas on this fire. "Coinciding with Eliot being way out of position?"

He eyed her, a storm settling on his brow like clouds forming over a distant butte. An apt description, with his chiseled forehead wrinkled like a washboard and those dark, dark eyes set so far back they were almost hidden. He grabbed the reports and fumbled through them, stopping to read here and there. She waited. "According to this," he gestured a page at her, "he *was* in position, verified by his GPS and patrol."

"He was out of position, sir," she said it firmly, quietly.

"That certain, are you?"

"Yessir, absolutely certain, despite what he says in his report. He wasn't there."

"And you base that on ..." his eyebrows rose and he turned his hand, inviting comment.

"The survivors' testimony, sir."

"Survivors?"

"Jones, Swift. And Rashkil." She purposely emphasized the last, testing for reaction, but the Colonel remained impassive. Great actor? How do you tell?

"So, there appears to be a conflict," he pursed his lips. "All right, I'll speak to Eliot." He stared at the papers for a moment more and then dropped them on top of a side pile, gesturing a dismissal.

She made no move to leave.

He ignored her well past propriety and she heard an edge in his voice when he finally said, without looking up, "Was there something else, Major?"

"Yes, sir," she paused. "The Reds had the patrol countersign."

He looked up sharply, a frown creasing his lips into an empty half-moon and she read, for a moment, confusion in his eyes. So, that's unexpected. Maybe he wanted to kill Collier, but not at the cost of security. Further proof of a traitor in the mix.

"How do you know that?"

She took a breath, "When Rashkil approached the entry, he couldn't raise Eliot on the radio. He called out and got the counter. When his patrol stepped out, the Reds opened up."

The Colonel glanced down at the papers, "That's in here?"

"Yes, sir." But not everything, of course. She had told Jonesy to leave that out of his report. Collier was the Colonel's obvious target, so why expand the list? Besides, it made Jones and Swift hold cards, should she need them.

"Rashkil must have gotten it wrong."

"That's not like him, sir."

Too quick, and the Colonel peered at her for moments way past comfortable, the caves where his eyes lurked sparkling and scrutinizing. She held herself tight but felt a tremor or two escape through her legs.

"Well," he said, dryly, "there's a first time for everything, Major, but I will look into it," and he gave a no-more-nonsense wave of his hand.

She blinked. Rather underwhelmed, wasn't he? Maybe this was just one more disaster to deal with and he needed to show calm, or thought it was just crap.

Push, Rosa.

"Sir," she said quietly, "have I given you reason to doubt me?"

He looked puzzled. "No. Why?"

"You seem to be doubting me now."

He sat back in his chair. "How so, Major?"

She gestured at the report, "I expected a little more

concern from you, sir. It's as if you're not taking this seriously."

A small grin gathered at the corners of his lips and the caves sparkled with amusement, "Major, I did say I would look into it. This isn't some kind of feminist protest, is it?"

What? Did he think she was a lightweight? "No sir, not at all, not even close," she responded tightly, her cheeks burning. "What I've told you demands elevated concern."

"And you don't believe I'm showing that? Perhaps you are misreading me."

Was she? She scrutinized him. His reaction was like Mom's, when Rosa had run teary-eyed into the den and told her that Poppy had choked to death in bed from that odd sickness sweeping through the building and Mommy, sitting on the floor, already wheezing just like Poppy, only nodded. Or like Rosa's, as she watched the last of her sisters go the same way.

She was struck dumb by the sudden rush of memories, flashing from one corpse to another, and he took her silence as assent. "Perhaps so. Perhaps, Major, you are overworked. We all are, I know. These days, staying alive is more than a full-time job but perhaps for you more than others, what with your," he paused significantly, "extracurricular activities." And he stared at her.

She rocked back, surprise showing full on her face but unable to contain it. He knows! She calculated how quickly she could reach across the desk and choke the Colonel out, find Collier and get away, just get away, before he recovered and had them clapped in irons. But the Colonel was a big man and there'd be a struggle and his guards would rush in and she and Collier would be ruined, shot at dawn, so stay your hand. Paranoia may be putting more meaning into his words than it should. She held her breath.

"You're undertaking far too many missions, of course," he said, throwing her into simultaneous relief and confusion because it didn't *feel* like his true meaning, "far too many. That's admirable because you are keeping us alive but there's a cost. Exhaustion, mistakes, and you lose perspective." He paused, frowning, his gaze going somewhere else. "Keep that in mind. I rely on you. Don't burn out. In the meantime, cancel all grabs until I figure out what's going on. And, put Eliot and Deavers on the north lines."

He might as well have hit her with a hammer. "Colonel, what?"

He blinked at her, some puzzlement on his face, "Was I unclear? Cancel all your grabs until I'm sure everything is fine. And Eliot and Deavers screwed up, so put them up north, where they'll do the least damage. Is that clear, now?" He turned to his papers again, and this was a dismissal she couldn't ignore.

She saluted and marched out smartly past the guards and down the hallway of this weird three-story house they used as a command post right here in the middle of Pemberton. Too damned close to the Red lines but sheltered by a hill and surrounded by enough people that snipers or suicide attacks weren't an issue.

She paused on the landing and did a Bugs Bunny head shake. WTF? Stop the grabs? Was he crazy?

Maybe. But, maybe not. She considered. Okay, the Colonel was blown away by the countersign information but couldn't show it. Didn't want to panic the troops, doncha know, so he'd look into it himself. Then he'd tell her to resume patrols, no further explanations offered, but there'd be a couple of staffers missing and best not to ask questions, Major. The Colonel had resources Rosa could only guess at, which was assuring and frightening at the same time. It meant there were things going on she didn't know about.

Like, an upcoming breakout?

She shook her head and went downstairs. The guards along the way eyed her but stopped well short of a leer because she'd break their necks in about a half-second. All that hapkido Poppy made her take. *"No, florita, no, no puedes abandonar, continues, hasta yo digo 'Basta,'"* even though she cried and pouted and her back and arms hurt and the bigger kids had thrown her around like a rag doll and she just could not understand why Poppy was torturing her. She did now.

She headed towards her office, staying close to the doors and away from the railing that overlooked the first floor and main entrance. Best not present a random target to some disgruntled guard or aggrieved sergeant. Such an odd building: all the rooms were on one side with the other open to the stairs. She shrugged. Jersey, what did you expect?

She opened the door. Corporal Awbrey sat behind his desk frowning at some papers. Dammit! She'd told him to leave before Taps!

"Corporal!" Exasperated. He looked up and jumped to his feet, still frowning. Nothing new there; Awbrey always frowned. If he weren't so damned efficient, she'd have shot him months ago simply for his air of gloom. "Why are you still here?" Gawd, he *never* left. A lot of officers would admire that, but the little twerp got on her nerves.

"I wanted to make sure you got the last reports of the day, Ma'am," he spoke more to the top of the desk than to her and she felt her irritation rising.

"You'll have to sleep in the office tonight, you know."

"Yes, Ma'am." Flat, uncommitted tone.

"Did you eat?"

He didn't answer and she sighed, walked over to one of her filing cabinets, and unlocked it. She fished around and located her late night stash: new issue MRE, mostly cornmeal and salt with a can of Spam inside. She tossed it to him and he caught it one-handed, rather deft. "That'll have to do for now, Corporal. You know where the Sterno is inside the bathroom? Good. Don't burn the place down."

He looked at the packet, then looked at her and there was a mixed sense of worship and anger in his gaze, as if he were deciding whether her largesse was true concern or just expediency. Bingo on the latter. Wouldn't do to have her clerk collapse from starvation. Still, she could have made him dip into his own stock of canned crap. But canned crap was harder and harder to find, even by world-class scroungers, and Awbrey was hardly in their league and hardly had the time to even look, since he seemed to spend most of his waking hours watching her. So, there was some compassion involved.

"Thank you, Ma'am," he mumbled, and gingerly placed the packet on the desk, as if it would fly away or something. She shook her head and moved to her inner office door.

"Ma'am," Awbrey cleared his throat.

"Yes?" she arched an official eyebrow.

"One of Rashkil's privates came by about an hour ago." Wow, the venom in his voice! "He said Rashkil was due back in the clinic at 1300."

Less than four hours have passed, and Collier wanted to see her again? Must have some really important information ... or a really bad case of the Rosa. She smiled inwardly as she casually glanced at her watch. An hour to go, then Collier would emerge from shadow and they'd both merge into shadow, joined, one, filled ... she looked at Awbrey, noted his narrowed expression, and mentally slapped herself. God, Rosa, are you getting sloppy or something? "All right, Corporal. Did the private say if Rashkil was cleared for duty?"

Awbrey shrugged, still eyeing her while she settled her breath and hoped her flush cleared. Need a distraction. "Was that a 'no,' Corporal, or an 'I don't know'?"

"I don't know, Ma'am."

"You should have found that out. We have other missions to perform and a dwindling supply of personnel to conduct them. Maybe you'd like to go on one?" He blanched and she almost chuckled. Awbrey was as far from field capable as Collier was office capable. She left him uncomfortable for a moment longer before saying, "Go eat, Corporal."

He looked at her fully, then scooped up the package and sidled out of the door, heading towards the bathrooms, which, another odd feature of this house, were separate from the apartments. Must have been some kind of hostel or something Before. She glanced around, ensured her door and everything else she controlled was secured, then slipped downstairs. She walked past the guard, ignoring his almost insubordinate, "Good night, Major," and stepped onto the midnight porch.

She stilled, listening for odd movements, took a casual stroll past the steps then suddenly dropped over the rail and into the bushes. She ran lightly, silently around the house and up the street, staying in shadows. Curfew did not apply to her, of course, but she didn't want other eyes on her, questioning, remembering, wondering. She didn't want to be seen. Except by one man.

She faded into the rubble of the church.

14

The stars were in their early spring patterns. Cold now, but not for long and sap runs and eyes open and faith and hope stir. Rosa frowned. She didn't feel much hope. Faith, yes, a spark of that, but she suspected it was more resignation than belief. No way this miserable existence, this unnecessary war, could last much longer. Everyone wanted to go home; whoever stayed could claim victory.

Okay, Reds, you win.

She chuckled. Would that be so bad? The Reds had odd and unworkable theories for organizing society, but at least it was organization; not like this ongoing kleptocracy of an American government, with its Byzantine palace intrigue. Sure, there'd be slave camps and forced labor and wholesale shootings. But at least the war'd be over ...

God, listen to yourself.

She shook her head. Rather die in a foxhole, bleeding and exhausted and out of bullets, than let someone else steal my life. Too many someones had already done so; some faceless, like the al-Qa'eda bastards who ended the world; some with faces, leering over her outstretched, stunned and just-raped body. Dying while fighting the faceless-and-faced is honorable. So is dying for the ones you loved who cannot fight anymore, and the ones still fighting, even if you end up a rag-tattered pile of bones, half-buried on some forgotten battlefield.

Feeling a bit down, are we?

She almost chuckled at that. Well, yeah. Things weren't going well. And they should be going well, should be, because they were the good guys.

Or, at least, they used to be.

She couldn't point out a specific day or event when things changed. It was gradual, like a fungus through a loaf of bread. Maybe it started with the running battle across Pennsylvania that had made them Ghosts, tattoo and all. She slapped her own, the one Collier put there after she'd come across Jonesy and him, flush with a successful combat, lancing it with sharpened ballpoint pens into each other's arms. She'd asked for one and Collier stepped right up and carved it, a blaze of life and triumph lighting his almond eyes. They'd made love the first time that night and, next day, ran towards Philadelphia, dodging, twisting, striking suddenly at an exposed Red flank, the Colonel directing them with an almost supernatural sense.

The resurrected Stonewall Brigade: starving, hurt, driven, but dangerous. A wounded animal, but not mortally so, slipping down forgotten trails and side roads, stealing marches on the converging enemy, striking from unsuspected directions and escaping into the dark. There, over there, the Colonel, standing at some hidden trailhead and we look at him with awe and silently raise our helmets in tribute as we ghost by seeking the next opportunity. The righteous armies of the Lord, reclaiming this blasted land, this broken country. And yet, they were the ones driven. Still hunted. Still losing.

Not because they were Ghosts. Because they were Blues.

The Blues, the Armed Forces of these once United States of America, which sends out Draft Gangs to seize children and old men as cannon fodder, grown women as front line soldiers, and young girls for the officers' tents. Forget the young men; they're Blues already, or Reds. Or dead. The Gangs confiscate a family's winter food, any working cars, and the last drops of hoarded gasoline for the Army, and a family's gold and jewelry and heirlooms for themselves, stashing them for easy retrieval when everything, finally, collapses. The Blues execute traitors, defined as anyone who disagrees with them, bulldozes the traitors' homes, shoots their relatives. And if a Blue wants a promotion, he kills the one above him, the ones below who threaten, and then forms alliances with like-minded murderers.

It's how you make general in the Blues.

She moved restlessly. The Ghosts had kept a lot of that to a minimum, which meant they were still blessed with competent sergeants like Collier and Jonesy. And they all threw a protective net around the Colonel. The Ghosts were a bright spot, a shining point of light in the ugly, evil thing the Blues had become. A celebrated unit, in service to an evil cause. Just like the Stonewall Brigade.

And how did that work out?

She watched a shadow in the shadows move stealthily across the moss, blending from tomb to tomb, making its way to her. It hesitated so she stepped out. Collier caught the motion and turned, trying to gather her but she held him off. He stiffened and looked around. "What's wrong?" he whispered.

"I don't know," barely audible, "nothing. Everything."

He crouched, peering hard into the dark, listening.

She sighed, "I don't mean right here."

"What, then?"

"I just don't know."

"Okay," he stood there, confused, but respecting her sense. She warmed. Completion, that's what she felt with him. Mommy had told her true love was everything in its place. With Collier, everything was.

"Are you okay?" he asked, after a moment.

"Yes. And no."

He nodded and looked away, disappointment radiating from him. She understood. She ached for him, too; even in combat she ached for him, but that was hardly the time.

It felt like combat now.

"Sorry," she whispered, after a minute, meaning … everything. A pause. "You called this meeting."

"After you gave us the mission brief, the Colonel told Eliot to change positions."

"What?" Hit her with a sledgehammer ...

... and then followed up with a maul. "Eliot didn't give the password to the Reds."

Stunned, speechless. "Who did?"

He looked at her. "C'mon, Rosa, it's obvious."

It was.

Some aspects of classified missions – like time and locations – could be deduced from general orders. Say, those prohibiting fire-support missions in sector whatever from 0100-0500. And also by logic: "Reds can read maps as well as we can." But not passwords. The only ones who knew them were mission members; in this case, the grab team, and Eliot. Deavers only knew the ones for extraction, which weren't at issue. The grab team didn't give them up. Eliot didn't give them up. Neither did she.

But the Colonel, who was not part of the brief, made surreptitious contact with Eliot. And changed Eliot's position. The Reds were there, instead. With the password.

C'mon, Rosa, it's obvious.

Which means ... her commander, the legendary Colonel Caldwell of the Ghosts, was in direct contact with the enemy.

No.

The world spun crazily, axes gone wild, the ground canting at wrong angles.

No. No way. She refused to accept it. She would not believe it. No. Absolutely not.

But *hija*, Poppy's voice whispered, the Colonel made you take Eliot. Then he changed Eliot's orders without telling you. And the Reds had the password. How else would they get it? *Hija*. Listen.

But, Poppy, for God's sake, why?

She looked at Collier's grim outline. "For God's sake, why?" she whispered.

"Like I said, two birds with one stone."

"No." She dismissed that. "Because there was no need to move Eliot."

"Maybe he likes Eliot too much to get him killed."

She didn't have to answer that, just cocked her head in a "Really?" angle.

"Okay, okay," he said, "so maybe he needs him for later."

"Later? To do what?"

"I was hoping you could tell me."

She nodded. Yes, you're right, Sergeant, that's my job. All right, *tranquiles*, *hija*, think. How does it benefit the Colonel to keep Eliot out of the ambush?

Let's see ...

A failed grab mission convinces the Reds that we're blind, at least for the short term, and now would be a good time to press our lines, break through, sweep into our middle. So they attack. As the Reds come screaming across the water, the Colonel springs a trap, collapsing the flanks on them.

Chancellorsville.

She blinked. Jackson's greatest battle, won by a flank march the Union didn't suspect. And, like Chancellorsville, secrecy was paramount: don't let anyone know what you're planning. So, send out a grab mission, but make sure it fails by not only putting a shovelhead like Eliot in a critical position but then ordering him off that position and tipping off the Reds. Not trying to save Eliot; trying to absolutely make sure the grab fails. Because … if the patrol gets killed and the Reds spur and storm across the creek, they fall right into the Ghosts' waiting arms. A regrettable sacrifice of good men on that patrol, but the results, the results … brilliant. She thrilled.

For a moment.

Because ... all of this was just so … unnecessary. Sabotaging the grab was unnecessary: all the Colonel had to do was open a little gap between Deavers and Collin that the Reds would certainly find. Put Collier and Jonesy and the rest of the hard-corps Ghosts about two echelons back of that. Reds surge across, are stopped cold, then the Colonel lays waste to the bastards with a pre-set artillery bombardment.

Except …

There's no pre-set artillery. There's no pre-set anything.

A chill ran through her. No platoons have been quietly pulled off-line and repositioned to blunt an attack. No stockpiles have been moved, no guns re-zeroed; no one, in other words, was in any position to take a sudden Red push. They were still deployed to meet an attack across their front; no depth, one measly reserve at the high school with the artillery and an even smaller reserve with Division at Wrightstown – paper pushers, so no help. A concerted Red effort now would break them in half. Not easily, of course, and the Reds would pay dearly, but break them it would. If the Colonel wanted a Chancellorsville, then it was too late.

Too late.

Her eyes narrowed. This wasn't a well-planned and brilliant Jacksonian maneuver. Not at all. This was something else altogether, and as much as she didn't want to believe it, could be only one thing.

Jealousy.

The Colonel was now the green-eyed monster. Livid, embarrassed, raging that you, *hija*, spend yourself with a lowly sergeant instead of him, him! An almost mythic leader. He cannot understand why. Isn't the Colonel desirable? Isn't he brilliant? In his roughened way, handsome? How could you resist?

Very simply, Colonel. You do not complete me. You do not.

So this becomes a Greek tragedy. And the Colonel rips out his own eyes.

She swayed. Collier caught at her and she folded into him, seeking the places she fit, and the warmth there.

"Oh, God, Collier, the Colonel did all this just to kill you. All of this, every bit of it. There is no sneaky little traitor. It's all him. All of it. He knows about us, he knows, and he's insanely jealous, and he's willing to destroy the Ghosts to see you dead," she whispered.

Collier was silent, then said grimly, "I'll see him dead first."

"No!" she whispered, harsh into his ear.

"But—"

"No!" she insisted, louder and more fierce, pulling him hard to her.

Clink.

The noise came from somewhere near the brick pile. It was probably just some rat, but they didn't hesitate. They pulled apart and melted into the dark, taking their separate, pre-planned escape routes without another word between them.

15

"Dropping off, picking up," Price said while handing papers through the passenger window to a suspicious private waving an M-16. A couple of other privates hovered behind a barricade of rusted cars and crap built right across the intersection of Little River Turnpike and Lee Highway, the barrels of two M-60s poking through and aimed right at Price. Took things a bit serious 'round here, did they? Price wondered if that was due to Reds or just being in the Zone ... ha, like extra security warded the Flu. Maybe some Breakout freaks still lurked in the ruins. That would certainly make *him* cautious.

The private was taking her sweet time with the papers, so Price settled and looked out the window. His two companions maintained silence, which suited Price just fine. He'd sized them up about four hours ago when they stopped for him on 340 just north of New Market: big guys, torn-up faces, surly. Goons. He'd seen them around, of course; after a few weeks, you see everyone at the truck park. But he didn't know them and was surprised that Leideig did; knee breaking wasn't the Colonel's style; a bullet to the back of the head was. They made him uneasy, and Price's hand kept drifting towards his pistol.

The goon next to him kept a finger on his own.

Another thing made him uneasy: the trip was uneventful. Price always ran into some kind of trouble: a Red raid or screwed up papers, sadistic MPs, something. Not this time. Only a ten-or-twenty-second delay at the eight or so checkpoints they hit on the way to Markham. Smooth. Amazingly smooth. Why was that?

Maybe because they'd avoided 81 and 66. Too many trucks careened all over those roads and the Reds loved to hit them, taking supplies, prisoners, and a few lives in the process. Command still didn't get it, still scheduled shipments along both routes. Must be the sight of those four- and six-lane concrete ribbons, long and inviting and still drivable, despite five years of neglect. Pricked a memory, he guessed – summer vacations and car trips and the sense of freedom – but they invited a rather unnecessary death now. Price used the unknown side roads, remembered from his days running with Pap, thereby reducing his encounters with unnecessary death.

But those side roads were disturbing. So many dead towns. Some of them, like New Market, were still active, troops running around and all. Others, like Luray, were ghosts. Nothing moved, not even dogs, and there was a hollowness to the streets, the houses just skulls. He could make a fortune from all the jewelry and art and clothing moldering inside them, but no. Price wasn't a grave robber.

The Event. He remembered it: Granny crying and wringing her hands in front of CNN for days on end and Pap beside her on the couch, silent and grim. Henry stayed away from the screen and its horrors, running through the woods, savoring the life there. But the Event was nothing compared to Breakout, when hordes of Flu-infected creatures poured out of the Zone, slaughtering and raping and spreading the virus. That had been the end of the world.

Henry was in the regulars then, shanghaied from the Provos all the way out to Kansas, already on 'special duty' with some little Major named Leideig who had just started his little business, when the hordes appeared. Price hid in a barn somewhere near Overlook, waiting out the creatures and the persons fleeing them and the waves of death both brought. He emerged, weeks later, sure the world was empty but, surprise, half of his unit, including Leideig, was still there. So he went back, because there was nowhere else to go.

No court-martial, no questions. The desperate shortage of personnel saved him, especially when the Korean and Saudi deployments came home, got mad, and joined the budding Reds. Weren't so budding after that. Leideig had carried him along the winds of Army vagary until here Price was, only 200 miles from home. Hadn't gone back there yet. He didn't want to see Pap's and Granny's bones tangled in the sheets of their iron-post bed.

Papers waving under Price's nose startled him awake. The private stood there, annoyed. "You want these or not?" Goon #1 glanced at Price with a hint of contempt and Price wrote himself a mental note to kick the craphead's ass when they finished the run. Goon had a point, though; letting someone get that close to the truck without noticing was stupid. Reverie gets you killed.

"Do you know where the courthouse is?" the private asked.

Price nodded and the private shrugged, stepped off the running board, and waved the barrier open. Price caught the driver's eye and pointed straight ahead. The truck lurched. Price glanced at the checkpoint guards: bored, no interest. Good.

Price pointed the way through the intersection of

Chain Bridge Road and up the winding hill to Main Street. Bigger checkpoint here, a sergeant in charge, but he gave them no more guff than the other places. "Go around the courthouse," the sergeant directed, "then take a left opposite the building." The sergeant stepped away. Price raised an eyebrow at the driver and, in moments, they had backed against a loading dock.

Price dropped down, heading towards the tailgate. Getting dark, which meant dinner was more on the minds of passersby than some after-hours truck. The two goons appeared on the other side and looked at Price. He nodded, and they slipped off to ensure passersby remained so.

Price walked up the steps and through the access door into a gloomy hallway filled with boxes and dust. He followed shuttered and dark offices along a passage that opened into a big bay with more boxes and crates, and even a dead forklift or two. Light and voices came from the other side and Price slid that way, keeping to the shadows.

Two persons stood in another entrance: Colonel Ostroff and some sergeant. Price scrutinized the area until he was satisfied, then stepped out.

"Ah, Corporal Price!" Ostroff called out, "Good to see you again!" Price responded with a wary nod. The Colonel was overly affectionate, always urging Price to stay overnight, take a room near his. No thanks.

The Colonel held Price's gaze for a moment and then nodded at the sergeant, who walked off. Ostroff smiled, "I trust it was an uneventful trip?"

"Yes, sir." Price kept his voice bland. No need to encourage the dear fellow.

"As expected." The Colonel walked over and patted Price gently on the shoulder. Price remained impassive, hoping the Colonel got the message because Price didn't want to hit him or anything. The Colonel was ... courtly, yeah, that's a good word, slight and effeminate with a narrowing face and dewy eyes and a gentle manner that made him a favorite among the troops and meant his tendencies were tolerated, even though this was a man's world once more and today's gays ran towards the rough and brutal, not the soft and caring. Heck, even women were no longer soft and caring, how much less a womanish man? Colonel Ostroff, though, was different, and Price doubted he lacked for bedfellows. He probably made his lovers feel safe, a rare talent these days. Maybe that's why he got the 3rd; he'd make them feel safe, that is, until they reached the deathtraps around the New Mex Territories.

The Colonel smiled a little wistfully and said, "Come along, then," and headed back towards the loading dock. Price fell into step. "We weren't really that concerned, you know," he said to Price as they stepped up to the big door, "there's been a drop-off in activity on the routes. Very few ambushes lately, and hardly any of those Reds. Mostly scavengers."

Hmm. "Any idea why, sir?"

"Not really, Corporal. G2 is puzzled but, of course, they're always that," and the Colonel brayed a contagious laugh that made Price smile. "There's some talk that the Reds are massing near the 1st, so they've pulled away from us, but there doesn't seem to be a lot of interest in verifying that." Ostroff reached into a wall panel and slapped something and overhead floods came on. He waited a moment and then walked over, pulled another switch, and the bay door rolled up.

A fully powered building, man, how cool. Price wasn't sure if they used generators or someone had managed to get the local power running, but he wouldn't ask. Curiosity killed the courier. Probably generators;

there weren't a lot of people left who knew how to run power plants, and those persons were assigned to Army headquarters, not pissant little supply depots.

Ostroff peered at the canvassed-closed truck backed against the dock and then glanced around suspiciously. Price hung back. Let the customer settle qualms. Ostroff undid the canvas and tied back the flaps. He pulled out a flashlight and played the beam around, satisfying himself that no one lurked. He then stepped inside and looked over the two crates secured next to each other. "Have you a crowbar, Corporal?" he asked and Price gestured to the back. Ostroff fished around, said "Ahh," and pulled one out, wasting no time prying the covers loose. Price was impressed. The Colonel was stronger than he looked.

Ostroff looked inside one open crate and then the other, a smile forming on his lips. He reached deep inside the first one and pulled out a package covered in paper. Slowly, almost reverently, he unwrapped it and peered at what looked to Price like an old vase.

"The Peacock Room," Ostroff whispered and set it gently back inside. He turned to the other crate and gestured to Price, "Help me with this, will you please, Corporal?"

Price glanced quickly around. This was the moment for a double-cross, but he saw no one and he helped the Colonel wrestle a very large framed item, probably a painting, out and across the top of the crate. Ostroff peeled back the heavy paper and shone the light on the picture: an explosion of color against a dark background, a beautiful face framed in long black hair.

"Know what this is, Corporal?" Ostroff whispered.

"Probably best if I don't, Colonel."

The Colonel snorted. "Nonsense, Henry, you've more than proved your loyalty and you deserve to know what a piece of history you've been carrying."

Price shrugged and the Colonel said, "Whistler."

Price was puzzled. Should be an old woman in a rocking chair, not a beautiful woman in a kimono. "His mom?"

"No." Ostroff chuckled, but not derisively. "This is *The Princess from the Land of Porcelain*. Exquisite, isn't it?"

Price nodded. It was that. "She doesn't look Chinese," Price pointed out.

"No, she doesn't," Ostroff agreed while admiring the painting. "How on earth did Leideig get these?" he whispered in some wonder. "The man constantly amazes me." He looked at Price. "We have a buyer, of course," and he carefully returned the painting, then loosely replaced the crates' covers. "I'll secure them later. Would you please get a lift?"

A lift? Price raised an eyebrow and walked back inside, looking around until he spotted one. He turned the key and a green "Ready" light came on. Amazing. There must be an engineer on Ostroff's staff.

Price guided the lift back to the truck and eased the two crates out and into the middle of the dock, the Colonel watching quietly. When Price settled the last one, the Colonel waved his hand. The earlier sergeant came down the long hall driving a forklift, carrying a wooden box. Price shook an admiring head. These guys were living large.

As the sergeant coasted the box to a stop, Price heard a shuffling noise and spun quickly, his hand dropping to the pistol. The Colonel had also turned, his eyes widening and the sergeant, taking a cue from Price, pulled at his own holster. The two goons were standing in the access doorway and watching them impassively. Ostroff paled.

"It's all right," Price waved the sergeant down. "They're with me."

"They're with you?" Ostroff turned, frowning. How could you, his girl eyes said. Price would have laughed under other circumstances, but he was seething. There was just no reason for those two idiots to be in here and Price braced for something to happen.

After a few seconds, when nothing did, Price looked at the Colonel, "Orders."

"Orders," the Colonel repeated, and his frown deepened and genuine lights of anger formed in his eyes. He stared at Price, weighing his truthfulness, and Price kept his gaze steady. After a moment, the Colonel nodded and turned towards the goons, his soft voice now steel. "All right, since you came in here uninvited, make yourselves useful." He pointed at the wooden box, "Load that into the truck."

The goons glanced at each other then at Price. "Do it," Price said tightly, still half-inclined to shoot them. They shrugged and walked over to the forklift, the Sergeant backing away into cover.

"Without using that," Ostroff added, pointing at the forklift.

Price nodded. Good idea, Colonel. That'll make it real hard for them to start some crap. The goons frowned at each other and Price pulled out his pistol. He saw the sergeant do the same. "Don't use the forklift," Price reiterated softly, while slapping the barrel against his hip.

The goons hesitated, realizing they were outflanked. They looked at each other, then reached for the box. They grunted and strained to pick it up and had to shuffle-step the five or six yards to the back of the truck, gasping for air the whole time. Obviously heavy. To give them credit, they set it down gently, but Price could see they were winded. He walked to the truck bed and stared at them. Now would be an excellent time to shoot them both, and he felt Ostroff move away, getting ready.

The goons just stared back, still impassive, and Price settled, feeling the tense moment dissipate. Okay. "Wait for me in the cab," he said quietly. They shuffled past him, not looking at the Colonel, and jumped down beside the truck. Price followed to the edge of the dock and didn't relax until the truck doors slammed and he saw both goons in the side mirror.

"Wasn't my idea, Colonel," Price said.

Ostroff still frowned, still upset, still betrayed.

"I know," Ostroff said, dryly, then peered around the truck to ensure the cab doors were closed. He nodded at the sergeant, who moved to where he could watch for more trouble. Ostroff stepped onto the bed and motioned. Price hesitated, not sure what the Colonel had in mind, perhaps some discipline for the goons' actions. But no: the Colonel's eyes were imploring, not vengeful, so Price took one long look at the sergeant and the area to make sure it wasn't a setup, then stepped inside.

"I want to show you this." Ostroff began worrying the top off the box.

"Colonel, I don't think—"

"Hush now, Corporal. It's important." He levered the top and let it fall beside the box. Price looked in, an inadvertent whistle escaping his lips.

"Precisely," the Colonel said, smugly.

No wonder the box was so heavy. There were five big gold bars in there. And, based on their position, probably five more underneath. Good Lord, ten bars of gold.

A fortune. An absolute fortune these days when wealth was measured in precious metals or gems or food or other forms of hard currency. With this much gold, Price could buy Farmville and turn it into a private kingdom, complete with his own army. The Kingdom of Price. Henry Land. No, Emmit Land, after Pap, who strode like a giant across those hills and had made Henry a prince. "Damn," was all he could say.

"Yes, damn, damn us all, Henry," Ostroff said as he replaced the lid and nailed it shut. "That's the payment for what you just delivered. And you're probably thinking I have lost my mind showing it to you because now you're at the same risk as Leideig." He paused, finishing off the last nail. "And you are, you are at risk."

Price looked at him, wary and attentive and had a crazy thought that the Colonel was about to do something crazy. But he looked so concerned, so worried, so ... like a woman warning her man of some danger.

The Colonel laid an earnest hand on Price's shoulder, "Henry," he said softly, "take warning. There is something going on, something bad. I don't know what it is but I think this Army is in real danger. No," Ostroff waved off Henry's surprised attempt to speak, "don't ask me because I simply don't know. I've seen some movements and shiftings that are too odd, including my assignment to the wretched 3rd. And now this." The Colonel gestured towards the truck cab, closed off to the bed by canvas. "Leideig sending these two is part of it. You must take care. You must consider getting out, saving yourself." Ostroff slapped the box twice. "Protecting yourself."

Price understood. Making off with the box would be all the protection he needed. Yeah, Colonel, real easy to say, real difficult to pull off.

The Colonel read his mind, "You're resourceful, Henry, you'll think of something."

The Colonel stepped out briskly and waved the sergeant over. Price followed after a second or two, troubled, wondering where to put his faith: in Leideig, larcenous and murderous but who knew a valuable asset and had always treated Price more than fairly, or in Ostroff, just a business contact, an infrequent one at that, who he really did not know.

No contest: Ostroff. Because Ostroff was in love with Price, and unrequited love was surer than larceny.

Yeah, Price, like you've had so much experience with love. He frowned. True, but some things you know without the necessary apprenticeship.

The sergeant walked up, taking one more careful glance around the truck and, wordlessly, handed a big envelope to Ostroff. Ostroff handed it to Price, who looked inside. Travel orders, gas chits, papers … everything they needed. He wondered if they would get the same casual interest going back as they had coming here. Hope so.

When he looked up, Ostroff was watching him closely, a sad, far-off expression on his face. Price was spurred to say something, anything, a kind word for an old queen who didn't have a chance in hell but who flattered Price by the interest. No, don't, just leave things as they are.

Ostroff seemed to read that, too, and smiled a bit. "Take care of yourself, Corporal," he said softly, and turned, placed his hand on the sergeant's shoulder, and walked with him back through the crates.

Without another look, Price closed the back, double-tied it, jumped down to the pavement and over to the passenger door. He pulled it open and launched himself into the seat next to Goon #1. He stared at both of them. They said nothing, sat looking straight ahead, not even acknowledging his entrance. "You two really fucked up," Henry said, "Now drive."

16

It took about five hours to reach Luray, what with blackout rules and suspicious checkpoint guards needing a little more baksheesh than usual to make them unsuspicious. Price used the time wisely, thinking hard on the problem Ostroff had presented – getting the hell out. And getting the hell out with ten bars of gold.

He considered the very simple plan of just shooting the goons and taking off with the truck. Go to Lynchburg, bury the gold down by the river, hide the truck on the old Liberty U campus, recon Farmville, make some contacts, and then retrieve everything with reliable help. Dicey, but doable.

Except for the proverbial ointment fly. Leideig.

Leideig possessed many, many attributes, chief among them relentlessness, and Price diverting a payoff this big would motivate the good Colonel into a search so intense it would make the Sundance posse look like a Girl Scout outing. When Leideig found Price, and he would, other attributes would emerge, like the Colonel's grim delight in prolonged, exquisite torture. No thanks.

So, out with the simple. He needed something a little more complex, something that would diffuse Leideig's rabid pursuit long enough for Price to ready the necessary defenses.

Obviously, then, he couldn't take the gold tonight. Leideig had to see and touch it then move it to one of his stashes, none of which Price knew because Leideig was one cagey bastard. That meant Price had, at best, a couple of days to locate the gold, move it without getting caught, hide it without being seen, and put the blame on someone else while ensuring his own alibi was tight.

Much to mull.

By about midnight, Price was pretty sure he had it worked out. Well, about eighty percent of it, anyway. Follow Leideig to the stash, no problem, get a truck, also no problem, but diverting suspicion, hmm. He glanced at the road-attentive goons, resisting an impulse to thank them for walking into the bay and scaring Ostroff. He could use that. Now, for the getaway.

Price racked his brains trying to remember if he had ever told Leideig about Farmville. He didn't think so. No one told their stories anymore because most of those still walking around had conducted most of the brutality of the past five years, so best not to give details. Maybe, though, in an unattended moment, Price had mentioned it. Should go elsewhere, then, but he didn't know any other place half so well. And besides, those dogwoods still beckoned.

They were gliding into New Market's outskirts by this time. The rendezvous, a derelict motel in the middle of an overgrown field, was coming up fast. "Cut the lights and pull in here. Now," Price ordered, gesturing at a half-grown driveway that still touched the road. Goon #2 swerved the truck onto the broken asphalt and goosed it towards the building, making for the back. Price watched Goon #1 closely during the maneuver. Do something stupid, asshole. Goon #1 acted uninterested. Good for him.

The truck rumbled to a stop. Price glanced around and saw no other vehicle. Okay, Leideig wasn't here yet. "You two stay put." He made a threatening gesture with his holster. "And I mean it." Neither of them said anything. They didn't even look at Price. Good for them.

He stepped down and away, peering hard into a darkness made almost impenetrable by truck-disturbed dust. Price scrutinized the open field that stretched from a wrecked swing set to the fence line marking I81. No lights, no movement, no sound. He took a breath and relaxed, fishing around in his pocket for a cigarette. Sure hope the Colonel gets here soon so he could fire it up—

"Hello, Henry," Leideig said quietly from his right.

Price almost bit the cig in half, whirling to the voice and reflexively going to the holster. He swore, then caught himself, "Sorry, Colonel, you startled me."

Leideig chuckled dryly, "More like scared you to death, Henry. You weren't expecting me?"

"I didn't see your Humvee, sir."

"That's because I didn't use it. I walked."

Walked? Hacking, wheezing, air-starved Leideig, walked? Mister I-still-suffer-from- Phase-3 so I have to drive even to the mess tent, walked?

Sumpin' ain't right, Pap's voice warned.

"Everything went smoothly?" Leideig asked and Price listened intently to Leideig's tone, trying to catch some clue. Nothing.

"Somewhat."

"Somewhat?"

Seed planting time. "Your two boys broke perimeter, came in when they shouldn't have. Looked over the cargo a bit. I stepped out here to see if they had a couple of friends waiting." He paused. "I coulda done this without them, Colonel."

"Hmm. Perhaps you're right, Henry. I may have made

a mistake. I'll deal with it."

Price nodded and warmed a bit inside. The Colonel had taken the bait. He couldn't see the Colonel's expression in the dim starlight, but knew Leideig's normally grey, virus-ravaged face was now flushed, showing signs of actual life, fevered and bright and insane. In a few days, should everything go right, Leideig would be showing that same face to the goons. They wouldn't find it very pleasant. He shook himself and fell in behind the Colonel, who was moving towards the truck. God, if he could pull this off ...

The Colonel slapped the cab as they passed by, "C'mon out, you two." He sounded pissed, and Price grew hopeful. The goons scrambled from either side of the cab as Price and Leideig reached the back, and Price stepped where he could keep an eye on #2. He noted the Colonel did the same for #1, hand already on his holster. Price swallowed. Not yet, Colonel, not yet. Need the goons alive. For a while.

The Colonel gestured towards the closed canvas. "Is everything here, Henry?" he asked quietly.

"Yes sir, it's all here," and he reached up to unhook the flap.

"All?" and Henry mentally smacked himself. Idiot! Should have said just "it's," not the unnecessary "all!" Must be more tired than he thought to make a mistake like that ... and then realized he'd made an even bigger one, that of position. His hand was too far away from his holster and he had taken his eyes off #2. He sensed a fast movement behind him and reacted but was just a second off. Damn.

Something heavy smacked him hard across the head and Price saw many more stars than the night sky held. That wasn't so bad, but the red hot spike driving to the center of his brain, was. He folded like the World Trade

Center, seeing, as he fell, Goon #1 standing beside the Colonel, relaxed and easy, like he and the Colonel were buddies. Price realized, as he hit the ground, that they probably were.

"Change of plans, Henry," he heard the Colonel say softly before the red spike overwhelmed him.

17

The madman squatted in his living room, tallying the damage: Ethan Allen couch now just rag-covered stuffing; Thomasville side chairs reduced to sticks and springs; rot and wrack and ruin. His wife, bless her soul, would be appalled, simply appalled. Good that the Event took her long before the soldiers appeared. They would have raped her over and over, which was soul-killing enough, but to see her house this way ... much worse. You're okay where you are, sweetheart.

He kept the wreckage orderly, cleaning it several times a day because dust and debris rained down almost continually from upstairs. Just this morning, a shell blew through the attic like a cannonball through Wile E. Coyote. The birds and raccoons would quickly find the new opening, as if they needed another way in.

The madman didn't go upstairs anymore. The steps were unsound, as was the flooring, and there were too many creatures claiming it now. Besides, there was no need; he could see the entire second floor through the gaps, all the way to the sky in some places. Lots of snow and wet got in and the first floor buckled, the foundation shifted and the house would collapse soon, but he wasn't moving. This was his place. If it fell, so be it. He would live in the rubble. He would live at home—

A noise. Too big for a raccoon.

The madman blinked. Someone was in his house again. He sighed inwardly. Don't these soldiers talk to each other, don't they know I've got nothing? He supposed the possibility of a dented can of beets or peaches or a random jewel kept them coming back, as well as the joy of deviling him. A crazy man squatting in the ruins spurred a lot of deviling.

The madman did not turn but waved a limp hand about the wreckage, "Look all you want, but you're wasting your time. I don't have anything."

"I don't want anything," a quiet voice replied and a chill ran through him. Not a looter, then: a murderer. Or worse, a rapist. He wondered if he should fight. Well, of course, but the fight would be out of him quick and the murderer or rapist would have their way. God, please let it be murder.

The intruder quietly stepped to the side. The madman gauged the distance. A sudden leap would bowl the murderer or rapist into the wreckage and, hopefully, onto something sharp. It would be unexpected. After all, he's insane, right?

"I just wanted to thank you," the murderer or rapist said, which was very un-murderer-like and the madman turned his head, curious. Oh, the sergeant, the one he pulled from the Creek. John's son. "You're welcome," he said.

They regarded each other for a moment and the madman thought how silly this looked, he all ragged and torn and pathetic, the sergeant all martial with rifle and pistol and fatigues, but looking embarrassed. Anyone happening by would consider this odd.

"You didn't have to do that," John's son said.

"Yes, I did. It was the right time." The madman was always drifting in and out of time. Like right now; it was a time when a civil conversation with a soldier was possible.

John's son smiled, "Certainly was, I would have drowned. I appreciate it. Anything I can do for you? I owe you, you know."

"No, John's son. I'm fine. You owe me nothing."

"Johnson? That's not my name."

"I know. It's Rashkil. You are John's son."

The sergeant stared at him. "That's it. That's what you said when you pulled me out of the water."

"Yes."

"How did you know that?"

The man pointed at the sergeant's blouse. "Your name tag. It's a rare enough name."

Rashkil looked down at the tag and nodded. "True. Dad said it was a bastardized translation of a German name, Tolkuhntod, or something like that. Means 'foolishly brave.'"

"I remember him telling me that once."

"Were you friends?"

The madman shook his head, "No. We saw each other at church."

"Church. Really."

"Yes."

"Which church?"

The madman pointed back towards town. "The Methodist one down near your headquarters. The one that's all smashed."

The sergeant chuckled a bit, "How 'bout that." The madman wondered at the hidden meaning, but mention of the church had started his mind on a different path. "I have something for you," he said, and wove through orderly piles over to the one intact piece of furniture, a sideboard, lots of drawers filled with useless papers – useless to looters but not to him – clips and notices, records of his lost life. He rummaged around until his hand closed on the book. "This," he said and offered it to the sergeant.

The soldier's eyes narrowed as he looked at the black binding and gold letters. "A Bible?"

"Yes."

The sergeant smiled indulgently, "Uh, thanks, but I'm not into it."

"Your dad would be disappointed."

"He was. We had these discussions, even after the Event. He remained faithful. I didn't."

"Your dad survived the Event?"

"Yes, but not Breakout," and the sergeant frowned and absently patted the bottom of his backpack. Must be a nervous habit.

"Then you should take this." The madman offered the Bible again.

"Why?"

"Because it was your dad's," and he took a step forward and handed it to the now startled sergeant.

"What?" The sergeant opened the Bible and quickly flipped through, examining the front and end leafs, stopping at a page densely covered in scrawled handwriting. "How in the hell?"

"He gave it to me before he left."

"Gave it to you? I thought you weren't friends."

"We weren't, but I was the last one of our group still in church. So he gave it to me."

"Why?"

"Your dad had some unusual ideas about God. I always found his arguments intriguing so he let me have his notes. That's all."

"So why wouldn't he just keep it?"

The man shrugged. "He'd moved on."

The sergeant stared at the Bible. "Unbelievable," he muttered. "Things just don't happen this way. First *The Shepherd*, now this."

The madman did not understand that comment, but didn't think he was supposed to. He was inspired, though. "Things aren't random, John's son. Everything is guided. Your dad believed that, but he believed the guidance wasn't necessarily for your benefit. It was all part of something larger and the individual could get overwhelmed."

"You tellin' me God is bringing me to these documents?"

"How else do you explain it?"

"Coincidence."

"Your dad—"

"I know, I know," the sergeant waved the Bible at him. "Dad didn't believe in coincidences. I'm still not buying it."

The madman nodded, turned and walked back to the couch rubble and squatted beside it. Nothing more to say. John's son looked perplexed. That first glimpse of God was rather off-putting, wasn't it? The madman smiled.

The sergeant shifted uneasily. "Well, thanks for this. Really, thanks. You've done me another good turn. I feel like I should do something for you."

The madman pointed at the Bible. "Then read that."

"No, I … should bring you something. You want a blanket or a poncho?"

"Someone will just steal it."

"You sure? You look very uncomfortable here."

"I'm fine. Just read."

"Okay. Okay, I will. I owe you, so I will. But, anything, people bothering you especially, let me know. I've told them at least a million times to leave you alone

—"

The madman stopped him with a raised hand. "I know. That's John in you, always looking out for others. You are his son," and he closed his eyes and rocked slowly back and forth. Prayer in this time.

The sergeant stood for a moment and the madman imagined the baffled look on his face. He heard the sergeant turn and pick his way through the orderly piles and then go. The madman remained in prayer. His heart felt light, even sang. He knew he had just done something very important.

18

The first thought Price had was, Backstabbed. The second was, I could really use an aspirin. Given the screaming, searing lump of tissue that was supposed to be his head, the second thought was more critical. But he doubted he was getting any kind of painkiller anytime soon, so best to spend a few moments with the first.

The "who" was easy: Leideig. "How" was even easier, and if his head weren't already throbbing, he'd smack it and call himself an idiot. Shoulda known the moment Leideig assigned the goons. He could just hear Pap railing at him, "Boy! You stupid or something? I always told ya, trust your gut. Now lookatchee!"

Yeah, lookatchee.

Okay, so, here you are, Henry, split head, sold out, thrown away, and beaten to the punch. All for a box of gold.

Incidentally, where, exactly, was "here"?

Price blinked, his eyelids sliding like sandpaper. Not the most pleasant of sensations but, along with his exploding skull, proved he wasn't dead.

Yet.

He nursed his head through a slow turn until he saw

dim lines of light. He stared until they made sense: a metal door, backlit by something, probably a kerosene lamp.

Price rolled towards it, discovering that he was resting on a burlap sack of some kind on top of a cement floor. Gritting his teeth against the multiple skull fracture he was obviously suffering from, he peered underneath, but all he saw was cement floor ending at an identical metal door across from him. Looked familiar.

Oh, yeah. The brig, an isolated self-storage facility near 301. He'd spent enough time here to call it a second home, usually after getting drunk and assaulting some non-comm. On those occasions, he could count on Leideig to get him out in the morning. Probably not the case today.

No, any getting out of here would be a self-initiated project, and one which needed doing rather quickly before Price outlived whatever usefulness he currently served. The headache suddenly receded as Price quietly reached for the doorknob. Action always made him feel better. He quietly turned it until the catch cleared then, slowly, pulled it towards him, but met resistance. Okay, there was a lock on the outside hasp of whatever storage unit they'd pitched him into. Not unexpected, but you don't know unless you check. Carefully, he released the knob.

He cast about, widening the search area as he found nothing. He kept on finding nothing: no cracks in the floor (well, not ones he could exploit); no furniture he could use as a weapon. There was a small drain hole in one corner that, based on its odor, served as a latrine but it was too small for him to squeeze his way into, even if he had the stomach. He stood, head notwithstanding, and made wide sweeping motions across the wall. Nothing, just nothing.

Now what? Maybe he should look again; never know,

might have missed something like a sledgehammer, a weapon, money, or a vehicle. He smiled. Keep that sense of humor going, Henry. Crack up the firing squad and they just might miss.

Footsteps coming down the hall.

Price scrabbled across the floor until he reached the burlap, burrowed under it and turned away from the door. He took several deep breaths to calm himself and, by the time the door scraped open, he was feigning deep sleep. Please come over and kick him, because then he could roll and take out some legs and, with a great deal of luck, fight his way out of here. Hey, dim hopes were better than none.

"Get up, Henry, I know you're awake."

Leideig. The dim hope collapsed.

Price stood, blinking at the very harsh light pouring in from kerosene lamps held up by a couple of guards. Leideig stood silhouetted between the lamps and Price could see two more faces hovering in the back. Quite the reception committee. Was Leideig that afraid of him? No. More likely, he needed the witnesses.

Price kept his face expressionless. Okay, Colonel, your play. Might be a sudden bullet through the skull, but at least that's something.

Leideig, the ever-present handkerchief dabbing at his mouth, peered at Price. "Henry, Henry, Henry," he said, shaking his head with mock sadness. "Black marketing, theft, and murder. And, of all people, poor little Colonel Ostroff. What possessed you?"

Price stared at him. So, Ostroff was dead. Three guesses, the first two not counting, as to who did that. And another guess, Henry old boy, as to why you're not dead, too.

Designated fall guy.

But for what? Ostroff had been a loyal member of

Leideig's little crew and, besides, was on his way south. Killing him was just ... unnecessary. And it was a pretty safe bet that Ostroff's pet sergeant was now mysteriously missing so, Leideig, you could've pinned it on him, lover's quarrel or something sordid like that. No need to bash Price over the head and accuse him of murder.

"There is something going on, something bad." Ostroff's words rang in his head.

Hmm.

Price looked at Leideig, saying nothing. Keep quiet. No protests of innocence. No protests of anything. Let's see how this goes. But, be ready. You never know what the gods of opportunity will offer.

Leideig returned the look, a tiny smile on his face, whether one of triumph or just appreciation for Price's silence, he didn't know. "Corporal," Leideig put on his official voice, "in a few hours, we'll have your court-martial. Then we'll shoot you." The guards guffawed at that and Leideig smiled with them. His eyes went to the door lock and lingered there, then back to Price, then back to the door lock. He wheeled suddenly, grasped the door, and slammed it shut. Price was back in darkness as the boots marched off. He stood for a few minutes more, listening while letting his eyes readjust.

What. The. Hell?

He blinked, then approached the door cautiously, listening hard for any sign that someone lingered outside of it. Slowly he turned the knob and pulled. The door opened easily.

Gee, what a surprise.

Obviously, the Colonel meant for him to escape. Made sense; Leideig gets a scapegoat, and the scapegoat's gone and can't be questioned. Could have accomplished the same thing by putting a bullet through Price's head, but bodies were so inconvenient. The opportunity gods have delivered. Let's take advantage, shall we?

He stepped into the hallway, crouched and tensed and ready to fight, but it was empty; at least, the weak light coming from somewhere far down to his right seemed to show. He walked cautiously down the hall and looked around the corner, but the guard station was also empty.

He smiled. Thanks, Colonel. So, let's slip out the front door, race around the south compound and across I81, through the hole Price'd cut in the wire and then dash over the remains of the New Market Battlefield and find the fourth tree in the third row of the overgrown apple orchard and pull out his stash – money and food and weapons and documents – and then go home, home to Farmville. He tensed, ready to make a dash.

"Boy, you stupid or sumpin?"

He froze, Pap's voice ringing hard and clear in his head. "You little punk," Pap continued, "you think he's going to kill you *in* the prison? 'Shot while trying to escape,'" Pap chortled.

Damn.

Price held his breath, trying to shrink into the dark pools, peering hard towards the death-trap exit. Now what? There was a door on the other end of the building he could probably force, but that would be very noisy and time-consuming and he'd bust through just to find Leideig's ambush had shifted location and was waiting. He strained towards the ceiling but it was too dark to see any vents or panels. And, besides, all he'd do was crawl around until someone found him. Great.

As previously asked, now what?

Well, one thing for sure, he couldn't stay here.

Price slipped back down the hall towards the open cell, peering back the whole time. He entered the cell and stood behind the door for cover, out of ideas.

Pap, I need some help.

Wait. What was that? A sound, a shuffling out of rhythm somewhere down the hall. Price froze. Someone else was in the hallway. He'd bet his stash it was one of the guards sent back to see what was taking so long, and being very stealthy about it, too. Probably wearing night vision. Be stupid if he wasn't, and Leideig is anything but stupid. So, guard boy's not seeing Price in the hallway and that's probably got him a bit baffled.

And he damn sure won't be expecting Price to still be in the cell, will he?

Thanks, Pap.

He braced behind the door, shoulder on the edge and hand on the knob. Here kitty, kitty. The shuffling got closer. Got to hand it to him, the guard wasn't taking chances. The shuffling stopped just outside the doorway. He's drawn to the only open door in the hall, but the prisoner can't be that stupid, can he? Curiosity-the-cat-killer will make him stick his head in for a quick check …

There.

Price saw an odd shadow and did not hesitate, slamming the door with all his force. "Uh*gch*!" The guard's skull crunched against the opposing jamb with clatterings and shatterings as the guard dropped a ready-held rifle and the goggles broke about his face. Price savagely hammered the guard's trapped head with elbows and fists. Don't let him scream!

He didn't.

Price dragged him inside, seizing the rifle and quickly stripped him of a pistol and some money and extra clips the guy had. The goggles were now worthless so he pitched them. Okay, got a weapon now, cool, but what I really need—

Clink. Hand grenade.

Almighty God, a hand grenade. He held it tight for just a moment, long enough to thank Pap again, and then he was loping down the hall. Okay, so, throw the grenade, let loose a couple of clips, run like hell through the yard. They might get him, but at least he'd go down fighting—

"No," Pap said.

Price stopped. He was at the corner. He could see the open doorway down at the end, where the ambush was waiting. A few more moments and they'll realize their buddy is down and they'll come charging in.

Pap grinned.

Happened faster than he expected. "Gates!" someone yelled, "Gates, answer!" and there was no answer and there were boots clomping and lights and shadows and muttering and Price threw the grenade.

Chaos.

Screams and guns firing as the grenade ripped the point men apart and Price allowed himself a half-second smirk of satisfaction before flying back down the hall past the cell and towards the other end. He hit the other exit door with full force and almost took it off it's hinges but, damn, the thing was tough! He hammered it again and again and, finally, with a major kick at the doorknob, it canted enough he could climb through.

Shouts and shooting behind him, still far down the hall. Nothing out here except starlight.

Go.

He raced around the next set of buildings, grateful he'd spent so much drunk time here that he knew exactly where he was: on the back of the lot, facing a ridge that overlooked I81. He was actually closer to his stash now – fortuitous, that – and it's time to get yourself over there and outta here—

"No," Pap said, "Settle this."

Henry paused. Yes. Settle this.

He peered in the opposite direction. The truck park was about a half-mile that way. He could get there in about twenty minutes, slipping in through one of his patented entrances.

Colonel, you're about to have visitors.

19

"Doin' some late night business, I see."

Price had the satisfaction of seeing Leideig, all lit up by a hanging kerosene lamp, genuinely jerk in true, unexpected surprise before grabbing at a holster on a wall peg behind his desk. "Uh, uh, uh," Price said as he, noisily, drew the bolt on the M-16. Leideig froze, then slowly withdrew his hand and raised his arms. "Why, Henry," he said, "I'm quite surprised to see you."

Henry hefted the rifle. "I'll bet."

"Oh, not that you evaded the trap," Leideig fluttered his fingers in a dismissive gesture, "but that you didn't take that opportunity to get as far away from here as you could." The Colonel glared at him.

"Need to clear some accounts first, Colonel," Henry pushed the barrel slightly towards Leideig's stomach.

Leideig's brows rose and he spoke softly, "Henry, are you going to shoot me?"

"Maybe. That depends on you."

"Does it? Well, then," and without waiting for permission, the Colonel lowered his hands, pulled a handkerchief out of his upper blouse, and dabbed at his mouth. He nodded at the office door. "I take it my guards are unavailable."

"You're gonna need replacements."

"Hmm." More dabs. "So, if you shoot me, you'll have plenty of time to get away before the cavalry arrives."

"Especially since the night patrols are all at the brig trying to figure out what the hell happened."

"Knew I should have stayed," Leideig said ruefully and Henry couldn't help chuckling at that. Leideig was, apparently, hoping for such a reaction because he shifted a bit and smiled.

"Watch it," Pap warned. Henry clicked the safety off.

Leideig froze, paling a bit. "Henry," he said, "there is no need for this. I did not intend you harm. I actually was helping you."

Price considered that for a moment, then gave a one-word answer: "Ha."

"It's true, Henry," the soft voice again, "but I do not blame you for doubting me. Perhaps, then, we can make a deal?"

"Well, sure, Colonel," Price waved the rifle. "I'm always up for a deal. Let's start with the gold."

Leideig chuckled and dabbed at his mouth, "Love to, Henry, but the gold is long gone."

"Uh-huh." Price shifted the rifle.

"It is. It was intended for others."

"I'm sure. So I'll take your cut, then. For my troubles."

"If I could," Leideig spread helpless hands and Price watched for any untoward move, "but I didn't take a cut. All of it went to something much bigger than my post-Army retirement and comfort."

"Which is ..." Price raised inquiring eyebrows.

"Assurance I'll live long enough to enjoy it."

Price let out a long-suffering sigh. "Right, Colonel, right. Just stop the crap and tell me where it is. I'll tie you up, come back and kill you if you lie, but leave you some if you don't. Deal?" Price waved the rifle threateningly, underscoring the generous terms on offer.

Leideig gave his own long-suffering sigh. "Henry," he sounded mournful, "I'd love that deal, but I'm telling you, there is no more gold. It is all gone. It went, every ounce of it, to buy certain officers."

"Okay, Colonel, I'll play. Buy them for what?"

"The surrender of the US Army."

Price blinked. "Surrender."

"Yes, Henry, surrender, the entire Army, all of it, in one day."

Price stared at him a moment. Then just laughed out loud. "Ri-i-i-ght, Colonel. Try another story, okay?"

"I know, I know, sounds ridiculous. I agree," Leideig coughed a bit. "I didn't believe it, either. At first. But, it's going to happen, Henry, and very soon."

"That Phase 2 gone to your brain, Colonel?"

"No, Henry," the Colonel said, rather coolly. "There's this group of Colonels and a couple of minor generals, all in very strategic locations. They're tired of this constant fighting, very tired, and don't see an end to it. You don't, either. Neither do I, and we're all just as tired of it as they are so I think you can sympathize. Everyone wants to stop fighting, but no one knows how. The Reds won't quit. We won't quit. So, something has to be done. This group is going to do it. They're going to decapitate the Army leadership, take over the government, and immediately cease-fire with the Reds and disband the Army."

Price snorted. "Nice try, Colonel. Give you a star for creativity. But ..." and he raised the rifle.

"Don't take my word for it, Henry. See for yourself," Leideig nodded at his desk.

"Trap," Pap said.

I know, Price responded, and took giant steps across

the floor. He drove the barrel into Leideig's chest, tipping him back hard against the back wall. "You even blink," Price snarled. Leideig's hands were back up, more to keep his balance than anything, but there was real fear in his eyes. Good.

Price pulled the top drawer open, one eye on Leideig as he shuffled folders around. Requisitions, orders of the day, lists of personnel, shorter each week, he noted. Nothing. "What's this crap?" he pushed the barrel hard.

"Ouch! Please, Henry!" Leideig shook. "My lungs are sensitive! Just keep looking." And he nodded at the drawer.

Price grabbed all of the folders one-handed and tossed them on the desk. He explored the bottom, which seemed smooth, unbroken. Wait. A notch. He scratched at it with a fingernail until it caught. The bottom came up. "Slick," he couldn't help admiring the handiwork.

"Thank you." The Colonel sounded pleased.

"Shut up," Price jabbed him and then pulled out two sheets of notepaper. He laid them on the desk. Both were handwritten, one covered in symbols and numbers, obviously coded in some way. The other was in Leideig's handwriting. Obviously the decode. He read:

Lieutenant Colonel Leideig,

Your services are recognized in this great endeavor and any concerns we may have regarding your loyalty will be answered when you have delivered the items to this location: here map coordinates were entered; somewhere near Philadelphia, if Price was reading it right. *Once we have proof this has been done, then all of the pending charges for your illegal activities will be dismissed. We trust you have ensured any lingering questions are put to rest by other evidence.*

Other evidence? Price blinked as Pap snorted in his ear, "Designated fall guy, remember, boy?"

"You bastard," he said to Leideig and kept reading.

All of this depends on the subsequent loss of the 1st. Since your future also depends on that event, we are assured of your confidence in this matter, while this letter assures your safety, as you requested.

Sincerely,

Lieutenant Colonel Frederick Kant

Chief of Staff, HQ

Kant's signature, a rather classical flourish, was on the coded page.

"Believe me now?" Leideig said.

Price read through one more time, thought for a moment, then whipped the stock of the rifle across Leideig's jaw.

"*Ack!*" the Colonel's head bounced off the wall and he slid like a giant sack of meat out of the chair and onto the floor. Price kicked him in the ribs then jammed the barrel against his head. "You fuckin' backstabber," he hissed.

The Colonel wheezed and flopped like a fish out of water and Price kicked him viciously again. "You sold me out and killed Ostroff because of some half-baked, stupid who's-the-president-this-week crap?" Price kept his voice controlled, even in his rage. "You actually bought this bullshit?" He shook the paper savagely at Leideig's groaning face.

"It's true," Leideig wheezed, "The 1st is going to be destroyed. The Army will surrender. The Reds are taking over. Please don't kick me anymore."

Henry kicked him again. "No way, there's no fucking way. I was just there, at the 1st, remember?" Another kick.

"Please, stop!" Leideig was flat-out crying, but also keeping it down. Such control. "The 1st is surrounded, Henry," the Colonel sobbed, "they don't know it, but their escape routes are all blocked."

"Bullshit!" a little too loud, that, but Henry was livid, "Bullshit, Colonel! I was JUST THERE!"

Leideig said nothing, just stared at him ...

... Ostroff: "There's some talk that the Reds are massing near the 1st."

Price blinked. Impossible. Just impossible. The 1st was some hard fightin' motherfuckers, led by that fabled Colonel Caldwell who'd made fools of the Reds for what, a year now? There's no way they'd allow themselves to be surrounded. There's no way they would surrender.

No. They wouldn't.

If they *were* surrounded, if a group of traitors, led by whoever this fucking LC Kant was and abetted by opportunists like Leideig groveling on the floor at Price's feet there, had allowed the Reds to envelop the 1st, cutting off all retreat, then the 1st would stand and fight. To the last man. And the shockwaves of their slaughter would be a blow the US Army could not survive. It would collapse.

But there's no way that Colonel Caldwell would fall into such a trap. He was too good at sniffing out Red intentions ...

"It went, every ounce of it, to buy certain officers," Leideig had said.

Price considered all this for a minute or two, keeping a foot on Leideig's chest. Then he slung the rifle, stooped, and put on his best, most sincere, "I'm-with-you" expression, placing comforting hands on Leideig's chest. The look of hope in the Colonel's eyes was almost comical. "I get it," Price whispered, "Caldwell had a price that only you could finance, and you get a 'get-out-of-firing-squad' letter in exchange. Brilliant." Leideig actually smiled at that. "Another one of your brilliant schemes, Colonel." Price paused. "You. Fucking. Traitor."

It took Leideig less than a minute to die. He didn't even struggle, either due to the inevitability or his inherent weakness, Price didn't know. Or care.

Price released his grip on the Colonel's throat, stood, and regarded the now-blue face. He kicked him again to make sure, then grabbed the papers, stuffed them in his coat, and slipped out the back.

Stars wheeled. Still early, maybe 0330, but the camp will be up soon. Gotta go. Price got his bearings, and looked in the direction of Farmville.

Not yet. Have to do a couple of things, first.

20

"Gawd, this sucks," Jonesy grumbled and spat an accurate stream of his discontent somewhere off towards Eliot's platoon.

"Not a morning person, Jonesy?" Collier asked.

"It's illegal to have us up this early."

"You should tell the union."

"Union," Jonesy cocked his head, "now there's an idea."

Collier smiled. Personally, he loved the early morning, this 0400 they were sharing right now with the rest of the Company. It was about the only time of day he was inclined to believe in a Supreme Being. Dawn was God cracking his knuckles, flexing a bit of finger, and stirring things up. Was there a passage like that somewhere in Dad's Bible? He slapped the bottom of his pack. Getting crowded in there. "The Reds have a union, Jonesy," he observed.

"Yeah, well, maybe they're not all that crazy."

Collier chuckled and turned his attention back to this loose gaggle that in no way could be called a formation. Galled his Fishburne Military School mind, it did. Troops at attention, squad leaders reporting up the chain in a series of choreographed callings and turnings, then a listening to the orders of the day. That's how you did these things, not squalling around a central point that more or less conformed to Captain Palmer, who was trying to pass on new assignments. Annoyance surged through him. An Army without discipline was just an armed mob.

"Hey!" He barked out in his ear-splitting parade field voice, "Shut the fuck up! Captain's trying to talk!"

There was a moment of stunned silence as the whole mass turned to him in surprise, then the muttering and glaring began. He glared back, eyeing down the hardest cases. They looked away.

"Nice," Jonesy commented.

"Thanks, man."

Palmer looked at him briefly, the gratitude clear on his face and Collier nodded slightly. Palmer was a good guy, a rarity among the officer corps. He was short and so barrel-chested his arms didn't hang straight, but his fighter's body was offset by a sincere baby face that accompanied a sincere belief in the Army's overall mission and the good intentions of the government, despite all contrary evidence. Naivety was a distressing trait these days, good guy or no.

"All right," Palmer cleared his throat, "here's the new postings. Eliot, Deavers – no change."

Collier frowned. "What the fuck?" Jonesy blurted. "They get to keep the north line?"

"Jonesy, Sector 4—"

"Shit, man, Mt. Holly. I'll be picking deserters and snipers out of my hair."

"Rashkil, Sector 3—"

"Looks like I'll be helping you pick from the Pemberton side," Collier commented dryly.

The assignments continued but they both had stopped

listening. "You believe this shit, man?" Jonesy shook his head. "It's like we're dead fucking asleep or something. Why the hell are we just shuffling in and out of the same goddamn line? Man, two weeks of this crap. Wasn't our goddamned fault that fucking grab went bad. Pulling our puds, man, pulling our puds."

"Preaching to the choir, Jonesy," Collier said as he stretched luxuriously and did his best to look like he didn't know what was going on. Unfortunately, he did, and Jonesy deserved to know, too. Perhaps a broad hint was in order. "It ain't us. It's command. Something is really fucked up."

Specifically, Jonesy old pal, we are, the whole bunch of us, at the mercy of an insanely jealous Colonel. At least, that was Rosa's conclusion two weeks (three hours and ten minutes) ago, about which Collier still had his doots. He'd tried to arrange another rendezvous with her to discuss things (among other planned activities), but she was convinced they were being watched, and if she was paranoid then he was, too, because her instincts were honed. That meant, of course, a drastic cut in his love life. He wondered what sacrifice of what animal to what god he needed to perform to resolve all this so he could, at last, "discuss things" with his woman. You hear that, Jehovah? Collier slapped the pack again. You need a sheep? 'Cause if this dry spell continues, I'm going to need one.

Jonesy was still talking, "No shit. You and I stuck on this side of the Creek and that asshole," he gestured towards Eliot, "gets the pussy-ass north. I don't like it, man, I don't like it at all."

"Makes you wonder, doesn't it?"

"No shit wonder," and Jonesy turned a baleful eye back to the front.

So did Collier and he immediately saw that Palmer

had stopped talking and was looking at Jonesy and him with the closest thing to a glare he was capable of producing. LT Whatever-the-fuck-his-name-was, standing at the front, had also turned and was trying to give them a similar glare. Oh, that's rich. Collier bore into LT Fuckall with murderous eyes. The twerp blinked and turned back in some confusion towards Palmer. Collier smiled. Worked every time.

Palmer hesitated for a moment then went back to reading the orders. "You got enough people?" Jones asked Collier.

"Had to shoot two last night, but I'm still at eighty percent."

Jonesy nodded. "You're actually doing good. You know I lost half a squad last week, don't you? Four of 'em got clean away. Bastards." He shook his head. "We're bleeding too much, Coll. This rate, we ain't even gonna be a swelled Battalion by the end of the week."

Collier shrugged, "Can you blame 'em? Get out while the gettin's good."

"Heard that." Jonesy lowered his voice, "So?"

"So?"

"Hey, man, don't fuck with me. Have you heard anything?" There was an expectation in Jonesy's eyes.

Everyone knew what Collier had done to Eliot and everyone guessed it had something to do with the botched mission. Jonesy didn't have to guess because Collier had told him what Eliot said, which led to an immediate effort by Jonesy to march straightaway to Eliot's cot and decapitate the asshole, an act barely averted by Collier's intense pleading along the lines of, "Dude, no. I need you. Don't get yourself thrown in the brig." Jonesy then reached the same conclusion Collier had: the Colonel was up to something, so he urged Collier to tell Rosa about Eliot, which was a relief because it meant Jonesy didn't know he had already done so, nor the circumstances of him doing so, which further meant Jonesy didn't know about them, and if Jonesy didn't know then no one knew and Rosa's paranoia was misplaced.

He hoped.

But Jonesy, being Jonesy, wanted follow-up and he expected it to come from Rosa through Collier, and that left him in a bad place. What could he say? Sorry, Jonesy old buddy, the Major has concluded, last time we spoke, that the Colonel has gone insane, courtesy of yours truly banging aforementioned Major on a regular basis.

Best to hold off.

"Later," he whispered.

"Cool," Jonesy responded and Collier "phewed" inwardly. That's one issue delayed, which meant he could attend to the next one on the never-ending list. Collier glanced at Eliot, half-hidden by some intervening troops. He could see the swollen jaw, but not the still-wrapped thumb, and he smirked with satisfaction. Eliot'll be eating soup for another week, at least. But it'd been a while since he kicked the shit out of the little fuck, and what had been the fallout? Nothing. Not a word. No retaliation, no Eliot goons layin' for 'im, no summons from HQ and another court-martial and stripe loss and short confinement, followed by the inevitable mindless act of bravery which led to his forgiveness and restoration, story of the last five years.

Why nothing?

"Any questions?" Palmer wrapped up his brief.

Jonesy's hand shot up, "Yeah, Captain," he called out without even waiting for acknowledgment. "What's the word from up north?"

"Nothing new to tell you, Sergeant Jones." Palmer intoned it like an old prayer, not even looking up from his clipboard.

"So why is that, Captain?" Jonesy's voice toned belligerence.

Palmer looked up, blinking, his face set to grim lines. You could almost believe he was annoyed at Jonesy for asking the question, but Collier knew better. He was annoyed because he really had no answer.

And, boy, did they need some answers. Like, why the hell were Eliot and Deavers still sergeants? Usually, you fuck up as bad as they did, you get to become privates again and peel potatoes for two weeks, not get, and keep, an important sector. He'd sure like to ask those two assholes what they were doing.

"Hey, Eliot!" Jonesy called out before Palmer could form a typical HQ non-answer. "You or Deavers hearing anything?"

Collier could have kissed him.

Eliot peered, with hostile and veiled eyes, over the shoulders of his blocking squad back at Jonesy, but said nothing. Deavers looked at Eliot nervously, then back at Palmer, but also said nothing. Collier moved where he could see both of them clearly.

"Hey, Eliot," Jonesy persisted, "'ja hear me? You and your butt buddy see anything? Hear anything? No? Are you even looking?"

The tension arced. Soldiers muttered and turned to each other and exchanged suspicious looks and comments flew between groups as hands gripped weapons.

Collier frowned. A bit touchy this morning, aren't we boys? Maybe they were asking themselves the same questions, and hadn't expected someone to actually voice them. "Hey," Collier yelped, "keep it down. We wanna hear this, right?"

Mutters of agreement outweighed by some unexpected "fuck yous," and Collier suddenly didn't like the way this was going.

"Perhaps we should talk afterwards, Sergeant," Palmer said, elevating his voice over the crowd.

Oh, boy, Captain, wrong answer, definitely the wrong answer, because now it sounds like you're hiding something, and the effect was immediate and volcanic. Soldiers whipped around to each other in either support or conflict and barrels raised while the dull mutter of discontent grew to a roar throughout the area. Surprised, Collier and Jones unslung rifles and went shoulder to shoulder to watch everyone. Collier especially watched Eliot's platoon, which formed ranks around him in a show of solidarity. Palmer paled.

"Hey!" Collier's voice boomed out, freezing everyone in place, "Calm the fuck down!" The roar subsided. Damnation, he thought, what's eating these guys?

"C'mon, boys, relax!" Jonesy backed up Collier. "We all want to know. Can't hear shit y'all jawin,'" and he bore down on Eliot. "Well?"

Eliot looked at his platoon, seeking support, and the determined look on their faces gave it to him, "We ain't had no orders," he yelled, barely understandable through his still-setting jaw.

"Orders?" Jonesy exclaimed, "What the fuck you doing out there, then? Jerking off?"

That got a laugh out of most of the assemblage, except for Eliot's platoon, and Collier saw their resentment escalating. He put a hand on Jonesy's shoulder in warning.

"Eliot's right," Palmer called out then, apparently reading the same tension. "They've been told to stay on our side."

"What?" both Collier and Jonesy reacted with simultaneous incredulity. Collier recovered first. "Captain, what the fuck?" he yelled while Jonesy spluttered incoherence.

"It's a command decision, Sergeant," Palmer replied in a brook-no-further nonsense voice. "It's felt to be too dangerous."

Now it was Collier's time to splutter as Jonesy cried out, "Dangerous? Jesus, Captain, getting up in the morning is dangerous around here! It's ten times more dangerous if we don't know what the fuck is happening!"

Uproar. Soldiers chose up, those who considered Eliot spineless lining up against the ones who considered him smart. Eliot stood center in the latter group, wide-eyed and turning from one furious knot of soldiers to another while his platoon stood grimly. Deavers had disappeared in the swirl.

"Shit," Jonesy muttered as he stood tensely with Collier, "Didn't mean to start a riot."

"I know. But, man ..." Collier didn't need to finish it. What an absolutely stupid decision to stop the patrols. Even the dumbest of troops knew it was stupid. Made no sense, no military sense at all, and if you're going to do something like that, you have to tell the troops why, even if it's just a simple "we're working on something, soldier, and it's close hold." They'd grumble, but they trusted the Colonel; hell, they'd get downright hopeful, given the Colonel's past brilliance.

Were they wrong, Colonel?

Collier gathered his breath, "All RIGHT!" he bellowed, "That's ENOUGH! We can't hear with y'all screaming like a bunch of old ladies!" He wondered, briefly, if the female soldiers would be mad at that. Sue me. "So shut UP a second!"

It was edgy and close and he got a lot of "Fuck yous" and "Asshole!" but there was still enough military discipline (or fear of him) around to drop the volume. Take advantage of the lull, Coll old boy.

"Captain, no disrespect," he called out, redirecting

energies, "but if we can't go out and look, are we at least hearing from others who can? Isn't the 4th south of us somewhere? Have we heard from them?"

The question intrigued the crowd and they all stopped and turned towards the Captain. Palmer looked around, frowning. "No," he sighed, "we haven't. We're pretty sure they're down there, but we haven't gotten a courier from them lately."

Collier inwardly rolled his eyes. Jesus H. Christ, Palmer, at least lie about it! The muttering picked up again and angry looks went in Eliot's direction. "No radio?" someone called out. Idiot. Everyone knew microwaves were down and satellite time was limited. Only HQ got satellite.

"How 'bout one of our helicopters, then, Captain?" Jonesy asked over the dumb radio comment, and that interested the crowd even more. Okay, Palmer, another opportunity. Ease our collective minds. Please.

Palmer shook his head, "We can't risk them. The Reds have Stingers."

Collier blinked hard as Jonesy, frustration notching his voice up an octave, said, "Well, shit, Captain, what are we saving them for? Evacuation?"

Yeah, good goddamn question, Collier thought. Stingers be damned, that's just part of the job, like crawling in the mud next to the Creek hoping to God the next potshot some Red took wasn't lucky enough to smack you between the eyes.

Why weren't the helos doing recon?

"How 'bout some jets, then, Captain?" Collier called out, the frustration making him reckless. "How 'bout HQ send us a couple, you know, the ones they're hoarding? Maybe actually drop a bomb or two, help us out a bit, you know? Anybody talking to HQ? Are they still there? Or have they taken the jets to Bermuda?"

Uproar again. Palmer stood at the center of furious soldiers repeating the same questions Collier and Jonesy had just posed, but at a much more frantic volume, and with fear-filled eyes.

Fear.

Collier smacked himself mentally. That's why everyone's so crazy this morning. They're scared, more scared than normal because we just don't know what's going on and now we know why: command had shut off patrols, wasn't even looking. That was wrong.

Very wrong.

But it's not Palmer's fault, so, fix this. Collier looked at Jonesy and shrugged and both of them waded through the arm-waving, wild-eyed shouting soldiers, knocking them aside with elbows, yanking others' backpack straps, kicking others' feet out from under them. They reached Palmer and wheeled to either side, forcing the more belligerent soldiers back. Collier quick-glanced at Palmer. His face was red but he looked calm, unflustered. Gotta hand it to him.

"Back off!" Jonesy shouted, pushing the front row with his rifle. "Give the Captain some room!"

"Shut your traps!" Collier roared with him. "Captain's got our questions, now give him time to ask command! Get back in line!"

"Fuck!" several soldiers roared back and a few of them expressed what Collier and Jonesy and Palmer could do to each other, but it began to subside. He and Jonesy eyeballed everyone back into the closest semblance of a line this bunch was capable of, and Palmer slowly, and coolly, looked over the half-assed formation. When it settled, he called out, "Dismissed!"

The troops looked at each other, uncertain, and a few of the real hotheads harangued their neighbors to just quit and go home, but those same neighbors smacked them quiet, and they all, in stages, shuffled away to respective postings. Bad eyes glared at the three of them as they did so, but that was a distinct improvement over fingers on triggers, and Collier felt relieved. LT Fuzznuts tried to get next to Palmer, but they all three eyebrowed him off. Soon, they were the only ones in the assembly area, the beginnings of rosy sunrise half-lighting them.

"You gonna court-martial us?" Jonesy asked Palmer.

Palmer shook his head. "No."

"I would." Collier observed.

Palmer just nodded, looking off as the stragglers headed around corners. "Can't be court-martialed for speaking the truth."

Collier and Jonesy looked at each other as Palmer faced them, "I've asked those very same questions, over and over. I'm getting no answers. None." He paused. "Something's going on. I don't know what, but it's not good, not good at all. Keep your people close. And be ready for anything." Palmer was struggling to keep his emotions in check, and not doing a good job. "Anything," he said again, then wheeled and strode into the morning dim.

They watched him go. Jonesy fumbled into his pocket for a cigarette and offered one to Collier, who took it wordlessly. "Shit," Jonesy said.

21

Shit, Collier thought, I'm off, off-tempo, out of step, unsynched. Was that even a word? Should be, because it explained why he was stomping up the barracks' wooden porch right now, instead of gliding through the iced-over weeds of Sector 3. Things were unsynched all over. After that fucked-up morning formation, it had taken Jonesy and him way too long to coordinate maps and AORs and flank connects and call signs and emergency responses and backups and well, everything. So he got off late, and while hustling the platoon up the trail that paralleled the Red side of the Creek, suddenly realized he'd forgotten the backup rations. Just plain forgot.

Unsynched.

Cursing, he'd put the-corporal-this-week in charge and warned him to set the patrol or he'd personally feed said corporal his own balls, then ran the two miles or so to retrieve the food stash. Couldn't send the-corporal-this-week or any of the privates, oh no, because they would either get lost or get shot or take a nap. If you want anything done in this hyeah Army, you damn well better do it yourself.

A freakin' sergeant doing slick sleeve work, Collier

thought, as he swung the door open. And why is that? Because they were undermanned, the men they had were crap, the assignments were crap, the Reds were crap, the Army was crap, so was the country, and he wasn't getting laid.

He paused in the doorway. The reason I'm off is … I'm not getting off? He chuckled. Nah. Rosa and he had gone through dry spells before, when suspicions about them had mounted or the Ghosts were running and gunning as they slipped around the Reds or doing something equally crazy ...

Equally crazy. He frowned. Things were crazy, all right. But not the normal crazy of an outnumbered Battalion escaping the traps set for it. No, this was a different crazy: patrols that no longer patrol and certain incompetent asshole-shouldn't-be-sergeants never rotated from critical points on the line and missions deliberately compromised.

Crazy crazy.

He stood there, unsynched, framed in the doorway, which was dangerous and stupid. Red snipers out there, not to mention residually pissed-off troops from this morning's formation and here he was, presenting the biggest, fattest, juiciest target imaginable.

So what?

Many, many hypersonic pieces of metal had been flung his way these past years, and it was only random placement of his body that had allowed them to pass, or, at least, smack only non-vital parts. Just random fucking luck. And random fucking luck would lay him low. So, go ahead, sniper, deserter, whoever. Take your best shot.

He waited a few heartbeats, but nothing. Collier shook his head. Apparently, random fucking luck ruled the universe. Dad's Bible notes seemed to back that up – Jehovah had Plans and Man had plans and rarely did the two mesh. So, a controlled randomness, then, which was a cancellation of terms. Uncoordinated randomness? What the heck is that?

One helluva theology you got there, Dad.

He let out a long, exasperated breath, reaching behind him to shut the door and end some sniper's golden opportunity. It was all completely fucked up. All. And he couldn't fix it, not now, not ever, not even if a thousand angels sprang to his aid ... so, fuck it.

He moved towards the storage shelves in the back. Okay, grab two or three bags of the plundered stuff, Vienna sausage and Spam, uhmm uhmm uhmm, then hightail it back out to the platoon before Palmer or LT Numbnuts or, God forbid, the Colonel, noticed he wasn't out there. But, hey, in for a penny, so swing by the hammock and grab another pack of gaggy cigarettes. Too bad all the cigars were gone. He glanced towards his hammock as he reached the shelves, and stopped cold. What's that? Some kind of odd shape ...

Crap. Someone was there, half-hidden by the post.

He rolled out, clearing the .45 as he went to his knees behind the lockers. He peered through the murk. The shape had shifted a bit, so whoever it was knew he'd been spotted. Deserter? Must be. Great, just great. A marvelous start to the day all around, t'weren't it?

Oh well ...

Collier moved fast, keeping as many of the lockers and hammocks between him and the deserter as possible. He slipped in a gap between the aisles and wheeled around the post, leveling the .45—

"Getting to be a habit with you, ain't it, Sarge?"

Collier stared at the short, squat, very dirty, and disheveled soldier framed in his sights. Big blue pop eyes, the completely undisciplined hair, squat body. "Why," Collier said softly, "it's Corporal Price."

"So, you remember me," Price grinned at Collier as he fumbled with an extra-long Maduro. "You wouldn't happen to have a light, would you?"

Collier hesitated, keeping the pistol on him. Price didn't look threatening, but he was a hired gun and might be trying to put Collier off before pulling a weapon and doin' him. And, face it, you're unsynched and maybe shouldn't put a lot of trust in your instincts right now. But Price's jacket was zipped, his holster inaccessible and, really, the guy looked flat-out exhausted. Collier depressed the pistol but kept the safety off. He recalled how touchy Price was, how very unpredictable. Be ready, Coll old boy. "We don't allow smoking in the barracks."

Price looked down at the cigar, "You did last time I was here."

Collier shrugged, "I get to. You don't."

"Bit unfair, Sarge." Price said and held the Maduro out. "Would you like this?"

"That's not the one I gave you, is it?"

"Oh, no, that one's long gone. I cured it in a humidor for a week or so, rum dipped it and it was real sweet. This one," Price gestured with it, "I got, along with seven others, from a townhouse near Conshohocken. They're not banded. I think they're Cubans."

"Cubans?" Collier's eyebrows rose. Price smiled again and pushed the Maduro at him. Collier took it, ready to fire should Price do something stupid. He sniffed it, savoring the bouquet. "Damn," he sighed, "that's nice." He tucked the cigar in his upper pocket. Screw the cigarettes.

"How was that letter?" Price asked.

"Letter?"

"You know," Price gestured at the hammock, "in the package. The one I got from Bill. The letter he wrote about your Dad?"

"You saw me read it. Apparently, I thought it was good." Understatement. Bill's letter had been on top of *The Little Shepherd of Kingdom Come*, an old schmaltzy book that Dad owned decades before Collier was born and which Dad just loved for reasons Coll could not figure out, and a map of the American University campus that Dad had marked up.

Collier's most precious possessions were the map tucked in the book and book tucked in backpack or back pocket all the time because there was no way he was going to lose Dad again, like he did five years ago in the middle of a phone call: Dad suddenly quiet then telling him the lights had gone out, that he had to hang up, that he had to go see what was wrong.

Never heard from Dad again.

Then, a few weeks ago, Price comes waltzing in and slaps the book and letter and even some of Mom's old jewelry (stashed in the old Pemberton High School because he'd get knifed for that, but not for a book) down on his hammock. Out of nowhere, just out of nowhere, like that crazy guy handing him Dad's Bible which had joined *Shepherd* in the backpack, although it wasn't as important. And, lookee, lookee, here's Price again, and he just gave Collier a cigar, worth its weight in gold, and goes straight to the letter.

Gee, you think he wants something?

"Okay, Corporal," Collier said, "We both know how much I appreciate—"

"You gonna shoot me?" Price interrupted, gesturing at the pistol.

Collier set his lips in a grim line, "Depends on what you are doing here."

"Running."

"That's obvious. You look like shit."

Price looked down at his torn and muddied uniform,

"Been a hard run." He suddenly looked up. "You said you owed me, right? Well, I need clothes, food, ammunition, maybe a better weapon."

Ah. Got it. Calling in a marker. Collier regarded him. "You deserting?"

"No, escaping."

"What's the difference?"

Price blinked slowly, "The difference is, you need to escape, too."

Collier let out a slow breath and felt his anger stir, "No, I don't. Because I'm not a fucking deserter. I don't like the way things are going, either, but I don't run. I see things through. If everybody runs, the Reds win, the 'Slams win, America's gone." He paused, thinking suddenly of Dad. "I'd rather die fighting, even if it's hopeless." He pressed the pistol into Price's chest, "And I shoot deserters. Without a qualm."

"Even if you're being sold out?" Price replied calmly, not a spark of fear in his eyes. Tough little bastard.

"What are you talking about?"

"You're being sold out," Price paused, fumbling with his pocket. "You sure I can't smoke?"

"No, you can't, and I'm getting damned impatient here, Corporal."

Price pulled in a long breath and Collier saw how worn he was, his eyes reddened and sunken, the exhaustion carving lines into his baby face. Yeah, definitely one bitch of a run. But why? There's no need.

Down where Price was, the Valley, where the 98th was attached to the 4th, there were lots of places to hide – woods and mountains and the Shenandoah itself. Stupid to come up here through Red territory. And then put yourself back at the mercy of a Reg unit? Really stupid.

But Price wasn't stupid. Unease drifted up Collier's spine.

"There's going to be a coup," Price said, "They're going to surrender the Army. And they're going to do it on your bodies."

Collier gave that about a half-second and then snorted, "Right. Sure. What crap. There's been a dozen or so half-assed coups. The Chief always stopped them."

"Not this time."

"Bull."

"Not this time, Sarge. They're going to do it."

"How do you know?"

"Can I show you something?" and Price stopped fumbling and moved his hand towards the inside of his jacket. Collier pressed the pistol a little harder, all the warning needed, and Price slowly pulled out two pieces of paper and held them out.

Keeping his eyes locked on Price's, Collier asked, "What's this?"

"Letters."

"From who?"

"Some LC named Kant at HQ. To my former employer," and Price smiled, no humor in it.

Collier's unease heightened. "Who's your former employer?"

"An accomplished financier." That smile again.

Collier blinked at him and risked a quick glance at the papers. "Get on the floor," Collier ordered.

"Not a lot of room down there, Sarge. And it looks dirty."

"Floor. Now," and Collier viciously jabbed the barrel.

"Okay, okay," Price went to his knees, keeping both hands out and flapping the letters as he lay down on his stomach. "Jesus," he said, "don't you guys ever sweep?"

"Shut up." Collier snatched the letters and looked them over while keeping one eye on the little twerp, pistol ready. He pitched the first paper, which was coded, and read the second. He read it again. Then again.

All of this depends on the subsequent loss of the 1st.

"This is bullshit," he said.

"That's what I said."

"It's just utter bullshit." Collier shook the letter and the pistol at the back of Price's head. "Why are you buying this?

"Because you're already surrounded, Sarge."

Collier started, "What?"

"Yeah, they got you, man. They're all the way around. About the only open spot is on the Delaware near some old battlefield close to West Deptford, and it ain't that open. Believe me, I crossed there, and it wasn't easy."

"That's southwest. We know they're over there. We're still open north."

Price shook his head, "Not anymore, you're not. I tried that way first."

"When?"

"Four days ago. Locked up tight. Had to slip south aways before I found an opening."

"That's BS. You came through there yourself just a little while ago."

"Yeah, Sarge, but I couldn't this time." Price squirmed a bit. "Sarge, can I get up? I'm getting tuberculosis down here."

"No," and Collier kicked him lightly in the shoulder. Price got the message and lay still. Okay, let's review: when Price first showed up, things were pretty normal ... well, for a war zone. Yeah, yeah, they were besieged but there was still movement, sporadic resupply and reinforcements, some mail, some contact with Army HQ, all from the north because they were holding the flanks okay. Not perfect, some leakage, but okay. They'd felt pretty good because they could always slip north, like they'd been slipping out of the Reds' grasp all along.

After all, they were the Ghosts.

But since then ...

The thwarted grab mission. Thwarted by the Colonel, please note. And Deavers and Eliot up there on the northern line weren't sending patrols out, apparently at the Colonel's order, please note again.

"Get up," Collier said and stood back to give himself a clear shot should Price come up with something other than a bad attitude.

"Thanks," Price said brightly and brushed at his clothes good-naturedly, coming up with another cigar, which made Collier grit his teeth. Jesus, sleight-of-hand expert; could have easily been a knife.

Collier shook the letter at him. "So, what? You fuckin' Paul Revere now?"

Price shrugged, "No. I can't go home yet, that's all. They're looking for me. They're going to kill me, so I have to hide someplace they'd never think I'd be, like right in the heart of it."

"Heart of what?"

"It! It!" and Price stabbed the cigar at Collier. "Aren't you hearing me? You're in the middle of a shit storm. There's a lot of Colonels involved. Hell, a lot of generals, too. They're going to give you guys up to the Reds, let the shock of all you getting massacred serve as their excuse for taking over. Pretty fuckin' brilliant, doncha think?" Price spat, bitterly.

Yes, pretty fuckin' brilliant, if it were true ... and if it were—

Holy crap.

Collier leaped forward and drove the barrel against Price's temple, tightening his trigger finger. This is your polygraph, you little bastard – flinch once, you're done. "What the fuck?" Collier hissed savagely, "How I know you didn't write this shit yourself?"

Price just looked at him like he was stupid, "Ya know, Sarge, I didn't come up here a few weeks ago just to see you. I came to see your Colonel. Gave him a letter, took a letter back. Don't know what was in them, but," he gestured at the paper Collier held, "I can draw conclusions. Besides, pretty elaborate way for me to desert, doncha think, Sarge?"

Yes, it was, Sarge. Collier frowned and pressed the barrel harder. "So why'dn't you just go to ground then, huh?"

"I told you, asshole, I gotta get someplace they wouldn't look," Price's color rose and Collier got ready because Price could just go off. "And I need help to do it. Figured you were a man of your word. Are you?"

Tableau, both standing there hard and violent, both a hair away from murder, and like that, instantly, Collier knew. The image blazed hard and harsh and stark right through Collier's brain: long lines of ragged soldiers standing next to open trenches.

He pulled the pistol back, watched Price for a moment, then lowered it, and was suddenly overwhelmed with a deep, deep weariness. Price could jump him but, you know, go ahead, you little fuck. Put me out of my misery. "You coulda gone on without stopping here," Collier said. "You coulda stole what you needed." Collier gestured at the cigar. "You obviously have talent."

"Trying to make me blush, Sarge?" Price looked away, then shook his head. "I had to make a stop first," that smile again, "and since I was in the neighborhood and don't want the bastards to get away with it ..."

Collier nodded and, after a moment, holstered his pistol. And, after another moment, pocketed the papers. "I need these." Price just shrugged and Collier looked at him. Little bastard, torn the million ways these last five years have torn all of us, our souls rent, our lives just fragments, anything human in us now mean and cunning and low. Yet, here he is.

"All right," Collier barely whispered it. He tilted his head towards the storage lockers. "There's a couple of knaps back there on the floor. They got food, so take 'em. There's weapons in the trunk next to the locker. Take some fatigues from that hammock over there." He pointed in the distance. "The guy's about your size. Make it look like another company ripped us off. Don't be here ten minutes from now. They inspect."

Price nodded, carefully tucking the cigar into his upper pocket. They stared at each other for a long moment, then Collier whirled and stalked towards the entrance, slamming the door hard behind him and pausing on the porch. He'd give Price a few moments cover, in case someone showed up. The sun was out, hard and brilliant but not warm. What was that line Dad always quoted? "April is the cruelest month." Yeah, that's it.

Looking across the compound, he spied a private skulking in the corner of the armory. Probably some fuck waste of Army meat getting out of a job. Good. "Hey you, Private!" he bellowed, "Get over here!"

The private started and paled and Collier grinned inwardly. The private hesitated, so Collier put a storm on his face. The private stood in front of him in seconds flat, shaking in terror. "Ye-yees, Sergeant?" his voice quavered.

Collier put absolute menace in his voice, "I need you to take a message to S2. And, if you fuck it up, I'll hang you with your own guts." The private kept shaking as he listened and repeated and listened and repeated until Collier was sure he got it, and then rocketed away from Sergeant Evil Incarnate as fast as his shaky legs could move him.

Collier watched him go. Without a backward glance,

he humped off towards Pemberton.

22

Rosa glared at the intelligence reports stacked on her desk. Might as well be from the Civil War. Useless, effectively useless.

Which made *her* effectively useless.

She stirred in frustration, pushing the papers away. If there was one thing she had never been since joining this Army, it was useless. She'd fought in the Mexican incursion, infiltrating small units deep into enemy territory and disrupting their lines, gaining a reputation as a fierce and unrelenting operator and getting a by-name request to the staff of some up-and-coming Major named Caldwell deployed in front of Richmond, arriving just in time for *that* godawful fight – and subsequent flight – across the Virginia Piedmont. Rapid promotions on the fly, and she became a Major and the Major became a Colonel and all of them became Ghosts, and she and Collier became lovers.

God, she missed him.

If she had an ounce of reckless courage, she would summon him, right now, into her office and slam the door and have at him in full hearing of Awbrey and whoever the hell else was within range. But she was not reckless;

indeed, she'd become overly circumspect, convinced the Colonel was on to them.

And was unhinged.

There was no other explanation for the Colonel's astounding disregard of the situation. He ignored her repeated pleas for the resumption of patrols, just sat in his office consulting an old Park Service tourist map showing the general location of hiking trails along the Rancocas Creek watershed. It wasn't a good map, more cartoon than anything, but, these days, you made do.

Hiking trails? What was he planning? Maybe a race across the front to hit the Reds in some unexpected place, then turn and hit them again in some other unexpected place until the Reds were so confused that gaps opened up and the Ghosts could rush out, out, free of this trap, long columns of soldiers and trucks and guns slipping up the Colonel's Park Service trails while she and Collier harried the Reds and confused them even more until the Ghosts simply disappeared. Again. Further north, to New York, or maybe back to Pennsylvania, then swing about and start the process all over. That'd be great.

But to do that, you have to know what's going on, Colonel. You have to know where the Reds are and what they're doing.

And you don't. Because I don't. And that's never happened before.

What *has* happened before: the Colonel hunkered in his office brewing up a miracle. But he'd still send her out to examine terrains and do probes, and from those, she could guess his direction and adjust her efforts accordingly. This was nothing like that. They weren't even doing the most basic of patrols, which was downright criminal. Maybe, just maybe, the Colonel had something in mind so radically different that conventional methods did not apply. But she had no inkling what that could be. She had no sense of pending brilliance, either, only a foreboding of disaster.

Because, the only way the Ghosts could slip along Rancocas trails unbothered was if the Reds had become static, emplaced, more interested in setting up strong points than attacking. She had no evidence of that. *Au contraire*, everything pointed to the opposite. The Reds had driven them hard for the past six months and would have caught them two months ago if the Colonel hadn't slipped their trap, but the Reds were still on them and had even managed to cut the Ghosts off from the rest of the Army. We can't reach the Valley. We can't reach anyone. One good push and they can drive us off this line. They know that. Why would they stop?

But, *hija*, they have.

They have.

The daily snipings and shellings continued, of course, but the probes of the Ghosts' lines had stopped. It looked very much like the Reds had, indeed, emplaced, gone to ground, and maybe that was the Colonel's spark, why now he hunched at his desk consulting Park Service maps.

Or the Reds were doing something else, like slipping around their flanks, as Collier feared. While the Colonel remained unhinged, as she feared. And an unhinged Colonel stops all patrols and takes counsel from his own madness …

You would kill us all, Colonel, just to kill one?

Chills ran through her. When did it start? Specifically, when had the Colonel figured out her true relationship with Collier, and the worm of it begun eating his brain? Had to be sometime in the last four months, when they were all exhilarated and high and ecstatic after the brilliant escape from the Reds and she got the tattoo and a lover and the Colonel asked her to move in, and she had said no. Dismissed the genius for the jock, had she? Was that enough to drive a man mad?

Apparently.

Think much of yourself, do you, *hija*? She chuckled. Hardly the woman to launch a thousand ships, but who can explain insanity? A bunch of frenzied hate-filled sub-humans had destroyed the world because of their insane desire to make everyone Muslim. Another group of sub-humans broke quarantine and launched horrific plagues across the country, because of an insane need to roam free. Could her choosing the sergeant make the officer equally insane?

"Mad," not insane, which implied gibbering and irrationality and believing he was the King of Siam or something. She could deal with that. Relieve him, gently place him in medical, tranquilize him, hope that Hoffman, the Phantom of the Opera, could keep the Battalion running. "Mad" is blindly self-absorbed and deluded, like those crazed villains in the Spiderman comics she'd loved, Green Goblin or Doc Ock, weaving plots towards some diabolical end that satisfied some grand illusion, some sincerely misguided lust. How do you deal with that? She couldn't very well web him and hang him from the ceiling.

She frowned at the useless papers. Madness trumps reality. A mad Colonel sees things that are, simply, not there. If he believes the enemy has gone to ground, then it has gone to ground, and he makes plans in complement. So, when he launches his attack, flinging the Ghosts across his Park Service trails at Reds he thinks are asleep, and the Reds prove themselves wide awake, then the Ghosts become the Light Brigade, this little crappy town, Gallipoli.

She couldn't let that happen.

Just couldn't.

Rosa took a deep breath. When not sure of the tactical

environment, force the issue. Shoot into the woods. Expose yourself. Get a reaction, no matter how personally dangerous.

Disobey orders.

She sat for a moment, then strode to the door and yanked it open, "Awbrey!"

The corporal came straight up out of his chair. Must have scared him half to death, and she suppressed a giggle. Stumbling, Awbrey turned and goggled at her, confusion across his face, like a dog whose mistress had come home in a bad mood. But, give him credit, the little spaz recovered quickly enough. "Ma'am?"

"I need you to get a runner and pass a message to Palmer. Have him report to me as soon as he can." She paused. "And be discreet."

He blinked at her, cocking his head. "Ma'am?"

"Discreet. You know the word. And tell Palmer to bring Jonesy. And Rashkil." She wondered if Awbrey could see her heart beat faster. Not only her lover's name causing that, but the treason forming in her mind: an illegal recon. To see if the Colonel was unhinged or not.

Awbrey shifted and looked away and she frowned because that meant something was on his mind. "What is it?" she demanded.

"Rashkil sent a message." He just couldn't keep the venom out of his voice. Couldn't keep the dislike off his face, either. "He said he had a casualty in Sector 2."

She nodded, keeping all emotion and reaction off her face because she was thunderstruck. What? An emergency meeting at 0200? Oh, Lord. "You've had this message how long?"

Awbrey fumbled at himself, "About an hour or two, Ma'am."

A pulse beat in her temple. "And you didn't think it important enough to tell me?"

He tilted his head again, somewhat puzzled, "It's a casualty report, Ma'am," and she could have smacked herself for an idiot. Yes, a simple casualty report, briefed as necessary, not when she sits behind her door, brooding. "True," she made her voice conciliatory, "and thanks for not interrupting me to provide it." The bone thrown, he eagerly grasped it, almost a smile forming on his strangely intent face. "What kind of casualty?" she said it as if disinterested, because it's important Awbrey think she was.

Awbrey shrugged, and she made a show of slight annoyance. "You should find out such details," she admonished. "After all, that's your job." She stared at him hard, ostensibly to bring home the lesson, but more to see if he suspected anything. No guile, just guilt on his face. Good. She wheeled, but then turned back. "Cancel the runner to Palmer," then entered her office to count the seconds until 0200.

23

"Rosa." A whisper.

She followed it towards three or four strangely placed gravestones about ten yards away. As she approached, Collier detached from the shadows and swept into her arms. She kissed him hard and deep, losing herself, alive now for the first time since ... the last time. He kissed her back, just as hard, and they were gone, carried away from this war and its harshness and misery and lost friends and family and the death, sheer death of everything. That is, until he suddenly pulled away, tense.

"What's wrong?" she whispered.

"Were you followed?" His tone was frantic.

"No!" She was sure of that because she had checked more than usual this time, and then checked and double-checked. Too many dangerous things were slouching in her direction. "No," she repeated, pressing his arm.

He looked off, peering into the darkness, and then dropped a set of NVGs strapped to his helmet. She stared. He never brought NVGs. They were hard to get, first of all, and harder to keep track of, especially in the throes of passion. Lose a set and see what happens. Which meant Collier wasn't just nervous, he was downright paranoid.

He never got paranoid. "Collier!" she whispered, suddenly afraid.

He looked at her, cockroach eyes dimly visible in the lenses suddenly disappearing as he pulled up the NVGs. "Sorry," he whispered back, but stayed tense, wary.

Threats slouching towards them both. "You feel it, too." She wasn't asking.

"Feel it?" his response was grim, "I'm way past that."

She nodded, "Me, too. Something bad is going to happen."

"It is." He reached out, pulling her to him, "It has."

She grasped his arms, "So you've figured it out." Of course. Collier was too sharp, and the Colonel's inexplicable, mad actions, too obvious.

"No. I was told."

Told? She blinked. "What are you talking about?"

He shifted his hands up to her face, "Price came to see me."

"Price? The courier from the 98th?"

"Yeah, him. I came off patrol today to get some equipment and he was hiding near my hammock. He looked like he'd been dragged through a field of stones. I was going to shoot him, but then ..." Collier jerked his head up. "Did you hear something?"

She stopped breathing, all of her now radar, probing the night. Paranoid or not, Collier was a Night Man, almost supernaturally attuned to the dark and could read its disturbances like most could read the day's. They both stayed intent, Collier leaving the NVGs in place and trusting his instincts, both scanning the area for moments longer than anyone approaching them could hope to remain silent. Nothing, but Collier did not relax.

"Go on," she whispered.

"All right, sorry." He leaned in, his lips touching her ear. "Price said we were going to be sacrificed."

"Sacrificed?" she reacted, but kept her voice low. "What does that mean?"

"Abandoned, then massacred."

"What?" That sounded crazy. "How?"

"We're surrounded."

"What?!?"

"Yes," his whisper ferocious, "we're surrounded. The little punk tried to come in from the north but couldn't, so he slipped across at West Deptford somewhere. Barely made it. Which means we're trapped."

"But ..."

"I know! How could they pull that off without us knowing?" He gripped her collar. "Because Headquarters is part of it. So is the Colonel."

"Huh?" Off-the-rails crazy now.

"They need a crisis." Dramatic pause. "For a coup."

Speechless, all she could do was place her hands on top of Collier's, letting him know he was hurting her. What the HELL? Some barracks thief sneaks in and tells Collier a story of coups and conspiracies and murder, oh my, and he buys it? Was there a brain virus going around? Ridiculous! Ree. Dic. U. Less! "You shovelhead!" She hissed between his hands.

He stepped back, surprised. "What? You don't believe it?"

"Believe it?" She threw her hands up in exasperation, her voice rising dangerously. "It's fucking impossible, Collier! There's just no way in hell it could happen!"

"That's what I said," he replied, quietly.

"Well, then?" she was still exasperated but a warning bell sounded in her head because Collier wasn't a shovelhead. He wouldn't buy anyone's sob story; he usually cut sob stories off with a bullet. Yet, here he was, grim and tense and downright scared, telling her something that, by all laws of common sense, he should have rejected. "Tell me why you believe him!" She almost snarled.

Wordlessly, Collier reached into his shirt and pulled out what sounded like papers. He handed them to her, useless in the dark, but then gave her the NVGs. So that's why he brought them. She fumbled the goggles into place, irritated with the focus and glow until she could make out both papers. She read them. Compared them. Read them again. "Who's this Leideig?"

"Price's boss."

"Who's this Colonel Kant?"

He said nothing because he didn't have to. It was apparent from the letters. As was Price's warning.

No way. Absolutely no way. "It's a setup." She rattled the papers at him. "Price is setting us up."

"For what?"

"For—" What? What on earth could this be a setup for? A Red attack, using the traitor Price as a diversion? Pretty stupid, since they were now alerted. A diabolical plot to expose her and Collier? Quite an elaborate and logistically insane method of doing so. She furiously raced through the remaining possibilities – wildly improbable practical joke, aliens – but there was nothing she could connect with this. Which meant, it could only be what it seemed to be.

No way. Absolutely no freakin' way.

Collier read her shock and indecision and spoke low, urgently, "Think about it. Price didn't have to come here. He could have run off somewhere else."

"Maybe he had no choice." She said that in the same desperate tone she'd used when calling it a setup.

"Oh, c'mon," he scorned. "There's a lot better hiding places than this. Nobody comes here, unless they've got a mission." Collier paused. "He did. To warn us. To save us."

"Why would he do that?"

Collier hesitated and aha! There! The flaw, the big glaring inconsistency that would break the punk's story and bring Collier back to earth. Wake up! The real danger is the Colonel's unhinged jealousy! We gotta fix that, somehow neutralize the Colonel and put everything aright and get at the Reds and maybe, just maybe, end this fucked-up war. There is no shadowy conspiracy involving hundreds of persons and mass betrayal and mass murder, Collier! There isn't! There is something much smaller, much more controllable, something that we can solve together. Please, see it. Please!

Then Collier spoke. Quietly, slowly. "For the same reason he hung on to Dad's stuff."

All the breath left her. In that, the proof: no ulterior motive, no scam, no intricate grift here, just the deep down purity of someone wanting to do the right thing, so rare these days, so precious that, when encountered, you knew it instantly. A sickness ran through her, wilting her nerves and sapping her strength as she rapidly listed supporting evidence – the failed grab, the changed orders, the lack of patrols, even Price's surreptitious meeting with the Colonel a few weeks ago. And she knew, as Collier already did, that the little thug was telling the truth.

"Oh, God, oh my God," was all she could say.

He gently, sadly, took the goggles back and buried his head in her hair. They clutched desperately at each other, blocking the night and all its dangers, too intent on each other to watch out, and were undone.

Sound, metal on stone, a large group rushing.

"Shit," was all Collier could say.

Several converging beams of precious battery-driven spotlights pinioned them, still holding each other, blinded and blinking, deer-like, as silhouettes quickly surrounded them.

"Well, well," the Colonel's voice sounded from the middle of one particularly thick mass of silhouettes, "I would call this an extracurricular activity, wouldn't you, Major?"

Rosa froze because she knew they were lost. Collier, though, didn't freeze, and, before she could stop him, lunged in the Colonel's direction. Stupid. The butt of a rifle caught him square on the jaw and he collapsed like a tipping pile of bricks. In the lights, she saw two soldiers, big and grim and triumphant, standing over him.

A hand reached out of the bright lights. "May I see these, Major?" the Colonel said as he took the papers from her. A flashlight turned his face into Satan's as he read them. He looked at her.

"Take them to confinement," he said.

24

Rosa had said nothing while the guards, leering and taking many more liberties than should be allowed, searched her, all the time making snide comments about "enlisted dick." They eyed her hungrily, no longer someone to fear. One of them had offered to leave the door unlocked if she would just be "friendly," and she stared him down until he snorted and said, "Don't matter, we getcha when the Colonel's done." The others guffawed as they trooped out, pulling the door closed and leaving her in complete darkness.

She wondered when the Colonel had assembled this little palace guard. Heck, when'd he coordinated a full-blown coup with the Reds?

She was on the third floor of the HQ building, in a small storage room at the opposite end from the Colonel's office. The staff used it to secure extra paper and rations, items so precious they'd installed locks to keep scroungers out. Now, the locks kept her in. There were no windows and the door was heavy and oaken and would easily take a pounding from her small frame. Some of the palace guard was standing out there, anyway, so, forget it.

She had spent five frustrating minutes tapping and

probing and even kicking at likely spots on the walls, all to no avail. Dammit. She had to get out of here. She had to warn the Battalion, had to find Collier, had to kill the Colonel, all in the next five minutes. She gritted her teeth and clenched her fists and thought seriously about a running leap at the door but, c'mon, that's stupid. *Tranquiles*, Rosita, *placido*, because frustration distracts and there is always a way out. Always. She stood quietly in the middle of the room, centering herself. Relax. Drift. Think things through.

Like, how it was a very good thing she and Collier had been intent on Price's information, instead of *in flagrante delicto*, when the Colonel caught them. That gave her some measure of defense. Yes, Your Honor, we were in the middle of a rather intense hug, but we were both so shocked over the Colonel's treason that we fell into spontaneous, meaningless consolation. Did I mention the Colonel's treason, Judge?

Did I mention treason?

A coldness took her. She no longer had any doubts about Price's story. And the Colonel, with those papers in hand, had no doubts about her lack of doubts. He's got to be wondering who else knows. He's got to be panicking.

Got to be.

Which was probably why he didn't just shoot them both right there. He needed to know who she'd told. News of their arrest must be racing through the Battalion like wild fire, convincing unknown others of his treason. So they would be safe, but only until (a) the Colonel figured out only Collier and she knew about it and, or, (b) the coup kicked off. Which was ... when? She didn't know, but it must be far enough off that he couldn't afford to kill them yet.

Which means, Rosa honey, you are in for a night of pliers, hot irons, rape and sodomy until the Colonel felt reassured.

The coldness became ice. Her very own methods turned against her; well, the pliers and hot irons, at least. She could break a soldier in about an hour; how long before *she* broke, especially when the Palace Guard lined up to pull a train? She'd been gang-raped before in the wreckage of New York City, but that had been different, and she ended up hunting down and killing the participants. She wouldn't have that chance here. The rape would go on until she fell at the Colonel's feet begging for mercy and swearing, swearing, that she had told no one, that Collier hadn't either, and then he *would* have mercy, a bullet to the back of the head.

Got to get out of here.

She almost launched at the door but a sharp command, "Rosita! No!" stopped her. Poppy was standing in her mind, arms folded, angry. Think, Rosita, think! What is going on outside that door right now? Well, Poppy, the palace guard is assembling various poles and clubs designed to ram up my various orifices, interspersed with their own male equipment, and sharpening bayonets to cut off my breasts and peel the skin from my face. Poppy frowned at her. What else is going on, Rosita?

What else?

The news racing across the Battalion like wildfire, of course, which meant a lot of interest in where she was and what was going on … and that made torture a little difficult to conceal, didn't it? Lord knows she couldn't keep the screams of her own clients from leaking out of this building's basement, an effect she actually encouraged for its lesson. So *when*, not *if*, the Battalion discovered her bent over a chair with rifles shoved up her, there'd be wholesale shock because, gee, Colonel, a bit excessive for officer/enlisted fraternization, doncha think? Which meant the unknown others she may, or may not, have told about the looming coup would know it was just a matter of time before she revealed their names and they had better do something about that, right now. Result? A big freakin' uproar, and the last thing the Colonel needed right now was a big freakin' uproar. She relaxed, suddenly relieved, but for only about two seconds.

Because, Poppy, the Colonel might *want* a big freakin' uproar. A really, really big one.

She stopped breathing. The Colonel was a tactical genius, almost prescient, always one step ahead. So what if, all along, he had known about Coll and her? Bide his time, choose the right moment and then, *wham*! There it is, an issue absolutely guaranteed to distract from the cancelled patrols and out-of-date intel. Which meant she and Coll were as much a part of whatever the Colonel had done (or not done) to arrange the Battalion's encirclement as anyone.

You idiot.

You complete and total idiot. You and Collier played right into his hands.

Jesus.

She sank slowly to the floor, overwhelmed. Oh God. Oh God in Heaven, they had been fish on the hook, dodging here and there smug and sure when, all the while, they were being led gently to the net. She suddenly felt stupid and foolish. You amateur.

They were lost. Completely lost. However much time remained before the coup – a day, two, thirty – there was absolutely nothing she could do about it. Incommunicado, unable to warn, unable to save the Battalion from enslavement and Collier from a bullet to the back of the head. And she would have her breasts cut off, her face peeled away, office furniture shoved up her, over and over, her screams broadcast throughout the entire Battalion because the Colonel needed a gigantic, distracting uproar.

Poppy, I have to get out of here.

She whirled, spinning a kick at a wall, getting thrown across the storage area and into a pile of boxes for her trouble. She sat up, pushing the boxes off her then changing her mind and probing them for something she could use: a pistol, a pry bar, a teleporter, anything, but it was mostly papers and MREs. Well, at least she wouldn't starve. The plastic sporks in them might make impromptu shivs—

Someone threw the locks.

She stood, facing the door and straining against the dark while a stab of fear skewered her to the floor. It was about to start, the palace guard lining up for a night's entertainment. The stab of fear went, abruptly, to cold anger. Kill the first two or three of them, make them fight, drag her down. Who knows, maybe she'd surprise them enough to force her way through, race across the compound and into her lover's arms until the Owl Creek plank fell. She centered, taking a deep breath, tan tien, the chi, flowing up her hands and powering them. Oh yes, come in, boys, you're in for a big surprise.

But not as surprised as she when the door opened and only the Colonel stood there, framed in the suddenly dazzling light, two of his thugs in the background. He looked at her coolly, probably detecting her readiness, and stepped inside. He glanced at the guards, who gave the Colonel a lamp and closed the door behind him. One of them couldn't resist a parting leer.

"It's time we had a conversation," the Colonel said, quietly.

She recovered quickly, using her officer's voice, even though her heart was pounding, "I can assure you, Colonel, that my relationship with Sergeant Rashkil is purely professional—"

He held up his hand, "We both know that's not true. But that's not what this is about." He paused. "I've come to make you an offer."

25

Collier sat on a cot in the middle of a dripping, mildewed, cement-block room he knew very well. Richmond, Culpeper, Pennsylvania, didn't matter, all these cells were the same. On at least a thousand occasions he'd slept in one while awaiting the results of various Art.15s for various things, mostly insubordination. Collier did not suffer fools well, especially commissioned fools, and often expressed that with a punch to the commissioned fool's nose. He usually got hard labor or confinement or stripes removed, whatever, but only until the next Red breakthrough, when his combat fury restored him to former positions and rank.

This time, though, his treasured fighting skills weren't going to save him; if anything, they condemned him. He'd ambushed and killed far too many Reds for them to let him go. Not that he'd want to live under a Red regime, anyway. Might as well be a 'Slam.

He supposed the Battalion was pretty much in a paroxysm of delight over his arrest, excepting Jonesy and Swift and maybe one or two others. He could hear it now: "Hey, man! Hard-ass Rashkil got locked up, that bastard!"

One of humanity's greatest pleasures was

comeuppance, and, no doubt, many thought he was getting his overly-deserved one. Since he'd meted out a lot of the necessary brutality this hyeah Army required, shooting deserters, beating malcontents, breaking a few bones, et cetera, et cetera, the many recipients of said brutality were now dancing with glee.

This hyeah Army.

He snorted. Look at this Army and tell me brutality isn't needed to keep it together. Just tell me it isn't. Draft Gangs tore most of the recruits from their mommies' teats and threw them into training camps not much different from Dachau, where subhuman DIs beat the recruits mostly to death as they drew sub-par gear and horrible food and were given even worse training and then thrown to the wolves. Like the meat grinder on the Saudi peninsula, giving the Boot the good ole American boot while turning Mecca into glass (take that, Mohammed!); more, Collier suspected, to make us feel good than serve a true military purpose. Oh, yes, don't forget the Border War, when Mexico decided this was a good time to take back half of their original country. The Texas Campaign, Alamo after Alamo. Then the Reds started their godawful terror bombing and then there was Breakout, timed almost perfectly with the return of the surviving Saudi and Korean and Afghan Regulars so that three-quarters of them – hell, three-fourths of the country – ended up choking to death on its own snot. Well, maybe not that many, but it sure seemed like it, and then, insult to injury, the Reds came pouring out of the mountains, slaughtering and enslaving with the peculiar enthusiasm of the self-righteous.

So tell me, in the last five or six years of murder and rape and slaughter, where are the genteel moments guaranteed to inspire, to keep this hyeah Army motivated and true?

This wasn't Grampop's Army nor Grampop's War, the good one, dubya dubya two, noble and heroic with flags waving and roses showering down and pretty girls in gingham clasping hands to breasts as our brave boys marched by. Hell, it wasn't even the surly drug-laced Army of Vietnam. It wasn't Dad's Army, either, or, in his case, Air Force, one of opportunity and brotherhood and the occasional brouhaha, like Grenada or the Gulf. No, this Army was a heavily armed and brutalized group of shell-shocked boys and girls desperately trying to stay alive while martinets and pinheads with general rank drove them from one ill-defined front to another, all the while stabbing each other and the president-this-Week in the back. Collier's Army wasn't noble or filled with grand purpose; it was just trying to restore some order, some security, so they could all go home without getting killed. Well, that's what *he* was trying to do, anyway. The generals, the presidents, the bandits, hell, the Reds, were all trying to take over. Collier didn't want to take over. He just wanted to go home. Couldn't he just go home?

So then, Collier old boy, can you really blame Caldwell?

He frowned at the dark. Could he? Here they were, going from one massacre to another, escaping one unbelievably murderous situation just to find themselves in another and the Colonel's gotta save our asses all over again and we're driven harder and farther from home and harder and farther from any kind of peace and there's just, simply, no end to it. Even a genius like Caldwell could get tired of this crap. The Reds had vision, purpose, goals, and intents and showed no signs of stopping. The Blues were floundering, running, abandoned, chewed up more each day and, eventually, they'd all end up on the wrong end of a Red barrel anyway, so what the fuck? Maybe he should bang on the cell door and offer Caldwell his services.

Not bloody likely.

Not even in the most remote fucking list of extreme possibilities was it likely. He would never turn, never join Caldwell's little coup. Indeed, it was now Collier's mission to shoot Caldwell between the eyes. See, Colonel, regardless of the murder and misery we've all suffered these past years, there was another vision and it didn't involve the Reds' stock and trade of slave camps and confiscations and dehumanization. Have you forgotten, Colonel?

Has everyone forgotten? Remember driving down interstates with your head out of the window and sitting by quiet ponds with fish pulling at corks and lying on white sand beaches and playing grabass with your buds in some alley behind the school and your first kiss and your first beer and fireworks and Playstation and movies and sneaking in way past curfew and Mom sitting there in the dark waiting to catch you out?

Don't you remember? Don't you want that back?

Collier remembered. Clearly. Springfield, a summer blue pool in the backyard and splashing and cutting up with Zeke and Darren and a hundred other kids. Dad barbecuing and occasionally throwing one of them in, Mom racing sodas back and forth and telling them to be careful which, of course, they weren't. Chasing girls on moonlit nights and skipping football practice and blowing off homework to the point Dad got really pissed and sent Collier off to Fishburne, which was okay because he ended up having such a great time there, learning so much, and making the best friends of his life. The Phantom Five, Juste and Kris and Mans and Perry and him. All of them lived through the Event because they were at Fishburne. All of them scattered because of Breakout and probably not a one of them was still alive because he would have, by now, run into them somewhere. But, they were still alive to him.

He wanted it all back, green days and silver nights and the sheer joy of just living. Enshrine those memories by fighting for them, or dishonor them by giving up, quitting, joining the enemy?

Stupid question.

Faintly, very far away, he heard Dad give a Homer cheer. He grinned.

And immediately stopped grinning as he wondered what was happening to Rosa.

Even though she was a fighter, a damned good one, some kind of martial artist, she was still a woman in the hands of prison guards and the righteously pissed-off Colonel who'd been panting after her for months. He hoped she gouged out a few eyes before they finally clubbed her down and took her. Sudden rage blasted through him. You better kill me, Colonel, because I am damn sure going to kill you. And every single one of you who touch her.

He pounded a fist into his hand, teeth clenched to the point of breaking. Dammitall! Locked up and helpless while his woman was being ravaged, tortured, weeping and calling out, "Help me, Coll, help me, why don't you help me?" He slapped his hands over his ears and squeezed his eyes shut to get the images out.

Out.

He'd carried far too many images over the years: Mom's Flu-ridden death mask, Dad's beaten and burned body, Uncle Art's moldering skeleton, bullet-riddled friends, raped and broken women. Most he had imagined, some he saw, and one, Dad's, was refuted when Price brought him the package. He did not want to add another: Rosa, crumpled, bleeding, and reproachful. My heart, my soul, no … don't haunt me like the others.

God, are You there, are You? Collier hadn't seen much evidence of Him. Quite the contrary: if the last five to eight years were testament, Lucifer was running things. Dad had wholeheartedly believed in God, long before the Event and even After; in all the troubles, clinging stubbornly to his faith while chiding Collier for his unbelief, saying that events were human but, weaving it all together, was the Unseen Hand.

Whose Hand is it, Dad? Because, from Coll's perspective, it was red, blotched, taloned, and cruel. If God did weave, He was maniacal at the loom, the stitch crazed and senseless. Where, in all of that, was any comfort? How, Dad, could you still believe?

He thought about Dad's Bible, no doubt carelessly tossed aside, along with *The Shepherd*, when Caldwell's goons stripped his backpack. The last of you, Dad, gone again. This time, forever.

It's just paper, Dad would say, don't worry about it. But think of this, Collier: how is it possible you got my book and my Bible, both items separated by time and distance, yet, somehow, coming together under the most impossible of circumstances? That's the Unseen Hand, Collier.

Is it, Dad? Or is it the smallness of things now? When there were millions of people, then the delivery of your papers would be miraculous. But when there are just thousands, it's only a funny coincidence.

I don't believe in coincidence, Dad said.

But I do, Dad, I do.

And even you, Dad, in your scribblings along the margins of your Bible, noted the remoteness of God, which I can summarize: God sees and hears but does not touch. He gives us our head and we build ovens for Jews and impaling stakes for captured peasants and guillotines for hapless monarchs and megatons for Japanese. You railed about that, Dad, saying it proves our need for God, and then wondering (quite angrily, if I'm reading your notes right, Dad) how many times the point has to be proven before He comes back to save us. And you wrote all that long before there were planes in sides of Towers and anthrax letters murdering millions in the name of God's vicious alter ego, Allah.

So how many more times, Dad? And why does Rosa have to suffer in the meantime?

Dad, shaking his head, "You are ignoring the central point, Collier, just picking and choosing what suits you. Remember the Guiding Hand. We are everything evil, going all the way back to the first caveman clubbing the second caveman for an extra piece of mastodon. Yet, cities rose, empires flourished, arts and letters grew and men sought God. Is it progress? No. Progress is an illusion. There are too many times in history when the Dark overwhelmed the Light, and that is, unfortunately, your part of history now. But there is light in that darkness and men still seek God. He is still there, Guiding, using you; yes, granted, in the most callous and brutal of ways, but His Heart holds a place for you and his Hand does touch you, even if you cannot feel it."

And the circle remains unbroken, Collier.

The conversation died and Collier was still. He didn't buy it, not really, but had to admit that somewhere, way down in what he guessed was his soul, something stirred.

Besides, face it, when there are no other options ...

"God," he whispered, "free her. Just free her." He didn't care if it was a miraculous escape or death during the eighth or ninth rapist, but just free her. Please.

Well, whaddyaknow, his first heartfelt prayer.

Yeah, yeah, he'd asked for passing test scores when walking into an English final or a straight line on a goal shot, but those were just utterances of fervent desperation (and obviously, from the results, received in the same spirit). *This* one, though, he meant. Free her. Prove Your existence to me, prove Dad's faith in You, and prove there is still compassion in the universe, some fairness, some justice, even love.

Prove it.

He kept repeating that mantra, a warding, driving off the images of broken Rosa, skeleton Mom, and burnt Dad, so they would not stand clear and vivid before him gibbering, accusing, reminding him that he'd failed. It was almost a pleasure, then, when boots pounded up the broken pavement outside and the door rattled and bolts slid rustily back. He did not move, kept his head clasped in his hands, but eyed the door through his fingers, tense and ready. Might have to make some sudden and severe moves, so best not to telegraph a willingness to do so.

One of Caldwell's cretin guards stood there shining an oil lamp directly into Collier's eyes, which was a pretty good tactic. It shocked his sight, preventing him from reading the situation and coming up with a quick plan; even more, it hid, for a few seconds, some short person standing next to the guard. Collier tensed. This must be it, the bullet to the brain. He was out of time, and he had to grab any opportunity, no matter how slight. A moment's inattention, some tiny distraction, anything that would give him a half-second head start, that's what he needed.

"Visitor, traitor!" the guard called out way too loudly, probably for the benefit of the two or three other malcontents locked up in here somewhere. Had to keep the lie going.

The short guy stepped forward and Collier recognized him. Awbrey, Rosa's mouse, little snippy impertinent craphead. What was he doing here? He was an S2 slug, insignificant, a gofer, a shifty little prick who was always too close to Rosa's locked office door when Collier was in there. Sticking his nose where it didn't belong, making snide comments whenever Collier showed up, in need of a good beating ... hey, wait a minute. Collier's eyes narrowed. Someone had to tell the Colonel where they were tonight, right? Why, you little bastard. It's always the guy you least suspect.

"I've got your charge sheet here, Rashkil!" Awbrey announced loudly, probably for the further entertainment of his neighbors, and Collier did the mental equivalent of "Huh?" while keeping his face impassive. Something was wrong. Charge sheets came from commanders in their tents during duty hours, not clerks in the dead of morning in a cell. And then announcing it for everyone to hear? Ah, I get it. Collier inwardly smiled because it was downright brilliant. "Rashkil went nuts when we gave him the charge sheet, had to shoot him, sir." So, this was how it would be, and from this guy, of all guys. Unbelievable.

"Never figured it'd be you, Awbrey," Collier said mildly, balancing himself on the cot. The moment the pistol cleared Awbrey's jacket, Collier would jump. He'd probably get a bullet through the gut, but he'd also get a full grip on Awbrey's throat and the satisfaction of dying while ripping out the little prick's trachea. At least get one of 'em, Rosa.

"You didn't figure out a lot of things, asshole," Awbrey snarled and whipped his hand up. This was it and Collier felt a surge through his legs and the sudden frenzy of action taking over his muscles ... and stopped, confused. Awbrey wasn't holding a pistol. He had a big overstuffed envelope in his hand, a homemade one, to be sure, but an honest-to-God envelope. The guard watched as Collier, his confusion evident, slowly reached out and took it. The guard's own brows furrowed because he had probably expected the same thing as Collier – pistol, flash, boom – and a crumpling to the floor. Things just weren't going according to script.

Collier squeezed the envelope as he took it. There were papers inside and something else, something hard. What the fuck?

Awbrey stared at him, still holding the end of the envelope and shoving it in such a way that Collier could not help but feel the object inside. Collier's raised eyebrows told Awbrey he had it and the little jerk stepped back, satisfied.

Collier watched him intently, wondering if the object was a bomb. But, then, why give it away? Awbrey stared at him more ferociously, if that was possible, and then said again, too loudly, "We'll be seeing you at the court-martial." Awbrey wheeled, then snapped at the guard, "Leave the lamp so he can read it, and be prepared to get his response when he calls for you." Then he stalked out.

"But—" the guard turned, hesitating, looking down the hall where Awbrey had gone. "Just do it!" Awbrey yelled and the guard hastily placed the lamp in the door and pulled it shut, then slammed bolts. Collier heard him walking down the pavement arguing and Awbrey arguing back.

Collier jumped off the cot and grabbed the lamp. He held the envelope up to it, but no, no wires, nothing unusual except for that hard object that did not feel like a grenade with its pin out just waiting for the pressure to be relieved. Collier tore the top off the envelope and peered inside. Papers, yes, mostly blank filler wrapped around ...

A knife.

A good trench knife, five-inch blade, deadly. He pulled it out. Did Awbrey intend for him to cut his own throat? There was a note wrapped around the hilt: "Don't waste time! She's at HQ!"

He blinked. Had to be a trap, had to be.

Yeah. So?

Collier grinned wolfishly. You're dead, anyway, old boy, so might as well go out in dramatic fashion, knife attack while screaming some ridiculous battle cry, maybe "Geronimo!" though more likely, "Kiss my ass!" He dropped the papers and hefted the knife. Let's see what this baby can do.

He waited an appropriate set of moments and then pounded on the door, hard and insistent, "Guard, guard, I've got my answer ready now! Get your ass down here!" Yeah, guard, that's it, run down here. Collier slid to the angle of the opening, listening to the guard cursing as he fumbled with the lock. Collier suddenly wondered if his prayer had just been answered.

26

"*So you're selling us out.*"

Rosa seethed inside because she sounded teary. Sometimes, when she was in a flying rage, like now, she got a bit weepy. Just like a woman, the Colonel was probably thinking, helpless little female all confused and stunned and disarmed. Keep thinking that, Colonel, especially the 'disarmed' part. It put her a step ahead.

"Those are rather harsh words," the Colonel observed. He stood before the chair she'd sunk into, his hips thrust forward, putting his crotch, the most marvelous of targets, within range. Just wait, Rosa, before you emasculate the traitorous sonofabitch, hear him out.

"We're ending an unnecessary war, Major," Caldwell continued, "not selling out. On the contrary, we're saving this Army. You can't call that a sellout."

Sure can. Probably not the right moment to get snippy about it, though, so stay in character. "But, Colonel ..." she blubbered. Wow, a bit melodramatic, that. His eyes narrowed, so she backed off. "... Colonel, that's what it amounts to. You can change the words, but it's still betrayal."

He reddened and she mentally slapped her forehead.

Exactly the snippy tone you wanted to avoid, idiot. The Colonel rocked a bit on his heels and she held her breath, afraid he would make some disparaging remark, spin about, and go. If he walks, I'm lost. All right, tease the man, then. She angled her head close to his belt and opened her eyes wide and questioning: just make it all better, Daddy. He was still red, but now for different reasons.

"That you say such things commends you, Major," he said, softly. "It proves what I've always known, that you are loyal and hardworking and feel deeply for this Army. I respect that. I understand that. It may not seem like it but I, also, am loyal and true to this Army.

"Let me explain," he waved a hand to forestall interruption, even though she'd made no such attempt. So, this was rehearsed, a dry run of what he intended to tell the troops as they were unceremoniously bound and gagged and buried alive by the triumphant Reds.

"For the past few years, we've been fighting our own countrymen. Our own, Major. What's the result? Nothing, not a thing, just slaughter. We're essentially doing the job al-Qaeda started. Why? Just to figure out who gets to rebuild the country? Because we still have to rebuild, and do so while facing other enemies, like the Mexicans, the 'Slams, maybe even the Chinese, we just don't know right now. If we stopped fighting the Reds today, there'd still be plenty of fighting for the next ten years. So why keep killing each other?"

"You know why, Colonel." Rosa couldn't help herself, although she remembered to sound pathetic. "Because the Reds would enslave us."

He made a derisive sound. "So they think. Given the cantankerous nature of the average American, Major, I doubt the Reds could impose a Communist regime. From each according to whatever," Caldwell sneered while becoming animated, surprising Rosa. This part, at least, he really believed. "Not in a thousand years, not if they had an Army five times this size with tanks and airplanes and a real Navy. It's just not in our nature, something those dreamers haven't figured out. But that won't stop them from trying, which means the war goes on."

He shook his head and thrust a bit closer, "Major, there's no way we can win this, at least on the battlefield. The solution lies elsewhere, when we assimilate their organization, take them over from the inside, get rid of their hardcore, and turn the whole Red apparatus to our purposes."

She blinked. "Is that what you're planning?"

He nodded, "Yes, Major. Here it is … we surrender the Army as a short-term action and get absorbed in the Red hierarchy. Gradually, we take control. I've recently acquired the means to do that." Here, his eyes glowed oddly.

She blinked. "Means? What means?"

He waved that away, "Unimportant in its detail, just know that the average Red is as greedy as the average capitalist. Once I've bought my way up, then we purge them. All of them. No more Reds, and we return the country to its former glory."

She didn't know if that was genius or insane. Always go with your gut instinct. "Colonel, that's insane."

His eyebrows rose. "Is it? Men of vision are always so regarded. Alexander, Galileo, Washington. We don't think them insane today, do we?"

My God, he just compared himself to Washington! "But," she sat back, exasperated, "the Reds aren't stupid, Colonel, they must smell a rat. Why would they trust you?"

"Because, Major, they're blinded by ideology. They think they have the mandate of history. They see my capitulation as a natural outcome of this war. Do you know much about the old Soviet Union? No? Guessed as much … you're too young and the schools during your time tended to whitewash it. They used to institutionalize their opposition, throw them in asylums, and subject them to drug and shock therapies. The Sovs thought anyone who rejected Communism was unbalanced. Our Reds think the same way.

"See," the Colonel waved his hands, fully pontificating now. "The problem has never been radical Islam, even after the Event and Breakthrough. There was no way Islam could get a foothold here, especially after we laid waste to their homelands. But Communism, oh yes, those people have always been here, ever since the Russian Revolution, and did not go away just because the Wall came down. They just bided their time, softening us with warmed-over socialism, little spoonsful at a time. And who emerged, after Breakout, as our biggest enemy? Not the 'Slams. No, Major, the Reds, the Reds!" His finger pointed skyward in emphasis.

She stared at him in utter disbelief. "But, then why are you joining them?"

"I'm not joining them!" he snapped, angrily, "They're joining me. Aren't you paying attention?"

Oh yeah, she was paying attention to the ravings of a madman. Obviously, this coup had been planned for some time and involved a lot of people in a lot of places and some of those people had convinced the Colonel he was the key. But he wasn't: he'd be bound and gagged and buried alive right beside her. Didn't he know that?

Apparently not.

A stone fell to her stomach. He didn't know, couldn't know and never would because he was a prisoner of his own hubris. Which meant there was no way to stop this. Which meant they were lost.

"What will happen to us?" She didn't have to make her voice quaver anymore.

The Colonel shrugged, his anger forgotten. "In the long run, not much. There will be adjustments, of course."

"Adjustments?"

"I won't lie. There will be some purges. A lot of purges, actually. Which is why I came to talk to you."

He paused. She could already see where this was going, and the stone became hot and heavy and burned her deeply as he said, "I'm giving you a chance to save yourself."

"What do you mean?" Her voice was low but she was just stalling while furiously plotting courses of action because she could guess his next words.

"Join us."

Bingo.

She looked down to hide her rage. "You know I can't do that."

"But I know that you can. Now that you know my true intentions, you can't refuse. That is, if you love this Army and this country as much as you appear to."

"Why would you even ask me?"

"Because you're smart and tough and offer so much. You would be an incredible asset."

She stared at him, the roiling stone suddenly the center of a terrible, righteous anger. She felt it surge through her, empowering her, and she knew, just knew, that the Colonel would not leave this room alive.

"Why else would you ask me?" Her voice became deadly.

He hesitated, but must have seen the certainty in her eyes, so he raised a placating hand, "All right, I will be honest. You have charms. I've made no secret of my attraction. Your unfortunate relationship with Rashkil aside, I still find you beautiful and sexy and strong. Your intelligence, and your beauty, must be salvaged."

She took in a deep breath and used it to feed her anger. That's what it always came down to, didn't it? Bed bait. Tough, smart, good at her job, but her appearance was always the deciding factor. All right, fine. It was that way long before the Event, so to expect more civilized behavior now was ludicrous. And dangerous. She had survived this long relatively intact (with New York exceptions) by killing enough men to make it clear she chose her own lovers, thank you very much. And she had always chosen equally tough, smart, good-at-their-jobs men who, yes, admired her figure, but her capabilities more. That's why Collier owned her heart. That's why the Colonel wanted to.

Which was the first of two errors: he assumed his want was sufficient to spark her interest. A lot of egoists confused their talents with desirability, their self-regard as attractive. It's not, Colonel.

The second was thinking she had no choice but to join him. Maybe if she was a frightened little girl, a weak powder puff as the Colonel assumed all women were (and, who could blame him for thinking that? These days, a lot of women just wanted someone to make it all better), but she wasn't. And she wouldn't.

Fatal assumptions.

Prepare.

"How will it happen?" she asked, her tone still low but now a sign of her murderous intent, which he could not read.

"We are surrounded."

She almost fell over at that, but held, needing to hear everything first.

"Yes, Major," he nodded at her stunned face. "That's why I stopped the patrols. Not as betrayal, but to save lives, whether you see it that way or not. They are going to hit us from the north, about noon today, which will shock everyone, panic the troops, make the surrender that much easier. It will just be token fighting, token resistance on our part."

So much was, suddenly, clear. "That's why Eliot's on the north."

"Yes."

"Deavers, too?"

"Yes."

"Their officers?"

"No. Too unreliable."

The Colonel got that right. Eliot's LT was worthless, regardless of which side he fought on. "Then what happens?"

"I surrender the Army."

"Then what happens?"

"Pardon?"

"What happens after you surrender us?"

"The Red commander knows who to spare and who not to. We go home."

Her heart stopped. "You gave him a list?"

He eyed her, a wariness showing deep in his eyes and she willed herself to be loose. "I did."

"Am I on it?"

"You can be." He paused. "Rashkil can't."

Parlaying his jealousy into murder while making himself look heroic … thank you, Colonel, one more reason to kill you. She checked herself quickly. She was primed, powered, ready to go. Now to lull him.

She began to cry.

It wasn't really that hard. Flying rage made her weepy, so just a little push and there, the tears. Always misread as weakness, always brought her enemies, sneering and grinning and triumphant, right into her circle of power. She looked down to hide the hard and deadly glitter behind the tears.

The Colonel just stood there. She could see the front of his boots. He was rocking a bit, hesitant, and she kept firm, letting tears fall. A step closer, Colonel, please.

But he didn't step closer. "I will give you some time. We do have some," he said quietly. "I will come back in an hour for your answer." He turned to leave.

Don't let him get away.

She groped out blindly, softly, with one hand, grasping his wrist, not hard, but imploring. He stopped, reading it the way she wanted him to, as surrender, a prelude to the passion he so wanted. He turned back and bent down. She felt his movement, his arms reaching for her.

The base knuckle of the first finger, the one inside the hand's webbing, is a powerful hapkido weapon. Its shape works against pressure points and nerves wonderfully, especially when driven by the whole body and angled in a manner to cause maximum pain. She did not hesitate.

She drove that knuckle into the side of his wrist as she stood and pivoted on the balls of her feet, spun, and was suddenly standing behind a quite surprised, but slow to react, Colonel. She brought up her left arm and locked the crease of her elbow around his throat, letting go of him with her right arm and folding that elbow around her left wrist, bracing her forearm against the back of his head and locking her arms tight about his windpipe and neck arteries.

Hatakajima.

She dropped to her knees, bringing the Colonel down to the floor hard and fast and on his side, knocking the chair out of the way with a terrible clatter that would bring the guards running. Didn't matter, they couldn't stop this.

The Colonel recovered quicker than she thought but

he made the same mistake everyone did: he tried to loosen her arms. Good. She took in a breath and leaned back. It suddenly became very clear to the Colonel that he could no longer draw air. It should also be clear, by the roar in his ears, that the blood flow to his brain had been cut off. The Colonel didn't know which problem to attack first, air or circulation, and made the wrong choice: air. They always did. He savagely attacked her elbow around his trachea, trying to loosen it. She, just as savagely, braced, preventing him from working his fingers in between. Go ahead, struggle, fight me, use up the few seconds of air your brain still has. Get a breath if you can, it won't save you. Your blood has stopped.

There was a commotion outside and she figured the sluggish guards had finally figured out something was wrong. She would be dead in about ten seconds. That's okay, the Colonel would be dead in five. She could not stop the Army's demise, but she could exact revenge. That's it, keep struggling, you traitorous bastard.

Caldwell went into a frenzy of kicking and clawing, finally realizing his only hope was in getting to her face. She easily dodged the groping fingers reaching for her eyes and tightened the collar around his neck. He became frantic, crazed, and almost rolled them over, like that would have done anything. She was locked on too hard for him to get out of this.

She wondered what his last thoughts were, probably something like, 'My God, murdered by a girl!' It almost made her laugh. He kicked hard once, another kick half as hard, and drifted away. Just drifted. She did not let go, but knew he was done. It was a merciful way to kill someone: they just go to sleep. Far more merciful than what he planned for them.

The door crashed open but she did not let go. She wanted to make sure there was no hope of resuscitating him, and she knew she'd reached that point when she smelled defecation. Dead people lose control of their functions. She squeezed once, hard, to make sure, and then pushed herself away and across the floor.

"I guess you didn't need my help," Collier said.

She looked up. He was standing over her, a bloody knife in one hand. She leaped to her feet and into his arms and smothered his face with kisses. He rocked back and took her in with one arm, keeping the knife away.

She leaned back, "How?"

"Awbrey."

"Huh?"

"Best I can figure, he's in love with you."

"I figured he was the one who told the Colonel."

"Probably was, but that doesn't mean he doesn't love you." Collier gestured at the Colonel. "How'd this go?"

"He told me everything," she stepped back, taking a deep breath, settling herself, and immediately a shock ran through her, "Oh God, what time is it?"

"About 0415."

She seized his lapel, "We have no time. They're coming at noon."

"What?" He shook with the realization. "Crap! We gotta get out of here!"

"We can't abandon the Army!"

"Are you nuts? We have got to go. Now!" and he turned towards the door, pulling her.

She yanked him back and then his head down to her level, "We can't!" she whispered fiercely and bore into him. He struggled, still trying to pull her out the door but she held on and forced him down. He stopped, seeing her now.

"Crap," was all he said. She smiled.

He looked back towards the door and then back at her, "What do we do?"

"We need to find someone to take over."

"Not Hoffman."

"Of course not. He's probably part of it."

"Weedon?"

"Killed yesterday."

"Damn," he muttered. "He was a good guy. Division?"

She stared at him. "Right," she replied, sarcastically, and he grimaced his response. Despair raced through as she considered, then discarded, candidates. Few competent field graders left, and, among those, even fewer the ranks would follow. This is what happens in a Byzantine Army.

"Let's put it to the troops," Collier suddenly said.

"What?"

"Assemble everyone. Tell them."

"That will cause a riot."

"Maybe. But they're owed it."

She blinked, the seconds slipping away. She felt him turning towards the door but the implications, telling everyone their revered Colonel had sold them out ... how could she do that?

How could she not?

There was just no time. No time. She looked up, pulled him to her, and kissed him long and hard. She knew it was the last kiss they would ever have. They broke apart and he looked at her, surprised and breathless.

"Let's go," she said.

27

Whoop! Whoop! Whoop!

Klaxon, the emergency air horn: an attack was imminent. Suddenly, whistles shrieked from inside the wooden warehouses, tin shacks, and grouped tents that served as barracks. Sergeants and corporals screamed, "Move! Move!" Main force troops hit floors and dirt and makeshift carpets, struggling into boots and grabbing packs and weapons, all the time cursing under their breath, "Not another goddamn drill!" hoping to God it actually was. The fuck happened to the patrols? Did the Reds get in? This *better* be a drill!

It seemed like chaos, the tramp and thunder of hundreds of boots as designated units rushed to prepared positions while the rest of the Battalion shut down, gathered up, and formed on their sections where sergeants, screaming and kicking and cursing, could run them through checklists and then surge platoons up the Pemberton/Ft. Dix road (or parallel it through the neighborhoods and fields) all the way to the artillery park, providing flank protection to the precious few trucks and carriers they kept here for just such an occasion. It wasn't as haphazard as it looked.

Collier stood on the back of a flatbed parked on the edge of the main assembly area, Rosa next to him, watching the organized craziness. The flatbed was almost dead-on perpendicular to all the activity, which meant everyone would be in shouting distance sometime in the next fifty seconds or so. Not that anyone could hear him above the din. Collier shook his head. Man, with all this noise, the Reds could easily zero a round smack in the middle of 'em all. That is, if they had the hardware. Collier doubted they did; otherwise, they'd have been shelled to oblivion long before this. Hell, the Blues used their own precious 105s sparingly, only on obvious and inviting targets like the screaming hordes of Reds that had chased them from one place to another over the past half-year. Thank God for those 105s.

"No one seems to have noticed us," Rosa said.

Collier grunted. "Give 'em time."

She snorted, lifted her newly appropriated M4 to the sky, and cut loose. "Crap!" Collier yelped, not expecting it.

Neither did the crowd, hitting the deck in a single choreographed move of downright panic. Couldn't blame 'em. Rifle fire this close meant either the Reds were here or some pissed-off troop had just gone postal. Maybe both. Couldn't blame 'em for their immediate, and quite murderous, reaction, either.

"Uh-oh," Collier said, as the now furious troops rose as one and turned their way, weapons lowered, bolts released, about to shred the both of them with 700 streams of variant .223 fire.

"Wait!" Collier called out as he hit the switch of a portable spotlight he had dragged onto the flatbed before setting off the klaxon. Suddenly, he and Rosa were brilliantly lit.

"Rashkil!" mixed with "Major!" and about five

thousand other exclamations of surprise, which merged with more dangerous ones. "Traitor!" "What the hell you doin', Rashkil?" "Major, baby, how 'bout me?" The troops surged forward, mean and bristling. No friendly faces, at least in the front row.

"This isn't going very well," Collier observed.

Rosa made a *tsk* of annoyance at him, then called out, "Listen to me!" her clear alto cutting across the mob and momentarily stopping them. Collier smiled inwardly. Ah, a woman's sweet voice, steak to a starving lion. The mob, still menacing but hesitant, focused on her.

She wasn't hesitant. "You've been sold out!"

The response was immediate and electric. Troops turned to each other almost simultaneously, yelling "What?" "What'd she say?" "What the hell is she talking about?" with eyes widened in renewed panic while the troops on the periphery turned suspiciously to the dark, looking for trouble.

"Maybe not the best thing to lead with," Collier said.

"You think?" she snapped, looking desperately at the quickly disintegrating scene. Groups formed and roiled around other groups and weapons were pointed while the babble of questions acquired ominous tones. Get control. "Listen to me! Listen! Your lives depend on it!" she yelped.

The groups stopped confronting each other and turned back to her. She went straight to the point, "The Reds have surrounded us! HQ has sold us out! We're going to be sacrificed!"

Throwing a road flare in the middle of gasoline wouldn't have been as volatile. Uproar, incredulity mixed with denials and sheer panic, and the roiling grew frenzied. Fights broke out, especially among the officers who had worked their way to the front and were now opposing each other: LT, Captain, the odd Major or two, all yelling about who was in charge. Things were reaching critical mass. If the officers didn't settle down, the sergeants would break and then the troops and that would be it. The Reds wouldn't need to overrun them: they'd overrun themselves.

Collier looked at Rosa. "What the hell do we do?" he asked but she just shook her head, staring in amazement at the scene. He scrutinized the crowd, frantically searching its borders for something, anything, to diffuse this.

And found it.

Palmer, standing just short of the front. Collier raised beseeching hands, and the Captain nodded, detached himself from the crowd of arguing officers, and jumped up beside Collier. He pulled out his Glock and cut loose a few rounds, which brought an instant and welcoming silence.

"Hey!" His parade voice carried across the area, "The Major's right! Listen to her!" and he stepped back, out of the direct spotlight.

Perfect. Collier gave him a grateful glance as a murmur came up from the crowd and the troops edged closer, scared and resentful but wanting to hear. "Put some lights on," Collier called out. A few troops jumped from the crowd and headed towards the generators and, moments later, the dim perimeter glowed. It was still dark and gloomy but he could see faces now. Collier peered at them, looking for expressions of hate, revenge, glee. Anything that meant trouble. Panic, yes, worry, definitely, but mostly just curious. Good.

Rosa stepped forward. "This will be hard to hear. You can believe it or not, but you know me" – a few catcalls at that point and Collier shook his head. Soldiers. – "and you know I won't lie to you. HQ wants to end this war by giving us up to the Reds." A gasp of disbelief went up.

"They want us slaughtered so they can call a cease-fire and then surrender the entire Army. It's very stupid, it's very wrong, but it's what they've done. They betrayed us to the Reds and let them surround us. They will attack us about noon. From the north."

"Bullshit!" one voice called out, clear and rising. Of course: Eliot, standing about four ranks back. "That's bullshit, Major! They're not up north. Where's the Colonel, Major?"

"The Colonel is dead, Eliot ..." Rosa spoke coolly, deliberately, and Collier's eyes widened as the shock of what she said coursed through the crowd and heightened the panic. Shouts again. "How?" "What?" "Who killed him?" – and Collier knew they were lost. It had been a good stroke to blame HQ, but telling them about the Colonel was madness. The man was too loved.

"... and *you* murdered him, Eliot!" she dropped her bomb as she pointed at him.

Collier could have hugged her right then.

There's nothing like a few thousand stunned and angry soldiers turning about and facing the designated scapegoat to enhance pucker factor, and Eliot went white. "What the hell? I did no such thing!" he screamed but the crowd knew him and knew Rosa and immediately was against him. Eliot's squad lowered their weapons but everyone else was lowering weapons, too, and they were all pointed at Eliot, who screamed again, "She's lying! She's lying! If the Colonel's dead, *she* did it!" Rifle barrels were shoved at his face and his squad energetically knocked them down while screaming threats at the shovers.

"Yeah?" another voice rose from the crowd, loud and vibrant and penetrating. Jonesy. "She's lying, Eliot? You were the motherfucker out of position on that grab a couple of weeks ago! Almost got our asses killed!" The uproar swelled and Collier spotted Jonesy standing to the right, near the crowd's edge with Swift and a few other reliables. Jonesy caught his eye and winked grimly.

"That's bullshit!" Eliot roared at Jonesy and pushed rifles away from his chest. But he couldn't hide the desperation in his voice.

"No, it's not!" Collier roared back, carrying over the crowd. "Y'all remember I beat the crap out of that little shit, right? He told me HQ ordered him to leave his position, leave us out there to get killed! He's part of it!" and Collier pointed an accusatory finger.

There was no reasoning with an enraged crowd and Eliot knew he was lost. He pushed against the group hemming him in, seeking escape, but a rifle butt stroked him across the head and he went down. His squad struck out with their own rifles to protect him and there was a mêlée of rifle butts. Bayonets and pistols emerged and this was heading towards massacre. Out of the corner of his eye, Collier saw Deavers and his platoon quietly slip away, into the dark.

"Wait!" Rosa, loud and pleading across the riot. "Wait! We can settle up later! We've got bigger problems now!" Fighting continued for a moment more but then her words penetrated and the riot slowly spun towards her again, weapons still out and murder still possible but not yet, not yet. Collier couldn't see Eliot, who was probably unconscious somewhere on the ground. She might have just saved the bastard's life. Dammit.

Rosa stood tall, eyes blazing, in control. "Right now, we have to do something about the Reds bearing down on us. If we work together, then we have a chance—"

"Chance?" a voice called out from the center of the crowd, "What chance?" Collier peered into the gloom but could not see who it was. He did not recognize the voice, either. There was motion and pushing and then some private Collier had seen around but did not know, stepped out. "What chance is that, Major? You tell me!"

Rosa looked at him. "We've got surprise, soldier, and that's big, that gives us the edge. We just have to get in place—"

"No!" The private slashed his hands out. "Get in place? Hell, no! Fuck, no! I've been 'getting in place' for six months now, and for what? For what?" He turned to the crowd behind him. "For WHAT?" he shouted again and there were answering shouts and stirrings from the depths.

"Damn," Rosa breathed and turned the M4 towards the private. Collier stayed her hand. "Wait," he whispered.

"Six months!" The private's voice was laced with passion. "Running for six months! And before that? We fought and fought and fought. For years! YEARS! We've been fighting too goddamn long!"

Cries of "Yeah, man!" "You tell it!" followed him as he turned back to the flatbed. The private's eyes flamed and Collier felt Rosa move the rifle and he stopped her again. "Major!" the private yelled, "All my friends are dead! My family is dead! Everybody's dead!" He jerked a thumb towards his own chest. "I'm it! IT! The last one! And now you're telling me those pieces of shit at HQ, who I've been fighting for all this time, sold me out? Well, fuck them! FUCK them!" and he brought his fists skyward, and over half the troops answered with a roar of approval. Collier saw Jonesy point his rifle at the private and raise an eyebrow. Collier shook his head and Jonesy nodded, backing down.

"And fuck you, too, Major!"

Collier almost grabbed the M4 and shot the private himself for that, but didn't. Rosa looked at him in astonishment but he set his jaw grimly and grasped her hand harder. "Wait," he repeated.

"Are you crazy?" she hissed.

"No, I'm not. Let this play out."

The private turned back to the crowd, half of which was dismayed by his bravado and the other half exhilarated. "Fuck this Army! Fuck this war!" he called out. "And fuck the Reds! I'm going home!" and with that he pushed a sergeant out of his way and shouldered through the crowd, back to the barracks.

As he passed, soldiers turned and watched and then huddled and one or two followed in his wake, then three or four, then dozens, while the ones who stood their ground pleaded and pushed them and were pushed back. It was like watching a hard tide suddenly break on rocks, with pools rolling and turning in one spot while the main current arrowed back out, a tide made of soldiers. Jonesy, open-mouthed, stood gazing at the retreating private and making jerky motions with his rifle, not sure if he should shoot or not. Collier noted that Jonesy was the center of the pools which stayed.

"Wait!" Rosa called out to the retreating troops, "You'll never get past the Reds!" Shouts met that, a lot of derogatory and descriptive comments mixed in, and fists flew and rifles came down and any second they were going to war with each other.

Collier stepped to the light, "Listen! Listen!" He barely made a dent in the uproar but he didn't dare fire his rifle to get their attention. That would trigger wholesale slaughter. Rely on the command voice. "He's right! The private's right!" he bellowed.

That was the last thing anyone expected to hear from hard-ass Rashkil. Even the deserting soldiers stopped and looked back at him in amazement. Collier couldn't see the look on Rosa's face but he was pretty sure it wasn't amazement: more like complete and utter disbelief.

"Don't stop him. Let him go," he continued, no longer having to shout. "Let them all go. Anyone who wants to leave, just go. We won't stop you. We won't shoot you. Take some of the trucks, some ammo, some supplies. Not everything, or we *will* start shooting."

The deserters looked at each other and then back at him and then at the private, who stood near one of the trucks. "Well, hell!" the private called out, "What are we waiting for? Let's go home!" and he waved the other deserters to him, giving Collier one long suspicious look. Collier just nodded at him. No tricks.

"What the hell are you doing?" Rosa was frantic.

"Wait."

"Jesus, is that all you can say? Our whole defense is bugging out!" and she made a desperate gesture towards the rapidly loading trucks.

"Just wait."

She gasped but Collier ignored her, watching the deserters closely. They had swelled to about three-quarters of the Battalion, a frenzied mass flowing into the barracks and sheds and tents and stripping them of weapons and clothes and food. The remaining three hundred or so – Jonesy and Swift and the other Spartans – gravitated around the flatbed, arranging themselves in a horseshoe in front of Collier and silently watching their former comrades rape the camp. Good. Very good.

Tugs of war occurred here and there among the pillagers, fistfights and a bayoneting or two as ownership was disputed. Collier let all that go. But there was one thing he couldn't let go and he scrutinized the mob …

There.

He jumped down and slid through the 300, who were startled and blinked but let him pass. "What are you doing?" Rosa called, but he ignored that, too.

He made straight through the mass of deserters. They

stopped and stepped back frowning, weapons up, wondering if the deal was now off, but he passed them without looking, intent on his one target.

"Hey, motherfucker," Collier snarled at a stooped soldier who was scooping MREs into a bag.

"Huh?" the soldier looked up and his eyes widened as he recognized Rashkil and also recognized he was vulnerable.

"What'd you do with my backpack?"

"Huh?"

"My backpack, asshole. When you and the rest of the goons grabbed me in the cemetery a few hours ago. Remember? Or do I have to draw you a fucking picture?"

"Oh." The solider blinked and looked a bit confused then back at Collier, wary. "I don't remember a backpack. I think we just left it."

"You just left it."

"Yeah. Pretty sure we just left it. We just wanted to get you locked up."

"You sure?"

"Yeah. Pretty sure."

Collier took a threatening step towards him and the soldier fell back on his butt, scrambling at a knife on his belt. Collier put his foot on it and ground down, getting a yelp from the soldier. "Motherfucker," Collier hissed, "if it ain't there when I go back and look, I am going to hunt your ass down."

"That ain't on me, man."

"The fuck it isn't." Collier kicked him then, partly payback and partly to prevent retaliation. "What are you lookin' at?" he growled at the deserters who had formed around both him and the soldier. The deserters shied out of his way and Collier spun and stalked back towards the flatbed. The bugout resumed.

"What was that about?" Rosa asked, as he jumped up

beside her.

"Personal matter," he answered, and she just nodded.

Didn't take long. The deserters got organized pretty quick, with the private turning into their de facto leader. They took five trucks, loading them up with supplies and the invalids (or fake invalids), while the rest of them hoisted packs and lurched left up Arney's Mount Road. It was getting light, but they could probably count on about an hour of gloom as cover. No doubt, runners had headed out to the artillery park to collect friends and spread the word and take a few more trucks and he wondered how the one or two competent officers out there would react. Badly, he was sure, ending up shot. Probably most of the crews would desert, too, but enough would stay behind.

He hoped.

Collier turned to Rosa, who watched helplessly as the last few deserters grabbed random stuff and raced away. "I know you think this is bad," he said, pitching his voice so the others could hear, "but those guys are no good to us. Never were. They're the grumblers and troublemakers, and probably would have skyed right in the middle of the shit, killing us all."

"Well, we don't stand much of a chance without them, Collier!" Rosa snapped.

Her voice was ice but, wow, "Collier." Right here in public. He shook his head, feeling warm, "We stood no chance *with* them. They didn't have any loyalty to begin with, and now, after they find out HQ betrayed them? C'mon. That private was right. There's been too much fighting, too much death, and, frankly, I'm just as sick of all this as they are. I want to pack up and go with them, try and find a life, the Reds be damned."

He paused, seeing the others press around, listening. "But none of us is getting out of here to find that life unless we stop the Reds' attack." Collier grabbed his sleeve and rolled it up, revealing the tattoo. "And, by God, we're the Ghosts."

There was a stirring and a ripple and the 300 looked at each other and looked at him and yanked up sleeves and stood with their Ghosts revealed. No words; none necessary, brothers and sisters all. They stood, tableau, the moments extending.

"I take it," Jonesy's voice finally floated up, "you got a plan?"

28

Kant stared at himself in the mirror. It was just a shaving glass, small and round, yet there were core members who considered even this spare thing decadent. Kant had little patience for those types: severe ascetics who wanted mankind to live in caves, graze like pigs on forest mast, and shave in the reflections of stagnant pools. More ecofanatic than dedicated cadre, and their obtuseness annoyed him. The wonders man had wrought – electricity and steel and skyscrapers – were proof of Godlike powers. Harness that, from each, to each, and we will conquer nature, the world, the universe. The ascetics could go hang, and they just might.

He smiled at that, which did nothing to change what he saw in the mirror. He looked so old, in his fifties, ten years away. The little bit of hair he left himself now grey and his eyes sunken and puffed, with wrinkles spidering out from them. The red veins stood out on his nose, his cheeks splotched with the moles and marks of too many years in the sun. He hid those with a half beard, General Grant style, but streaks of grey were in that, too, and he wondered if he should cut it off. No, the beard made him look tough, just like Grant, and he needed every advantage, even of appearance, as things spun into place.

You indulge in vanities, comrade.

He smiled at that, too, because he had long ago concluded vanities were the real motivation of the human soul. Marx had gotten that completely wrong (like he had gotten so many things wrong): man did *not* have a deep altruistic drive to share his production with the brethren, a drive exploited and crushed by the capitalist system. *Au contraire*; man was a meat bag of vanities, all of them demeaning and self-destructive and rendering Marx's system of shared production impossible. But, a *supervised* production that fed the vanities while diffusing the self-absorption inherent in them … yes. Keep man controlled and working and single-purposed, while allowing harmless things like clothes and makeup and entertainments. Man would be docile, happy, easily led. By shepherds such as him.

He had distressed Pai with these heresies. Pai was orthodox, as were most of his generation, drunk with Allende and Che and Castro. They could not, or just refused to, see the dichotomies in Cuba's poverty, Che's ridiculous foco theory, or Ortega's hypocritical structure. They were as narrow as any fundamentalist Christian, and ten times more violent. Kant could still feel the bruises and cuts from the first time he'd been questioned.

That was when, 1982, 83? Something like that, when Kant was thirteen or fourteen. It was summer break and Pai had taken them all back to Brazil, as usual, but not to idle the days poolside and the nights in wooded parlors of scented coffee and rum discussing high theory with the professors and government secretaries.

No, Pai had dressed him in his school uniform, blazer and tie and gold emblem, and had him walk the favelas to mark the contrast, to make him grateful, and obligated.

"See?" Pai had said, "See what the capitalist structure

builds?" And Kant had seen: the disease, the cravenness, the subhuman wants of the lumpenproletariat as they eyed, with lust and murder, his fine linen pants and handmade leather shoes and $100 haircut. But he had also seen something else: the Coke cans, the Adidas T-shirts, the Walkmans, and an idea had struck him hard, obviating fear.

"The police murder the children to hold down crime," Pai was discoursing, "for the comfort of the nortes." Pai had almost spat that last, which was odd, because he made a home among them.

Kant, in the throes of his revelation, had completely ignored Pai's mood, which was unfortunate. "Look at what they have, Pai," he'd said.

Pai had turned to him in surprise, so Kant gestured at a group of street rats kicking a half-deflated pelota at a three-legged dog. "They're all wearing Nikes and they're drinking Coke. Give that to them, and they'll follow!" He had said it brightly, enthusiastically, with the force of the very young with a very new idea.

Pai had stared at him, speechless, then reared back and brought a bony hand hard across Kant's cheek, as was his wont, but this time vicious enough to open it. Kant had stumbled back, stunned, as the street rats, equally stunned, stared then suddenly jeered and threw rocks at him as Pai stalked away. It had taken all his strength to stay up with Pai and out of the clutches of the rat pack that tore at his clothes and hair. He'd been crying and bleeding and exhausted by the time they reached the limo and, even then, Pai almost left him behind.

That night had been one long harangue, one long beating, one long session with *Das Kapital* while his beautiful Mama Natalia, with the long silver hair and kind face, wrung her hands outside the door. Pai had slammed the book with his fist, and then Kant with both book *and* fist, while reading aloud the passages covering surplus cost of labor and exploitation. "This, this!", Pai screamed, "this is what enslaves them! And this is what will FREE them!" and Kant had cried and shrieked "Yes, Pai! You're right, Pai!" and he was unworthy and a failure and a disappointment.

He had learned two things: the orthodox were brain dead, and a right idea remains. Even weeks after Pai's punishment (and the numerous follow-ups designed to wring out the last trace of heresy), Kant still could not shake his developing sense of man's vanities. If anything, Pai's overreaction had solidified it. He learned some peripheral things, too, like how to hide his true beliefs in the face of torture, and how to organize the like-minded in secret as he found similar disaffection among the sons and daughters of Pai's peers. The vanguard, both north and south.

And he had learned contempt. As the last of the Wall fell beneath the sledgehammers, Pai sank into himself, and Kant walked about with a face worked into a sympathy he did not feel. Months later, when the USSR collapsed, when the Sandinistas faded, when Pai's friends, one by one, repudiated their beliefs and the old man withdrew to his darkened library and poured over suddenly irrelevant texts, an alchemist facing Descartes, Kant no longer hid his contempt. Pai could not accept the evidence laid before him, could not adjust his thinking, and now it was Kant's turn to rail at him. Daily.

A few weeks later, in that same library, Pai blew his brains out.

Pathetic.

A weak old man, ultimately, but one from whom he had learned many lessons, and so Kant's contempt mixed with respect. Especially as Mama Natalia, gasping out her last breath of Phase II but still looking proudly at her handsome son in a lieutenant's uniform, said, "Remember his dream, *filho*. Bring it about." And I am, Mama, I am, from my early, secret efforts to build the now powerful Red Army, to my fifth column damage here among the hated, corrupt enemy, just days away from collapse.

At a movement in the mirror, Kant's hand slid down to the ever-present pistol on his lap. Treachery rode the wind these days. As his own plots moved to culmination, he grew wary of counterplots, not only from the moronic Blues but from Kant's own cadre, some of whom felt their leadership would be more efficacious than his. Finger on the trigger, he watched Captain Quesnell's anxious face poke slowly into the tent flap.

"Colonel!" the Captain hissed.

Kant shifted, the pistol ready and eyed the Captain hard. Could he have turned? That would be unexpected: Quesnell was unimaginative, slavish, and fawning, which were great assets in a lackey. He was, also, quite frightened of Kant, which enhanced those assets. Still, men were variable, and one must always guard against sudden ambition, even among the ambitionless.

Kant gestured, ready to shoot if necessary, and the Captain hurried in, worry wrinkling his face. Alarm grew in Kant's chest. Something has gone wrong. At this critical point, only hours away from the crisis which would implode this government and deliver the President and the whole country into his hands. He grabbed hard at the rising alarm and forced it into submission. After all, if everything was lost, what would be the result? A mere bullet to the back of the head.

Peace.

"What is it?" Kant asked with calm and dignity.

The Captain looked around the empty tent, his eyes wide with fear. "Colonel," he whispered, "I am so sorry to bring this to you, but there has been no response to the signal."

Hmm. Kant frowned. "How many times have you sent it?"

"Three times! Nothing! So I sent it three more. Still nothing. I have sent it every five minutes since, and *still* nothing!" The Captain said that last with a panicked note, betraying his fear.

"Atmospherics?"

"I tested the wavelengths, sir, and everything else is getting through." The Captain's shoulders and head bobbed in worry, because Quesnell's date with a bullet coincided with Kant's.

"Movement?"

"Nothing detected, sir."

Kant let out a long breath and leaned back in his chair, tenting his fingers, purposely forgetting the pistol. That should help ease Quesnell's mind.

So, this was one of two courses. The first, that the treacherous prove themselves so. His poodle had turned Doberman, a snake in his bosom all along, and was actually luring him to destruction. The second, a test of faith. Everything remained on schedule and this was a mere glitch: a failed radio, a signal gone astray, even something as stupid as dead batteries.

He furrowed his brow. These were the moments that proved the steel within, the correctness of a vision, the mettle of a leader. How much confidence did he have in his plans, his picked men, his judgment? There will be no more information than what you have, so choose wisely.

It only took a minute to the Captain, but a year to Kant. He looked up at Quesnell's sweat-beaded brow, "Things proceed. But, release the reserve forces."

The Captain's brows went up in surprise but he read Kant's look well enough to stifle the protest. "Yes, sir," he gulped, and bowed out of the tent.

Kant watched him go then turned back to the mirror, noting the small smile on his face. When he wrote his memoirs, either from the Oval Office or a prison cell, he would credit this moment with its proper drama.

29

What was that quote?

Collier shifted his weight and peered down the barrel of the M-16, checking the view. Something like, "Getting hung in the morning really focuses the mind." Not quite right, but conveyed the sentiment. Dad said it on appropriate occasions, like just before Collier had to take the SATs or a driver's test. It definitely explained the last three hours of frantic activity by a bunch of exhausted and frightened troops as they slapped together some halfway decent fighting positions. Were they good enough? We'll see, we'll see.

There was a shuffling somewhere behind him and he turned in the trench, keeping his head below the lip and bringing the rifle around. Just what he needed about now, a Red recon stumbling over him. Jonesy's face popped around the corner, and Collier relaxed.

"Good to see you're awake," Sergeant Jones said, "The last group signaled. Everything's in place."

Collier nodded. "Guns?"

"Got three."

"That's it?"

"Yeah, but they're 105s," and Jonesy smiled

wickedly.

"Wow." Collier was impressed. "I thought we'd only get mortars."

"I can be real persuasive, my friend."

"So I gather. Helicopters?"

Jonesy snorted, "Please. The two that could fly bugged out with Division a few hours ago. Didn't you hear them?"

"Yeah, but I was hoping. Everyone know what to do?"

"Briefed and happy."

"Cool, Jonesy." He paused. "We're going to get our asses handed to us, aren't we?"

Jonesy shrugged. "Probably. You want to live forever?"

"Actually, yes."

Jonesy laughed. "Yeah, well, uh-rah, motherfucker," and he crawled away.

Collier smiled and sneaked another look. He was in some woods on the west side of the Catesville Road, about three hundred yards from its intersection with the Pointville Road. The woods extended on either side of a small creek that ran all the way back to Pemberton. Thank God. Since this was going to be a run-and-gun, Collier and his squad would need the cover as they merrily leap-frogged ambushes, slowing the Reds down and giving the Ghosts a chance (a ghost of a chance, yuk, yuk). And *that* depended on where the Reds showed up.

If they came this way, fine, everything was ready. If they came down Ft. Dix Road instead, Collier was screwed. He'd have to hustle up Catesville, with all the available cover on the wrong side of the road, to support Palmer in front of the old high school, which had so many buildings to it the Reds could deploy with little interference and roll them all up quite efficiently. Since the high school was the Blue artillery park, a smart Red commander would want to seize it before someone not privy to the Colonel's agenda resisted the idea of surrender and got the guns operational.

Collier had pointed that out to Rosa, who agreed but simply said, "When have the Reds ever been smart?" And that was a good point: the Reds were pretty much straight-at-you kind of guys, relying on numbers to overwhelm. Buncha Cossacks. It would do them just as well to get between Battalion and the arty, and the only way to do that was down Pointville, which was Eliot's old sector. "Where would a Red Army like to make first contact?" she asked, "At an arty park that may react badly, or through the welcoming arms of a traitor?"

All good points, but, either way, Collier had a lot of running and gunning ahead of him.

He glanced left, then slowly peered towards the right, barely making out the top of some soldier's helmet about ten yards away. He took out a mirror and flashed sunlight at it and, about a minute later, got two answering flashes. Good. His first team was alert. The Wilson brothers had a squad further up Pointville next to the Fort Dix gate, but they were too far away for Collier to see them. They had a radio, though, and were calling every five minutes. Collier wished he could turn his radio off between checks to preserve the batteries, but life did not run in five-minute increments.

So, now, waiting. That was half of war, waiting for something to happen. In this case, though, they knew what that "something" was. The attack would come; it was just a matter of from where and how close to noon the Reds and the Colonel had scheduled. Collier wondered where the Colonel had planned to be so he could pull off this charade. Probably HQ; that gave him a central point to issue a cease-fire. But Caldwell was a lead-from-the-front kind of commander, and Eliot's perimeter was right here, across Pointville, south of some farm ruins near the intersection. Deavers' perimeter was next to it, all the way past the high school, so Caldwell could have been anywhere along this line.

How would it have worked? The Reds show at Eliot's line, he puts on a demonstration, Caldwell comes rushing up and broadcasts a couple of conflicting orders, opening up several lanes for the Reds and, next thing you know, they're at the compound disarming the troops. Caldwell makes his speech, then lines of soldiers are marched out and fall into ditches. As the Reds expect.

Surprise, motherfuckers.

He grinned then took in a deep breath and blew it out, taking another impatient look across the field. Where else had American soldiers braced for attack? Guadalcanal, Khe Sanh, Riyadh ... quite a list. Soldiers hunched down in jungle or woods or sand, scared, tired, tense, knowing all hell was going to break loose and there was nothing they could do but fight hard and hope to survive. He remembered a trip, back when he was a kid, to the Antietam battlefield. Collier had jumped into the Sunken Road and lain down, looking over its edge at the top of the next hill from where the Irish Brigade had come roaring down on the waiting Confederates. Imagine, flagpoles rising over the ridge followed by a massive line of very angry blue-clad people heading straight for you. Gulp. The result was a fierce, horrible, unrelenting massacre, the dead piled five deep. Dad, looking down at him, had said, "We're harder on each other."

How true. Let two Americans reach an impasse and the resulting fight was brutal and bloody with no quarter asked, none given. America laid waste to Japan's armies and radiated its cities and flattened Germany and absolutely obliterated Saudi Arabia, but that's nothing compared with what Americans did, and do, to each other. Who invented the drive-by shooting, after all? Look at us now, all because we dislike the other guy's social organizing principles. We conduct wholesale genocide of ourselves, simply because of an idea.

The nature of who we are, Dad pointed out. We are the only country ever formed around an idea. Every other country in the world was formed around land or ethnicity or power, but not this one. No, we stood up and declared our name and said every single one of us was an independent and free person who owes no one, has no kings nor rulers, and can go where we please and do what we want as long as we remain in the natural law. The Indians didn't like that, so we wiped them out. The South said black men were excluded, so we wiped out the Confederacy. The Brits took a dim view, so we wiped them out. Twice. And we wiped out the Mexicans and the Spanish and Noriega and the Republican Guard and all of Arabia because they, also, contested the idea of an independent, free people.

There seemed something particularly heinous, then, about a subset of Americans, raised here in privilege and riches and option, who sniffed contemptuously at bourgeois concepts of free will and opportunity, embracing, instead, with great enthusiasm and joy, a foreign structure that imposed top-down control.

People are very suspicious of freedom, Dad had said, because they're afraid someone will get away with something. Well, it's a lot cruder than that, Dad: everyone wants to tell everyone else what to do, to the point of concocting hare-brained Utopian philosophies designed to make everybody, except the concoctors, of course, toe a very restrictive line.

Like these Reds, the latest iteration of those tired old Commies or Pinkos or Cong, whatever, mouthing the same tired clichés about brotherhood and equality, all the while digging mass graves and building camps and salivating over the riches and power they anticipate from our bent backs. All for your own good, you pathetic little peasants. We persons of great intellect and insight, so much smarter than you, are far better equipped to make life decisions for you. Shut up and dig that ditch, or we'll shoot you.

Let's see who shoots who, motherfuckers.

He thought he heard Dad chuckling behind him somewhere and he smiled and slapped Dad's book and Bible. Found the backpack right where that jagoff said it was, in the cemetery. Saved him the task of running up North Pemberton Road to find said jagoff and slice him in half. Nope, instead, gonna stay right here and get meself sliced in half, killing as many Red assholes as I can before they overrun my position. About 1000 yards from your hometown, Dad, which, if you think about it, is kinda funny. We'll have a good ole laugh about it, that is, if your God exists, and if He has a sense of humor. And is willing to overlook some of Collier's past exuberances …

The radio cracked. "Sarge," Wilson #1's laconic voice.

"Go."

"Comanches."

Well, that answered the question of where, didn't it? Good thing he didn't bet Rosa on this; he'd be polishing her boots for a month. Collier keyed three times, which was the Wilsons' signal for "Give 'em a show." Any Reds listening to these brief but cryptic exchanges would be a little puzzled. Let's hope they're so confident of the Colonel's betrayal they don't give it second thoughts.

He flashed the mirror and saw the soldier look over. He hand-signaled and the soldier flashed a mirror back and ducked out of sight. That group was now heading towards Pointville.

He keyed the radio. "Papa 1."

Palmer, "Here."

"One minute," Collier replied and Palmer keyed twice. Okay. Palmer should now be gathering his group and falling in behind Collier's position, about the middle of the woods. Wilson was the bait, Collier was the surprise, Palmer was the spoiler. If this all worked out, sometime in the next hour or so, a very mad and confused Red Army should be hot-footing up North Pemberton Road in pursuit of that huge crowd of deserters, while Collier and Rosa and Jonesy and whoever else managed to live through this, tippy-toed south.

Live through this? It is to laugh.

He peered through the woods at the ruined farm about three football fields away. He could see the road clearly between the wrecked buildings. Figures slipped furtively through the trees: his other team getting into place. Okay, Wilson 1 and 2, any time—

A sudden burst of fire off to the left, some distance away. Collier smiled. Damn, boys, did you read my mind?

"Baker! Baker! Baker!" the radio suddenly screamed. "Incursion, Sector 3, point 240, we are in full retreat!" Wilson broadcasting standard Blue code, which should ease any Red qualms. The firing swelled and fell off and there was an answering roar, ten times louder. The Reds were responding. Good. If things were going according to plan, the Wilsons were now racing down the south side of Pointville, in full view of the oncoming Reds. The Reds should follow, hounds to the hare, and think it all great sport because there had to be *some* Blue show of resistance, if only token. The Reds should be thinking all is good. They should be relaxed. Should be.

But no plan survives first contact, and there were so

many things that could go wrong. Like, the Reds ignore Wilson and go straight for Pemberton, or one of Caldwell's co-conspirators alerts them the jig is up, whatever.

Oh, knock it off and get moving, will ya?

Collier rolled out of the trench and ran across the road, crashing into the woods and following a rivulet south along the ditch until he reached the outskirts of the farm. He saw, and heard, his own fire team fanning out either side of him. As he entered the yard, one of his people took position at the southernmost point and waved him on. Collier raced over and slapped the private on the shoulder as he passed. He looked back and saw both teams, all twenty of them, arraying about the half-collapsed big white barn. Perfect. Collier crawled to the edge of the rubble and cautiously peered around the corner.

He could see a good distance down Pointville Road. There. Movement. He strained his eyes but it was hazy today and weirdly warm and he could not make out a lot of detail.

"Through," Jonesy's voice came over the radio quietly and Collier keyed once. Good. Wilson had made it past Jonesy's position on the other side of Catesville and should be now heading towards Palmer. This could be a critical moment: Jonesy's transmission, coupled with the odd lack of panicked and crazed calls from Blue HQ asking what the hell was going on, might cause the Reds to get suspicious and hold up. Collier peered down the road. Nope, still coming.

Look at 'em down there, soldiers in varied green fatigues and mostly black boots, with some of those weird desert-colored ones mixed in, all US Army issue like Collier's, but stitched in red. Only way to ID them, since the Reds looked as ragtag as the Blues. Some of them wore Post-Event stuff, the shoddy workmanship evident even from here. He wondered if they had their own depots or just stripped the dead.

The Reds were in loose formation, as though on a road march. Some were on point, but way too close to the main body; they did have some flankers out, but not far enough. The first ranks were bunched up with what looked like command vehicles. Overall, too close together and too relaxed ... a sense of relief flooded through Collier. The Reds had bought it. They have no idea what's coming.

The first rank reached the intersection, then the second rank ... now. Collier turned and waved a hand and pointed left. Half the team broke behind the barn and scurried into the overgrowth bordering the road. Count twenty seconds ... there!

Wham WHAM!

The two grenades went off on this side of the Red formation as the crack of rifle fire suddenly rose, intensifying into a single long burst as the team brought to bear on the startled Reds. The Reds reacted, the ranks closest to the attack dropping and returning fire while the ones behind and to the sides bolstered them.

Now, guys, follow the Red tactical manual ... bingo.

Half the ranks on the right flank broke and headed into the brush on the south side of Pointville, emerging moments later in the intersection itself and rushing up Catesville to outflank the attackers. The other ranks backfilled them, a classic turn and loop designed to catch any attacker in the side.

Which put the bulk of the Reds right smack in the middle of the intersection.

The first rank of Reds laid down suppressing fire and the supporting ranks backed that up with even more fierce fire into the woods from where the team had triggered the ambush. The team should no longer be there … ah, yes, fast movement through the trees, which had to be the boys and girls skedaddling. Collier looked back at his relay. After a moment, the relay flashed a mirror twice and bolted across Catesville to join her quickly fading comrades. Collier turned back to the Reds and saw the flanking maneuver piling up past the intersection, heading towards him. The Reds were now in place.

He keyed the radio. "Thunder," he intoned, and pressed himself flat into the rubble.

It took, at most, five seconds, although it felt like five years. Collier heard the distant *thwumpthwumpthwump* of the guns firing, but only because he expected it. Probably some of the Reds heard it, too, and probably had just enough time to say, "Oh, crap."

Ker-whoom! *Krawham*! *KaCRAM*!

The first rounds landed dead in the middle of the road and a wave of heat and rubble washed over Collier, motivating him to burrow deeper. His ears popped with the sudden pressure but he heard screams, just the same. The second and third salvos arrived seconds later and it was Armageddon. Collier couldn't risk a look until the last wave of hot air blew past him.

He shook himself, getting the debris off his back and head and then poked at the rubble in front of his eye until he had an opening to see smoke and flame and things falling back to earth no more than three or four yards from the center of the intersection.

Good shootin', Tex.

He keyed the radio, "Step five, east, fire for effect," and he rolled over and scrambled through the wreckage, running as fast as he could for the woods. He reached the first team member just as the next salvo arrived, diving into the ditch and pulling his helmet down hard. This set fell farther up the Red column, but it was still close enough for him to feel the concussion and to hear shrapnel whizzing by.

"Everything good?" he asked the private who grinned and gave him a thumbs-up. Collier nodded.

He rose and waved his hand forward and the whole team, about fifteen of them now, stood and centered on him. He turned and ran back towards Pointville through the wood screen, crouching and looking for an opening as they all reached the edge of the west woods. Collier stepped up where he could see down the road.

Chaos and utter destruction. The intersection was a blistered moonscape of strewn body parts and weapons and asphalt. More explosions volcanoed up the road and Collier saw the rounds walking through the now ravaged Red column, one-two-three, one-two-three. Collier grinned. He didn't know who the gunners were, but Jonesy had picked them well.

The Reds were running here and there, obviously stunned, but not in full retreat yet. A command car about a hundred yards away on the edge of the first set of craters, had an officer standing next to it and talking frantically on a field phone connected to the cab. The officer was there for only a moment as another salvo bracketed him, atomizing the man and turning the car into scrap while knocking Collier on his butt. The team cheered, laughing at him at the same time, and Collier couldn't help but join them.

"Okay, boys and girls, they know we're here. Let 'em have it!" and he lowered the barrel and cut loose. It was indiscriminate wide field of fire, no specific targets selected, the purpose to sow more confusion and terror. The M-16s sang all together in varied pitches of staccato bursts as they hurled lead down-range into the surviving Reds. It was simply murder.

And it was, simply, all they needed. Any vestige of

resistance or rally among the surviving Reds dissipated and they turned heel and ran, Collier's fire team giving them all the encouragement possible. The scrambling Reds retreated into the next salvo but they didn't care; they stood a better chance dodging the rounds than engaging whatever force had emerged to their front. The M-16s sang and the artillery roared and it was a symphony of death and carnage with absolutely no chance of survival.

Collier grinned. This was going better than he hoped.

He signaled a halt and the rifles stopped. He squinted through the smoke left by the just-delivered salvo. Off to his right rear, he heard cheering, which had to be Jonesy's team, and Collier's team picked up on it. He let them because that should help send the Reds along. He keyed the radio, "How'd we do?"

"Beauteous," Jones responded, "How many'd you lose?"

Collier did a quick head count, "Six."

"Not bad. So, any changes?"

"No. Go to the next phase." Jonesy keyed acknowledgment and Collier waved his team in. "All right, good job. We might actually get through this. They're going to shake themselves and come back mad and hard so we gotta reach the first site post-haste and get ready. Here's what we'll do ..." and he paused, frowning. There was something odd in the air, a trembling, very familiar, but he couldn't put his finger on it. The team members heard it, too, first looking at him and then each other. They all looked up at the same time.

With a high-pitched roaring scream, three jets flashed by overhead, rocking the woods with their wash. Collier almost fell down in shock. F-16s! Good God! The ground shook hard and then, geysering up in the distance where the artillery should be located, a tremendous cloud of fire and smoke erupted. Collier rushed onto the road, heedless of the exposure, and looked back towards Pemberton at three smoke contrails peeling right and left from where they had merged over the guns. Damn all the angels, the guns were gone! One of the jets broke away and slipped back to the left. Collier saw it skimming over the treetops, menacing and sleek and deadly.

"Get down! Get down!" he screamed and dove into the drainage ditch by the side of the road, his team piling on top and beside him. The ground bounced hard and a fire wind roared over them, a hurricane of shrapnel and flame and shattered trees and rock. The soldier on top of Collier was lifted up and out of the ditch in the tornado created by the falling bombs. A wave of broken tree limbs and pavement washed over the side of the ditch and pummeled Collier, something huge and heavy smashing into his helmet and momentarily stunning him. He shook his head hard, despite the pain. Got to gain control. Somehow, he still gripped the radio. Instinct. "Jonesy," he called.

"I'm here," his voice flat.

"You guys all right?"

"Missed us. Didn't miss the guns, though. Didn't miss you, either."

"I know." He looked around as the surviving team members stirred out of the debris and staggered about. He did a quick head count. "Lost half," he replied, grimly.

"Damn. Want us to come for you?"

"Break," Palmer's voice came over, tense and high, "Were those 16s?"

"Yessir," Jonesy answered.

"Jesus!" Palmer's voice sounded as pale as he probably was, "I thought all the jets were out west."

"Apparently, Captain," Collier replied dryly, "we're deserving of special attention."

"Break," Rosa's voice came through, harsh and commanding, "This is no place for discussion! You're giving yourselves away. Sergeant Rashkil, it's your call," and she keyed off.

Collier's lips tightened. She was right, the shock of the counterattack had blown their discipline apart, and they simply had to move, jets or no jets. He eyed his team, which was bewildered and shaking and terrified. Could he blame them? In this whole war, none of them had experienced a bombing. Helicopter attacks, certainly, an occasional tank or two, artillery and even rockets, but such high-tech weapons as jets were supposedly beyond the Reds' capability. Supposedly, only the Blues still had them and were used sparingly because they were just too precious and their pilots too few for wholesale commitment along the fronts.

Supposedly.

He frowned. This conspiracy must run deeper than he thought if jets were involved.

And coming back. Collier heard the uptick of tone and the swelling sound of jet engines as the 16s swung about, probably to make another run at his position. Just how many bombs did those damn things carry?

He didn't want to find out. Collier keyed the mike, "All units," he said calmly as the jets got louder, "run like hell."

30

"Report." Rosa's voice was flat and colorless. Collier stared at the long, deep, and pulsing red scar that ran from the bottom of her chin to just below her right eye. Must be a shrapnel wound from the jets' plastering of Pemberton a while ago. "You should fix that," he said, pointing at her face.

She looked at him, her eyes fire and war and murder, the Aztec Princess aroused. "I said 'report'!"

Collier immediately dropped into military mode. "Major, we've lost over half. The jets caught us as we were abandoning the Arney's Mount ambush site. Palmer is dead." He paused at the flicker in her eyes, but just for a moment. That's all the grief present circumstances allowed. "Everything was working fine up to that point. The Reds pursued us on a parallel down Pointville exactly as we wanted, and were north of Arney's Mount as we came out of the woods. It was just unfortunate timing that we did so as the jets came back."

"Damned unfortunate," Jonesy muttered. He was sitting on the ground, his back against a pine tree while a private finished wrapping a plaster bandage over his shoulder, hooking it to the shattered remnants of his elbow. An M-16 round had caught him somewhere back at the third ambush and this was his first chance to get it fixed. Jonesy looked drawn and tense, obviously hurting despite the morphine syrette. Didn't stop him from fighting, though.

Didn't stop any of them. What was left of the Ghosts was spread along the woods southeast of their old barracks area, between the remnants of a neighborhood and a bunch of overgrown fields to the north. It was about the only untouched area between Pemberton and Pointville Road, which explained better than anything how the various, separate units had all managed to show up here over the last half hour. The woods were thin enough for Collier to see everyone in tableau, like every painting and picture of a battle's aftermath: torn-up men and women sprawled all over as their lesser-wounded comrades attended them with plasters and needles and bandages, a lot of those makeshift. About a hundred and fifty, give or take, smashed and hurt and ripped and exhausted, so thirsty they drank the shallow brown water from a little rivulet bisecting their position, not caring if it made them sick or not. Collier gingerly touched the spot where a bullet had slashed across his abdomen. We're all hurt, all bleeding, all spent.

But, by God, we're alive.

The jet sounds trailed off towards the east and Collier looked up. Smoke from the firestorm that was once Pemberton washed over the sky. Well, that was one benefit of bombardment; they were now hidden from aerial observation. Collier guessed the jets were running low on fuel and bombs and heading back to wherever they had staged, probably somewhere near Trenton. Couldn't be anyplace closer, not even that old air base near Wrightstown – McGuire, yeah, that's the name – because the Ghosts had holed the runways when they took over

Pemberton to prevent its use. No one had jets anymore, but why take chances?

No one had jets anymore.

He blinked at the smoke. "I didn't plan on jets," he toned.

Rosa blinked at him. "What are the Reds doing?" she asked.

Collier shook his head. "I didn't see them, Ma'am. The terrain blocked me, and then the jets."

"I saw them." Wilson #1 sat against a pine tree away from Jonesy, picking at the remnants of his sleeve as he tried to pull out a splinter lodged in his upper arm. Wilson #2 was holding his brother's arm, a steri-Pak at the ready. "They were bunched up at the top of North Pemberton Road."

Rosa regarded #1, then pulled a map out of her tunic and spread it over a stump. "Show me," she said.

#1 hauled up, with the help of his brother, and walked over, his brother hopping alongside. #1 stared at the map and placed his finger on a spot. "Here. Looked like they were heading straight for Arney's Mount."

She frowned, "Were they coming our way?"

Wilson shook his head, "I couldn't tell, Ma'am, but they stayed on the north side of the road."

"No flankers?"

"None that I could see."

Collier and Rosa looked at each other, arriving simultaneously at the same conclusion. "They've gone after the deserters," Collier said, quietly.

Her hand went up to her scar, wincing because she probed a bit too deeply, using that gesture to ward off the gesture she wanted: throwing her arms around Collier. He had leaned forward a fraction, anticipating the hug because of the sudden joy in her eyes, but no, not here, not yet. Later.

Jonesy didn't wait. "It worked, man!" he said as he slapped Collier's calf from where he was sitting on the ground.

Collier buckled a bit and then smiled at him. "Yeah. Looks like we pulled it off." He turned a palm out, taking in everyone. These guys pulled it off. This Corp, this core, we happy few.

The Ghosts.

A motley, torn-up remnant of surly, ill-disciplined, malcontent whiners, the buncha 'em, but they did it. They did. Collier felt something funny in the back of his throat and pressure in his eyes and was overcome by a swell of emotion. My God, was he about to cry? For a sorry bunch of derelicts who never quit, who fought grimly through the most horrific butcheries this continent had seen since the 1860s, who never surrendered and always, always, kept the dream of home, of what it all used to be, in front of them?

Yes.

They were barely a coherent force. If the Reds descended on them now, that'd be it. As an Army, they were beaten, but as men, as women, they were unbowed. Defiance gleamed at him from every eye, resolve lined every brow, and there wasn't a soldier here, no matter how badly hurt, who would quit. A remnant, tested in fire, forged by it, hardened and trued, a cadre that would rise and fight again.

Someday.

Rosa tapped her map to get his attention. "Is this the runoff we're standing next to?" she asked.

Collier stepped closer and peered at where Rosa's finger rested, on a thin blue line squiggled just north of Pemberton. He looked at it and then at the rivulet, then spun slowly to get his bearings. Nodding, he said, "That's gotta be the one, Ma'am."

She stayed on the blue line, frowning, as she traced its connection to the Rancocas, then slapped the map hard. "That's our way out," she said and stood up straight, staring into his eyes. Desperation and sorrow and fear all there, but, also, hope. He felt a similar hope surge in his heart

Rosa took a few steps back. "Listen to me!" she called through the woods, "We've got a chance."

The remnant looked up from its various wounds and ministrations and focused on her. The hope in her voice immediately reflected in their eyes and Collier saw them gathering, restoring, renewing. My God, look at that, look at the pure raw power in them still, the stubborn and fierce refusal to die. They are hurting and bleeding and exhausted but will jump to arms and turn and face hell itself at Rosa's word.

Brothers. My brothers.

"It looks like the Reds have latched onto the deserters, "she said that last word with some venom, "and are going after them." She turned and gestured at him, "Sergeant Rashkil's plan worked." There was a smattering of applause and some calls of "All right!" and "Good work!" Collier waved an acknowledgment. It was better than a medal.

Rosa continued, "That means we've got some time. About half of us bought that time, dying back there in Pemberton and up the road." She paused. "We can't let them die for no reason."

Silence as the survivors thought of friends and lovers and comrades now lost. Collier caught her eye and nodded imperceptibly. Good tactic. They'd, somehow, find a reserve, that last bit of energy, to do whatever Rosa asked. Their dead demanded it.

She pointed at the water. "It looks like this runoff will lead us west to the Rancocas, which you all know flows back to Mt. Holly. We'll be south of the Reds chasing the deserters.

"We can reach the Delaware by slipping between those Reds and the ones on the other side of the Rancocas. Cross into Pennsylvania and, from there ..." she spread her arms out. From there, anywhere.

The remnant looked at each other and then back at her. In seconds, there was commotion and murmurings and movement. They hurriedly tied dressings and then helped the wounded to their feet and grabbed backpacks and weapons and checked them ... the normal activity of an Army getting ready to move. Nothing more to be said, no further pleadings, no arguing. This was the situation and they simply had to leave.

Rosa smiled. "I guess we're going," she said to him.

"Yeah, what the hell," Jonesy said as the Wilsons pulled him up. He winced while he tested the sling. "Might as well. Can't stay here."

"So, how are we going to do this?" Wilson #1 asked.

"We should use infiltration tactics," Wilson #2 offered. "Break into five-mans, stagger the groups, use flankers."

Jonesy and Collier both shook their heads, "Take too long," Collier replied, "By the time we got everyone assigned it'd be a couple of hours, the wounded taking even longer. We just need to go."

"He's right," Rosa said. "The Reds are probably screening Pemberton as we speak, looking for stragglers. They might be on us any moment. We just need to go."

"A column?" Wilson #2 looked dubious, "We'd be strung out along the creek. Easy to hit us."

"But it's the fastest way to get going," Rosa pointed out, "short of running away. We don't have the time for anything else. We'll designate point and flankers, but we just need to form up and go."

Collier nodded along with her words, silently encouraging the Wilsons to comply. They were good soldiers but usually needed some prodding to get the point, so Rosa was firm but fair, letting Wilson #2 know she had heard him and considered his point but she was now, by elimination, the commander, and she had, by God, made her decision and, guys, you need to fall in right now, right now before the jets … and then it hit him like a lightning bolt. "Oh, no," he breathed.

It was just loud enough the command group, because that's what they were now, turned to him in some alarm. "What is it, man?" Jonesy asked.

"It won't work."

"What?" Rosa.

"It just won't work. We just can't form up and go. Don't you see?" and he pointed up. "The jets."

Jonesy caught it first. "Fuck," he said quietly, and then the others blinked and their jaws dropped as the realization hit them, too. The ever-widening gyre, the patrol sweep of the jets, would find them spread along the Creek running for their lives. The jets would blast them and then call the Reds down on the survivors and they would all be lost.

All.

Too much distance, too little time, too many wounded: which meant they were all dead.

All.

Collier's jaws clenched in frustration. They'd never had to think about jets before, never had to worry about them. How did the old armies deal with aircraft? Simple, with other aircraft. He bowed his head.

Rosa, eyes wide, shook her head fiercely. "They shouldn't be a problem. They'll be with the main Red group, after the deserters."

He looked at her. "Then why are they still coasting

around Pemberton, blowing the place to crap?" He paused for a dramatic moment. "I'll tell you why … because they've got another mission … make sure no one escapes to carry the tale." He didn't have to say what tale.

"But, we're in the woods! We'll have tree cover!"

Collier slowly looked up, deliberately focusing on a barely budded maple tree above them. "In a month, we'll have cover. Not today."

Rosa followed his gaze, growing visibly paler. "Maybe then," her voice betrayed her desperation, "we could just go straight south, run like hell through Pemberton and out into the woods across the Creek, put some distance between us before nightfall. The dark will cover us."

Collier shook his head, "The Red screen out there will pick us up, call the jets down. Besides, even if we busted through, if they've got jets, they've got infrared. They'd find us."

The sudden consternation among the command group spread quickly among the troops and they hobbled and limped over to form a grim, silent circle around them. None spoke. They knew their lives were being decided, but it was the measure of how much they trusted this group that they immediately didn't turn into an arguing rabble. Well, maybe it was really a measure of their exhaustion but, nonetheless, Collier was overwhelmed. He had always felt responsible for himself and his own, like Rosa and Jonesy, while the rest of the Army could go hang. Now, all these people were depending on him. It was staggering.

An argument broke out between the Wilsons and Jonesy with Rosa listening; not a virulent one, but intense, just the same. Jonesy wanted to stick with the rivulet while the brothers thought a violent push south would be effective. Collier was quiet, considering, listening, weighing the arguments while his mind worked furiously. There was always an option, always something that could be done. They had already faced and escaped far too many other seemingly insurmountable traps to believe otherwise. Yeah, true, that was courtesy of the Colonel, who, until Rosa so abruptly ended his plans, had been happily plotting to sell them out. But still, the lesson remained: there is always a way. You just have to figure it out.

And just like that, he did.

He held up a hand, "We have to make them think we're still here," he said.

The others stopped, turning towards him. The surrounding soldiers shifted their attention, waiting. He paused a minute. "They have to think we're still here," he repeated.

"Explain," Rosa said, quietly.

"A diversion. We fix their attention on where they least expect us to be. Right here," and he swept his hand back towards Pemberton. "It'll surprise them. After they get done rampaging the deserters, they won't be expecting anyone to be left here, especially anyone still spoiling for a fight. They'll be stunned, then really mad, and come at us with everything." He paused. "Jets included."

Rosa looked at him blankly. "But we can't win that."

"Of course not," Collier agreed. "But there won't be a 'we,' just a few of us. As the rest head down this rivulet," he pointed at it, "to the Rancocas and then the Delaware. And Pennsylvania." He folded his arms, finished, and let it sink in. After a moment, he turned and said softly, "I need volunteers."

The remnant stared at him with steel and then shuffled forward as a group. "No," Collier said, "just ten. That's all. Just ten. But," and he felt the emotion choke his voice, "thank you."

He felt movement behind him. "And not you," he said, pointing at Jonesy and Rosa. "Not you two."

"I'm staying, man," Jonesy stood defiantly. Rosa stood just as defiantly next to him.

"No, you're not, neither of you."

"You can't stop me," Jonesy was belligerent.

"I won't leave anyone behind." Rosa was just as belligerent.

He loved them, loved them both, the ache in his heart soaring with the pride and humility that these two people, these two wonderful people, wanted to die with him. God bless them. Please, God, bless them.

"No," he repeated quietly," and here's why. Jonesy, I need people who can move and shoot and you're too hurt. Besides, you're the best trail guy in this Army and can get everyone out of here before the jets come back and start searching. And you've only got an hour to do that."

He turned to Rosa, "And you are the only person even close to being a commander. You are the only one who can keep the Ghosts together, the only one. If you stay with me, this Army," and he gestured back at the remnant, "will dissolve and we will have no hope, no future, and all of our dead comrades are so, for nothing."

He paused, his eyes silencing both their protests. "You know I'm right. You know it. And you know there is simply no time."

Objections still formed on Jonesy's lips and his eyes were hard and furious but he was a soldier, he could size up a situation, so he stopped the coming words and looked away. Rosa, defiant and tight-lipped, shook with the passion and fear that overcame her, but she was more of a soldier than either of them. "You're right," she whispered.

Wilson #1 looked at Rosa then back at Collier, "You go, man," he said softly to Collier, "My brother and I will stay."

"No. Not both of you. There aren't any real brothers left."

Wilson #2 stepped up, "That's why we're staying, Sarge, don't care what you say," and the brothers shook hands.

"Me, too," said a voice behind him. Collier turned and there was Swift leaning against a tree, tall and raw and with his ever-present off-world stare. Relief flowed through him. "Thought you were dead," Collier said.

"I am," Swift replied laconically. "So are you."

Collier turned back to Rosa, who was frozen, tears forming pools in her eyes, "There is no time," he repeated.

She stood, uncertain, unmoving, torn in half by two desperate needs, as commander and lover. Commander took over. "How will you arm? We're almost out of ammo."

Collier looked off towards Pemberton. "We'll collect what we can from the barracks and armory. It's probably all a wreck but we can dig around and pull out what we need. The heavy weapons are probably still in the safe, unless the jets got lucky and hit it direct, but I don't think they did. I'm hoping they didn't," he said, hopelessly.

"But it's just ten of you," she said, gesturing at the volunteers who had now formed around Swift. The Wilson's were helping them set packs and collect ammo from the wounded.

"Yes."

"You'll be killed."

"Yes."

They stood a few feet apart, tight, tense, folding into themselves and struggling. There had always been this possibility, a stray bullet, a stray artillery round, a firefight, a promotion move, hell, a crazed private could have killed either of them at any time. *That* they were steeled for, ready to grieve and remember and then move on. But this, a deliberate parting, with one of their deaths certain, was not anticipated. There had been an unspoken promise between them that, if they both survived this war, then they would, hand in hand, go find a safe place. Collier watched that promise dissolve and drift away in the breeze.

There was nothing more to say.

She flung herself at him, clawing and entwining her hands through his cropped hair, pulling tight against him. Her lips found his and she pressed hard, despite the wound, kissing with desperation, trying to mark this kiss with the stamp of forever. He rocked back and then folded her in his arms, returning her kiss just as hard.

Some moments become eternal. The first dance with a woman you love, the first solo night drive, the first time you sleep with someone … the world stops and makes an eddy around you, flowing for everyone else but leaving you unmoved and excepted, the rules of time not applying. The feelings and touches and soaring spirits loop back into themselves and create their own world, free of the real one, and, if you remain undisturbed, then the moment can last forever. It will last forever in your mind, at least.

But something always disturbs. Collier felt it, not just the startled ripple through the soldiers gathered around them, pausing in their preparations to stare for a moment, then look at each other, then back at the two of them. No, it was something relentless, something big and ugly bearing down on them. The real world loomed, tapping its watch impatiently.

She just as suddenly pulled away, the tears flowing easily down her cheeks. She stared at him for a moment, her eyes wide to take in as much as she could remember, then turned to the amazed remnant. "Let's go," she barked, her voice a bit shriller than usual. She scooped up her pack and rifle and strode down the water's path. She did not look back.

The remnant hesitated, then bustled about grabbing their equipment and shaking hands with some of the ten and adjusting packs and moving into position and then there was this undulating line, slipping onto the path and bunching up at the top, then a fitful movement, and then they were actually moving, a tattered caterpillar, flowing down the creek.

The late sunlight lanced in through the trees, spotlighting green camouflage or black rifle muzzle, like a million camera flashes picking out a favorite view. Collier stood quietly, arms folded, trying to appear calm while he screamed inside. He peered hard towards the front but she was lost to him now. Lost.

Someone stirred next to him and he glanced over. Swift stood there, laconic and loose, watching the column move away. He looked at Collier. "We all knew," he said.

Despite the searing knife slicing his heart in two, Collier grinned. "Just can't keep secrets in this Army, I guess."

"Um," Swift grunted. They both stood watching the tail of the column recede. Rosa, his heart screamed, Rosa, but she was gone.

"You got a plan?" Swift asked.

He turned. The Wilson's were busy piling up the heavier weapons that the remnant left for them, some RPGs, an SAW, a couple of LAWs. Hope they could find the Stingers. Hope they still worked, since they hadn't broken them out in several months. The Reds had learned to keep their helicopters away, and who knew they had jets?

Collier stirred and squatted by the pile, examining the

heavies. "Sure," he said. A simple one.
    Buy time.

31

Collier nursed the canteen, judging by its slosh that he had about two mouthsful left. That should do for the ten minutes or so of breathing he had left. At least he won't die thirsty, but it'd be real nice if it were cold water. Well, the Rancocas was off to the right there somewhere and it was running high with snowmelt, sooo … maybe jog over, recharge the canteen, get brain freeze?

Get shot.

He chuckled and peered at a jet banking through the thick smoke northwest of him. It whipped over to the left, making another run at Pemberton. Go on, drop a few more bombs, heck, drop 'em all and then go back and rearm and talk about the fire you're taking and what a tense situation it is. Your commissars will have fits: "That double-crossing Caldwell! Load up and go again, and again! Destroy Pemberton! Destroy Caldwell! Meanwhile, we'll send more troops!" And they'd scramble around trying to find a spare Red unit or two but, really, who'd they have left? Just some REMFs and clerks, and precious few of those, courtesy of Collier and the boys.

About an hour after Rosa and the others disappeared

up the trail …

… disappeared …

Collier led the team up Arney's Mount towards Juliustown and found the Red rear guard laughing and grabassing around some command vehicles. Took about three minutes to set up, and then *wham*! A barrage of 81s smack in the middle of the grabassers. Those Wilsons could sure shoot some mortars. Collier and the others thoroughly enjoyed the show, then opened up with rifle grenades.

Armageddon.

The few Red survivors skedaddled up Arney's Mount, and Collier took advantage of the lull to make adjustments for the expected company. Sure enough, about ten minutes later, probably two hundred or so Reds came roaring back to see what the hell was going on. Mortars, rifle grenades, .223 … rinse, repeat.

Lots of fun, but all the ruckus brought the jets back, and then it was Collier and friends' turn to skedaddle all the way back to Pemberton while dodging bombs and the Reds' attempts to catch them. Collier kept circling back to hit the Reds on a disorganized flank or in the rear, while the Wilsons' set up the mortars somewhere past the church and kept the rounds coming.

It had been a very interesting afternoon.

But, it was coming to a close. They were down to seven; six, really, because one of the Wilsons caught some bomb shrapnel in the calf and was immobile. Could still load mortar rounds, though, and the brothers were stubbornly popping off every few minutes, taking direction from Zach, one of Jonesy's corporals, who was somewhere near North Pemberton Road with an SAW and RPGs, still scaring the bejesus out of the REMFS and clerks now hunkered down and crying for their mamas. Collier and Swift had ended up south on the Browns Mills

Road, hidden in a ditch on a long hill above the old college, armed with all kinds of interesting toys they'd dug out of the armory, and still itchin' for a go.

See what a half-dozen, highly motivated people could do?

See, also, what reputation can do? The Reds expected a surrender and got, instead, classic Caldwell, pulling them into a trap while making good his escape. Whoever this Colonel Kant was, he had to be eating his own entrails about now. How much more so when he finds out it wasn't Caldwell at all but a few stubborn Ghosts using Caldwell's rep to keep the whole friggin' Red Army at bay?

Poetic.

Eventually, though, even the dullest of commissars will start smelling a rat, and, since the main Red units were still up there past Mt. Holly somewhere mopping up the deserters, will start looking around for more REMFs and clerks to send off to Pemberton and see what's what. The closest group of *those* was in the Red blocking force south of the Creek, which had to come this way. When they did, Collier intended to grab their attention. He patted his SAW. This would certainly do it.

He also patted the sore spot on his shins. He had managed to trip over a rake while he and Swift were racing through Pemberton. A rake, a fuckin' rake hidden under piles of crap in the middle of the yard where that crazy guy lived and Collier, running hell-bent for the south, had laced it through his legs, whipping his shins as he tried to detangle and cursing up a storm because, geez Louise, fella, even crazy people put their tools away! Swift had actually laughed at him. If the old coot had popped his head out about then, Collier would have shot him, Bible or no Bible. Maybe the jets, or the coming Reds, would do it for him.

That's not nice.

Collier internally shrugged. No, it wasn't. He owed the poor old guy. But a tidal wave was coming, cruel, remorseless, swallowing helpless old men who once knew Dad, as it came for Swift and the Wilsons and Rosa, and Collier did not have time to be nice or considerate or affable or anything because he had to divert the wave, keep it here, and give his lover time.

Time.

Buy more time. Every minute they could get, as the sun dropped lower, was another minute Rosa and Jonesy and the remnant were away. If they could keep the Reds guessing, reeling, venting their rage on Pemberton until past sundown, then there was a better-than-even chance the Ghosts would reach the Delaware before morning – unbothered, unbombed, intact. When the Reds finally figured out they'd been had, they could gnash their teeth and kick Collier's body all they wanted. His would be a death well served.

Because of Rosa, standing on the steep banks, the wind whipping her hair and veiling her face in the sunrise. He caught his breath. My lover, my soul. Live.

Live.

Collier peered at the sun, descending too damned slow for his taste. Wasn't there some Bible guy who asked God to stop the sun until he could finish a battle? Well, how 'bout this, God: make the sun speed up. Bring on darkness right now, freezing everyone in place while the Ghosts, his lover at their head, silently pad along the Delaware's bank seeking an unguarded point. That'd be cool, God, an oldie-but-goodie miracle with a modern flair. So do it, God. You hear me? Do You?

"Do you believe in God?" Swift suddenly asked.

Collier blinked in surprise and whistled a few bars of *The Twilight Zone*. "How very uncanny. Are you a mind reader or something?"

Swift shrugged, "No. Just thinking about it."

Made sense. Odds were greater than even that two or more persons facing the immediate prospect of bombs dropping on their heads would dwell on the subject of God. Nothing X-Files about that.

"So, do you?" Swift asked again.

Collier shrugged. "Once."

"No more? Why not?"

Collier just snorted in derision.

Swift reached over and pulled at a newly sprouting weed, some kind of Johnson grass. He put the thin reed into his mouth. "I gotcha. But you should."

Collier looked at the corporal, "You're not about to get all Holy Roller on me, are you?"

"Nah, Sarge, just preparin'." Swift stretched and checked the road then looked at the sky. "I was born in Nebraska, Sarge."

"Yeah?"

"You ever been there?"

"Don't think so."

"You'd know. You'd remember. It's real flat. Lots of people think that's bad but you can see a long way. Seems like forever sometimes. You can see heaven."

Collier checked the SAW for the umpteenth time and then looked at Swift. "What's it look like? Heaven, I mean?"

Swift frowned around the reed, "Shouldn't make fun, Sarge. You make fun of something, you can't understand it."

"Uh-huh."

"Yeah. Well, you know, I had a pretty good life there. It was all farmland and I did a lot of farm stuff ... that's what you did out there ... and I hunted and fished and had some good friends, even a girlfriend. I wasn't ever going to leave. I just loved it."

He paused and Collier watched the off-world look creep back on him. "The Event," Collier said.

"Yeah, the Event," Swift grimaced. "I was fifteen, something like that. I mean, the Towers was bad enough, but the whole East Coast?" He shook his head, "Man, I was so upset, I just couldn't believe what was happening and then the government getting all Nazi on us and taking everything and the other stuff they did. It was bad, you know?"

"I know," Collier peered down the road but didn't see anything there. He saw other things: the news flashes, scenes of DC and the dead bodies everywhere, Fishburne locking them all down, him trying to sneak out but falling out the second-story window and breaking his heel. Dad calling him out of the blue, weak and practically dead, trapped in the Zone.

"Yeah," Swift peered just as hard down the road, seeing his own pictures. "My mom died during Breakout. Everyone did. My dad was already dead, shot by a looter, so I joined the Army. Was about to get Draft Ganged anyway. Missed going overseas, but fought the Mexicans down near Texas until the Reds showed up. Fought them ever since."

"We telling each other's stories, Swift?"

"Yeah," Swift kept staring down the road. "Tell 'em now. That way, when we get to heaven, we'll already know them."

Collier chuckled, "What makes you think we're going to heaven, Swift?"

"Just do."

"Why?"

"Because," Swift glanced at Collier, "we're God's Army."

Collier *tsk*'d. "Yeah? Then how 'bout God drops us

some reinforcements, a couple of extra divisions, say? Or some anti-air? Hell, I'd settle for a ham sandwich."

Swift shook his head. "That ain't the way it works, Sarge. You have to prove yourself. You earn you a place. Then you at the table with all your buddies."

"I think that's Valhalla, Swift."

Swift shrugged, frowning at the dirty bandage still holding his previous wound (three weeks ago? three years ago?) together. "Whatever you wanna call it."

Collier blinked at him. "So, let me be sure I've got this straight … you're sitting here about to get your ass blown off because you think it guarantees you a place in the Hall of Heroes?"

Swift nodded.

"Okay," Collier said.

Swift turned back to the road, the slight smile still there, saying nothing. Collier saw him go off-world again.

Whatever floats your boat, Swifty. Whatever half-baked weird-ass mythology you can come up with to prepare you for that final, screaming moment of death, when hot metal shreds your heart and body and the last of you gasps its last bloody and frothy breath, here on the side of some road near some pissant town, dying ugly, dying alone, quickly forgotten … okay. If it gives you peace.

Peace.

Peace came in many forms these days. There was peace in murder, in destruction, peace in self-delusion about a benevolent God who ignores slaughter and war and misery and pain, Dad, and peace in thinking your warrior ethic earns you a horn of ale and a Valkyrie, Swift. Or seventy-two virgins.

There is peace in someone you love.

He saw Rosa again, this time on a windswept plain with the river flowing by and the land empty and beckoning. Looked a lot like the Shenandoah near Front Royal. Good spot. Safe, no soldiers, no war, no more fighting. Her being there was peace.

There is peace in God, Dad whispered to him.

No, Dad, there is not. There is only blame.

Blame.

Collier shifted the SAW into a more comfortable position and thought about blaming someone. How 'bout Mom? She was always on him about his homework and his friends and he had doubled his wastrel efforts just to get back at her and if she had been more understanding, more lenient, he would've been at home when the Flu struck, not safe at Fishburne, and would be with her now, side-by-side, six feet deep in the front yard, instead of sitting in a ditch about to get shredded. Blame Dad, too, for calling every night after the Event and telling him there was hope, or a reasonable facsimile thereof, in the very act of living, so live, Collier, live.

Sorry to disappoint, Dad, but that's not gonna happen.

Who else to blame? How 'bout the 'Slams, because they mistook Kali for Allah; or the old government, which thought it knew everything (it didn't). Let's go with every president since the Event, one falling right after another and taking thousands with them each time; or the Reds, dusting off failed philosophies and sincerely murdering thousands more to invoke their Better Way. And the Army. Price. Caldwell. The Wilsons.

Blame everyone. Blame no one. Blame yourself.

Blame. Yourself.

Let's conclude that everything that has happened was the fault of one Sergeant Collier Rashkil, born December 1985 and now 24 or 25 years old (lost count), son of John and Teresa Rashkil (nee Smith), both of New Jersey, of Pemberton, where their son, coming full circle, would finally die. He was just as much to blame as anyone.

And if you're to blame like everyone else is, then you can't really be mad at anyone, can you?

Not even God.

"There it goes," Swift said.

Collier turned and saw an F-16 banking frantically out of the grey smoke cloud as a white smoke contrail reached up and slammed hard into its tail. Stinger. There was a blast of fire and metal and the jet careened over, two flame-shrouded sections tumbling crazily over the town, arcing south and down and out of sight in seconds. They did not hear or see the secondary blast.

"Good shot, Wilson," Collier commented.

"Yeah, too bad we ain't got no more."

Collier shrugged, "We were lucky to find that one. At least it went to good use."

"S'pose that'll piss 'em off?"

"S'pose."

"Wilsons ain't getting out alive."

"None of us are, Swift."

"Yeah." He paused. "How much time you think we got?"

"Why, you got a date?"

Swift chuckled, "Just wondering."

Collier looked at the sun, "An hour. Tell your God to expect us about then."

"Why don't you tell 'im yourself, Sarge?"

"You have more clout."

Swift smiled and looked down the road. "All right," he said.

Ten minutes, they said nothing, and the sun dropped a bit more and the shadows stretched. Collier watched one in front of them, generated by a big tree to their right rear. Slowly, leisurely, testing each inch of ground before covering it, the shadow was taking its sweet-ass time. What's it been, three, four hours since the attack down

Catesville Road? He shook his head. Seemed so much longer. Time was supposed to fly when you were having fun, so he guessed this wasn't really fun. Just busywork.

"Something's coming, Sarge," Swift said quietly.

Collier shifted, flattening himself, and stared down the road. The sun illuminated the landscape as though preparing for a snapshot and he could see the base of the fallen water tower off to the east and the ruined government buildings north of that. Excellent. He would see what was coming long before it saw him. But he couldn't see anything yet.

"I don't have it," Collier said.

Swift tapped an ear and Collier turned his head a bit, straining. All he heard were birds and wind, that stuff. The popping and explosions from the burning town behind them, okay, got that, too, but nothing else. No more jets after the shoot down, not even distant gunfire or mortar shells. Why, it was almost a drowsy, late spring day. Collier smiled. Then he heard it.

"What is that, a truck?" he whispered.

Swift shook his head, "No. It's too big."

The increasing rumble had real substance to it: a dinosaur lumbering along the landscape, shaking the ground with each step, the natural result of very much material moving very fast. The little dinosaurs scurried for cover because they didn't want to meet the thing head on. They didn't want to meet it at all.

Can't blame them.

Movement beyond the water tower, something thin and horizontal like a splinter set sideways in the distance, dancing a bit side to side and then up and down because something big was pushing it out of the New Lisbon Road, where they had started the grab mission so many weeks (years, centuries) before. The splinter hesitated and shook itself against the base of the water tower, canting at a crazy angle and Collier realized it was climbing the wreckage. Then the sun caught the rest of it and the clear air gathered the detail and presented it, almost with glee, to Collier's eyes.

M1A1 Abrams Battle Tank.

"Shit fire," Swift uttered in awe and sudden fear. Collier just nodded, his heart jumping to his throat.

The Abrams hesitated and Collier guessed it had reached the top of the water tower rubble and was at tip-over. The driver was feeling his way, so he must not be that experienced. But, hey, how much experience do you need to drive 70 tons over a crap hill?

The Abrams suddenly fell down the side like an avalanche and hit the ground with a jolt that had to rattle the crew's teeth. It paused, no doubt so the crew could pick themselves off the deck while the commander called them a bunch of clumsy oafs. Definitely not experienced, which made sense. Most of the real tank crews disappeared into the Saudi deserts five years ago, and the lack of trained mechanics and the right fuels and oils had pretty much sidelined what was left.

Pretty much.

"Where'd they get a tank, Sarge?" Swift couldn't keep the fear out of his voice.

"Same place they got the jets, I suppose," Collier hoped he kept the fear out of his voice.

"But I thought only *we* had running tanks, and I thought they were all south."

"And I thought all the jets were out west, Swifty, yet here they are," he paused, watching the tank slowly spin on its tracks and line up with the road, "Guess a lot of people switched sides, huh?" He paused. "Including Caldwell."

"What?"

Collier nodded, "Sold us out, Swift. Was going to

surrender us all today."

Swift stared at him open-mouthed for a moment, "Sonofabitch," he said quietly.

"Yeah, sonofabitch."

They were silent, watching the tank. It had stopped and little figures danced on top and beside the tower rubble, sliding down and running over to the tank, forming up on it. Of course, standard tank doctrine required ground force escorts, unless you were blitzkrieging across the desert to meet other tanks. This wasn't the desert, and the Reds knew there weren't any tanks opposing them here; heck, there wasn't *anything* big here. About the only armor the Ghosts ever had were Apaches, and Division took those with them. The way things were going, Collier wouldn't be surprised if those same Apaches showed up about now, decked out in Red colors.

The tank lurched a couple of times and the ground escort winged to either side behind it, taking the banks on the sides of the road. Smart. The tank would be the focus of any ambush, drawing initial fire that it would just brush off the way Collier brushed off gnats. The patrol would then collapse to the side away from the ambush and use the cover of the tank to flank, driving the ambush out of position, cutting off retreat, and then shooting them like dogs. Maybe the tank would drive over them as a final gesture of contempt.

Swift looked at him. He appeared calm. "What do we do, Sarge?"

"Could run. Wanna?"

Swift shook his head. Collier smiled. "You're as dumb as you look, Swifty."

Swift smiled broadly and they both knew, instantly, this was the place, this was the time. Gonna heft an alehorn at God's table tonight.

Collier rolled off the lip of the ditch and dropped to the bottom. Swift turned to watch him, keeping his head down and out of silhouette. Collier squatted and pawed at the three M-72s. Okay, these'll help, but this ... Collier lovingly stroked the AT-4. He'd stumbled across it in the armory's rubble and almost left it behind because it was too heavy and bulky and pain-in-the-ass, and, really, wasn't gonna need it. Boy, was he glad he overruled himself. He grabbed the extra four belts of SAW ammunition and passed them up to Swift, then handed him a box of M40 grenades. The 72s went next.

Collier laid the AT across his knees, studying it. He had fired one before, or rather a simulated training round, in basic at A. P. Hill the summer after Breakout. He was already a corporal then because of Fishburne ROTC and because he had joined willingly, not dragged in kicking and screaming by a Draft Gang. He was sure he would end up in the desert, since that's where the majority of the Army was about then, stymied before the Zagros Mountains. He had wanted to go there because he wanted to kill 'Slams the same way they killed America. The Reds were just some half-assed home-grown revolutionary movement and roundly ignored; that is, until they rolled into Richmond with three columns, surprising the bejesus out of what became the Blue Army. Collier fought those initial battles around Richmond and, well, come to think of it, just about every one since. Never got a shot at the 'Slams. Oh well.

"You know anything about these things?" Collier asked, peering at the tube.

"They're supposed to work real good against tanks," Swift sounded hopeful.

Collier hefted the AT. "Yeah, Russian tanks. I'm not so sure about an Abrams." He handed up the AT and then rolled back to the top of the ditch. He looked at the tank, which was slowly coming towards them. Still about three, four hundred yards away, but looming like it was right there. Collier wondered how much terror was affecting his perception.

"How we gonna do this, Sarge?"

Collier pointed. "The road dips there. When the tank crests, its bottom will be to us for a few seconds." He paused, thinking, then gestured at the banks next to the dip. "See how narrow it is there? That'll make the escort bunch up, come real close to the tank." Collier pulled the AT to him, then laid the ammo belts beside the SAW and the 72s next to that. "All right, I'm going to blast the tank with the AT. When I do, you start firing 40s on either side of it, one right after the other, drive off the escort. I'll get the SAW running right behind you."

Swift gestured at the AT. "You fired this before?"

"Once."

"Really?"

"Yeah, but only a practice round."

"Damn," Swift muttered. "Don't miss."

"You seen the size of that thing?"

Swift grinned. "Yeah." A pause. "Will it work?"

Collier let out a long breath, measuring the distance to the closing tank. "Don't know. Abrams are tough. But they've got two weak spots, where the turret meets the chassis, and the treads. It's hard to get at the treads because of the skirt and you can't get to the joint of the turret unless you get to the side of it and you can't hurt it there unless you get a lucky shot." He paused, "The bottom of the tank lets us at both. Something should happen."

Swift nodded, then gestured at the radio. "Should we call the others, tell 'em what's happening?"

"Battery died an hour ago, Swift."

"Oh. I was wondering why it was so quiet. Why didn't

you tell me?"

"Didn't want to worry you."

"Worry me?" Swift laughed, "Yeah, Sarge, I wouldn't want to be worried."

They both chuckled at that as Collier slapped Swift lightly on the arm and they both settled on the slowly approaching tank. "Sarge," Swift said, after a moment, "I haven't heard the mortar in a while."

Collier nodded, but said nothing.

"Guess it's just us, Sarge."

"Guess so."

"The last two soldiers in the entire Army."

"With a few exceptions here and there."

"The Alamo."

"The Battlin' Bastards of Bataan."

"Custer."

They looked at each other grimly and Collier nodded. "Custer. That's it."

Collier watched the tank reach the dip. They probably had about two minutes.

"What'd you want to be when you grew up?" Swift suddenly asked.

"A rock star."

Swift snorted. "You and everyone else."

"No, really, it's what I wanted. I played pretty good guitar ... hold on." Collier stared. The tank had stopped. Collier saw the commander's hatch pop open.

"Shit!" he grabbed Swift's shoulder and pulled him down, both of them sliding to the bottom of the ditch.

Swift was startled. "Sarge?"

"Bastard's checking us out. Damn!" Collier prayed the hardware on the ditch lip was sufficiently covered to look like nothing but debris in the tank's binoculars. Please, Lord, no gleam of metal in the sunlight, please.

Minutes passed. Collier watched the sun perceptibly

drop, the bottom of it now touching the tops of the trees behind them, silhouetting the ditch and the weapons on the lip. Might as well be a spotlight. Collier cursed quietly under his breath. Should have dragged everything along with them.

Shouts from somewhere near the tank. Collier strained his ears but the tank rumble was constant. What are they doing? "I'm going to take a look," he said. Swift nodded, still staring at the sun. Collier hoped he was praying to his Valhalla God for some assistance, and that the Valhalla God liked Swift enough to send some. Slowly, Collier lifted his head to the ditch rim, careful not to disturb any vegetation.

The tank was in the same location, right before the road's dip. The tank commander, leaning out of the hatch, gestured at some soldier standing near the treads. Both waved arms and pointed up the road at Collier's position. The rest of the patrol was on either side of the tank. Apparently, they hadn't spotted Collier and Swift yet or the tank would be lowering the 120 for a shot. The same sun that Collier worried had betrayed them was probably blinding the commander's view through the binoculars.

Thank you, Valhalla God.

The guy on the ground gestured a bit more, then turned to the patrol members standing near him. The commander sat back in his hatch and watched, occasionally looking back up the road. Someone peeled off from the patrol group and ran around the tank to the other group and repeated the same gestures as the first guy. The escort broke apart and scattered to either side of the tank, joining up in front. The first guy stood there, yelled something, and about ten of them stepped off, heading up the road. The rest remained around the tank. The tank did not move.

"Shit," Collier said as he tumbled down the ditch.

Swift looked at him. "What?"

"The patrol is coming up. They're going to check us out before the tank moves."

"What do we do?"

Collier thought furiously. "We gotta get the tank moving." He stepped back up and looked. The patrol was out of sight, probably in the dip right now. The tank was still there, idling. Swift pulled up next to him.

"Okay," he pointed towards the road. "When the patrol clears the dip, we'll open up, just with the rifles. Leave the SAW out of it. We don't want the tank to think there's something bigger up here. Don't launch the M40s, either ... throw frags instead. The tank commander will probably shoot at us once or twice but then figure he can just use his support weapons to take us out, so he'll drive up. Once he's up the dip, I'll fire the AT into him, then we open up with everything."

"What if he hits us with the main gun?" Swift asked.

"Then you can tell God you had a good plan."

Swift chuckled and moved farther down the ditch, pulling out some grenades and laying them on the top. Collier moved to the right and checked and charged his 16. Spread out like this, they might look like a bigger ambush. One 120-round would get them both, of course, so he hoped the crew was as inexperienced as he believed and would miss. Please.

Collier watched the helmets of the patrol bumping along the dip, a couple of faces peering over here and there. Not stupid. They knew this was a good ambush site. The tank was directly behind them on the rise, in line. In line. Collier suddenly smiled. The tank would have to shoot through the patrol to get at them, even with the secondaries. No patrol sergeant would stand for that. When Collier and Swift opened up, the tank would have to move.

"We're going to be all right," Collier said. Swift looked at him but said nothing. There was an odd cast to his face which Collier had seen before: Swift's battle mask. Quite ugly. Quite effective.

A couple of the Reds moved up the sides of the road, crouching against the banks and looking a bit frantic. Yep, you're very exposed. After a moment, they waved and the rest of the patrol emerged from the dip, as if they rose out of the ground. Collier could see the stitching on their uniforms. He sighted along the chest seam of the first patrolman. Thanks for choosing red.

A little closer, a little closer ... there!

Swift actually beat him by half a second, ripping off a stream of bullets on the group to the left. Collier saw his own target dissolve at the end of his tracers and then he guided them across the front of the right-hand patrol. Body parts, uniform parts, blood spray caught in the sunlight, examined, considered, then discarded. There, they took out half the patrol with that initial burst. Collier was quite satisfied and slowed down, calmly lining up the fleeing Reds and shooting them two or three times in the back, watching their fronts explode, entrails preceding the body. Swift kept throwing grenades at the two or three on the left who refused to run and stubbornly fired back from cover, although they didn't have a real fix on Collier and Swift so the shots went wild.

And now for the tank.

Collier peered at it. The commander was gone, of course, buttoned up as soon as the firing started. The escort had scattered, now firing at Collier from behind the tank, but they had even less of an idea where he was. At least the closer guys were occasionally spraying the ditch lip. Collier pulled the AT to him. C'mon big fella.

The tank moved. But not the part he wanted.

Collier's eyes widened as the 120 lowered, lining up

with his head, aiming right between his eyes. "Swift! Swift!" he called. The corporal, in mid-charge of a grenade, stopped and looked at him. Collier screamed, "Get down. Now!" and Collier dropped to the bottom. Swift did not hesitate, sliding down with him.

Sequence. The flat crack of the gun firing, followed by the whoosh of something fast and sharp over their heads, almost like a frenzied ghost moaning as it whipped by, then the high-pitched *kapow*! as the round exploded somewhere in the tree line. All that took about a second, but the three sounds were so distinct Collier could easily separate them. A shower of branches and leaves fell around them. Collier looked up and saw the smoke column, branches still flying in it, about 50 yards behind them.

They looked at each other. "Shootin' a little high, ain't he, Sarge?" Swift observed.

"'Pears that way." Collier said and pulled himself up to the ditch lip. The tank had canted, the recoil probably forcing the driver off the controls. It came back on position and the gun centered where it had before. Collier stood his ground, watching. There was a sudden flare of flame and smoke at the gun's end, followed by the same sounds. Collier flinched but stayed, turning just as the trees and debris geysered behind him, about thirty yards to the left of the first shot.

"He thinks we're in the trees," Collier said.

Swift nodded and pulled himself up. The escorts' rounds were also moving to the trees, believing the commander saw something they didn't. Perfect.

Collier stood and eased the AT back to him. He settled it on his shoulder and sighted down the road, clicking off the gradations. All right, you Commie sonofabitch, c'mon down.

The turret moved back and forth, then stopped.

Suddenly, the tank lurched forward, hesitated, then lurched again hard, like it had skipped a couple of gears, its engine roaring. Collier's eyes widened as the tank leaped. Wow, fast! Collier braced the AT. Get ready.

Dust and rocks and crap suddenly sprayed him as bullets kicked up around the ditch. "Dammit," he spluttered as dirt shot into his mouth. He dropped back down, taking the AT with him. "Swift!" he yelled, "those bastards on the left spotted me. Keep their heads down!" Swift leaned on the lip and ripped off several streams of fire, staying there as the Reds shifted on him and rounds tore up dirt at his front. Swift's eyes were manic, the battle rage on him, an insane killing lust that made him such a machine in a fight. He screamed as he fired, something that sounded like, "Two on!" Well, yeah, they were two on the Reds, but no need to advertise that. Unless that's Swift's way of announcing entry into Valhalla.

Collier braced against the ditch lip, ignoring the rounds that spattered around him as he sighted the AT. The tank's gun had already cleared the dip and the massive body lifted into view, but so fast, so freakin' fast. Panic momentarily gripped Collier as the bottom of the tank, exposed in the sunlight and laid out and ready and so big and beautiful and terrifying, presented itself. Shoot. Shoot now.

He pulled the trigger.

There was surprisingly little recoil. Collier guessed that was due to the open back of the tube. Anyone standing behind him would have caught hell, he supposed. Time actually stopped and he swore he saw the fins deploy on the missile as it streaked towards the tank, but that had to be his imagination. Or wishful thinking. The missile traveled the distance in less than a second, and there was no way the human eye could follow that.

The missile exploded and the concussion washed over them, causing Collier to reel back a bit, even though he was far out of blast range. Where the tank had just been was now smoke and flame and Collier could not see what happened.

But it seemed like it worked.

"Two on! Two on!" Swift screamed at the top of his lungs, his eyes gone, completely gone, redded over and gleaming with an unholy light. But it did not stop him from slapping open the 203 and loading a 40 in one fluid movement, a dance of such beauty, such art, that Collier wondered how ballet masters had ever missed it. Swift fired and loaded, fired and loaded. It was cold and steel and terrible in its smoothness and Collier heard the sharp, horrid blasts of the grenades slapping the air and detonating somewhere in front, one after the other. Marvelous.

Collier took position behind the SAW, lined up the right side of the road, and cut loose.

It sang, just sang, a burr of noise and death like a powered scythe, the Eternal Reaper, reaching out with metal and murder and rhythm and song and carrying all before it. The belt rattled through the chamber as Collier guided the barrel lovingly through its death arc.

He was the Destroyer of Worlds, Galactus, the Horsemen, and his death chant roared from the barrel as the belts belled their lust for blood and he blessed them and their holy work. Die, you fuckin' Red enslaving bastards, die and meet the blackness of eternity, discover that all you fought for, all you believed in, was wrong, was evil, was worthless. Scream in your lost, hollow places, forever.

Die. To save Rosa, save Jonesy, Price, the last true lovers of freedom, save all of them.

Die now.

Explosions punctuated the searing white line Collier drew across the front of the escort's last position. Swift was marching 40s along the same line of fire, so Collier turned to the left where the two Reds with the courage to stay and fight had been, and there was nothing to see there but smoke and fire but that didn't stop him and he pressed the trigger, stitching the clouds with tracer and lead. He swung wildly back and forth, Swift and he crossing and re-crossing their fire in a manic, frenzied dance, the caller in their ears directing mayhem and slaughter with a rhythm defined by the SAW's high tenor and the 40's rumbling bass. Flowers of fire and shock jumped high along Swift's path while Collier lasered among them.

Death bringers.

Murder sang within him and he could not help it, a maniacal laugh rose from his chest and soared over the battlefield, carried by a sense of lustful rage and pure, white-hot vengeance. He danced on the end of the SAW, screaming his joy, revenge a living thing, a searing explosion in his heart that pounded at him, demanded release, and he added it to the bullet streams, charging each round with poison and retribution. Every shot true, guided by righteousness to the very hearts, very souls of his enemies.

And Swift, delivering compact death that blasted holes in the air and the ground and the very universe, still screamed, "Two oooooooon!"

Collier's belt ran out as Swift reached for some scattered 40s, so there was a momentary pause. This was as good an opportunity as any and Collier turned to the corporal, "Swift, what the hell are you yelling?"

Swift stayed in motion, sweeping the 40s to him and loading as he looked at Collier, his eyes white and insane, "Tu'an! The survivor! The one who carried Partholon's tale!" and he turned back to his work, as if that was sufficient explanation.

Collier blinked. "Who?"

Swift leaned into the ditch, slapping in another 40. "Partholon was the first man of Ireland. Defeated the demons and died of plague."

Collier gestured for him to go on

Swift looked at him, "Sarge, I'm Irish."

"Yeah?" Collier said, expecting more.

But then the world ended.

Something huge and heavy and hot slammed across Collier's face, grabbing him by the back of the neck and tossing him hard into the other side of the ditch. He smacked his chin into a rock and saw blackness and stars dance before his eyes as his face opened up in several places. A tidal wave of dirt and crap showered down on him. He bounced off and fell straight back in what had to be an almost perfect imitation of a boxer falling to the canvas. In between the stars swirling in his vision, he watched the SAW cartwheel over his head and out of sight. He landed hard and tried to shield his face but his arms would not respond so he just shut his eyes. Rocks and dirt pelted him, and the five or six places now bleeding freely on his face stung with it.

It would have been really nice to just lay there for a while but something told Collier it was very important that he move. When he no longer felt crap pelting him, he opened his eyes, or at least one of them. The other one refused to budge and he gingerly probed around it with a finger. He felt warmth and liquid and didn't have to look at the finger to know it was covered with blood. He probed upward and was rewarded with a stabbing pain. So, a huge cut over his left eye was pouring blood into it, sealing it shut. Okay. Yes, and there's three more huge cuts, one on his left cheek, another one on his jaw and, let's check a little higher ... yep, there, another one on the scalp line.

Guess he wasn't pretty anymore.

He turned his head slowly, surprised that he could actually do so, and squinted towards Swift's last position. There was a lot of dust swirling in the air but he could see the corporal, sitting with his legs splayed out and staring stupidly at his bloody hands. Looks like he lost some fingers. Collier turned his head side to side, trying to clear the blood so he could get the eye open, but no luck. He stared at Swift. "Still doesn't explain Tu'an," he croaked.

Swift looked up, blinking, then back at his hands. He shifted his legs and pushed to a kneel while fumbling around in a blouse pocket, pulling out a cloth that he immediately pressed to the bleeding shreds of fingers of his left hand. Collier nodded. Training always told, which reminded him that he should probably get up and see what the hell just happened. He rolled a bit to get the crap off him and then sat up, immediately vomiting all over his pants. He stared at it. Great. The last pair of Pre-Event fatigues he owned and he has to ruin them. He slipped off his backpack, rolled over and rubbed in the dirt to blot the puke then stood up, his ears roaring and the stars swirling like sparks from a campfire.

He peered over the edge at a moonscape. The front of the ditch was twisted and smoking, which was just not at all the way they left it a minute ago. The SAW was gone, of course, but a couple of its belts were still there. Where were the 72s? Collier looked back in the ditch and was surprised to see them piled up at the bottom, covered with dirt, but looking undamaged. How 'bout that?

He couldn't see very well and that wasn't because he was only using one eye. There was just too much smoke and flame out there, all the way to the dip in the road, swirling and casting in the small eddies made by fire. It would clear up momentarily, of course, and he could get the tactical picture. Not that he couldn't figure out some big round had just dropped on the front of the ditch, but it would be really nice to know where it came from. Artillery, which meant the Reds had a spotter and something mobile to fire with. Probably a howitzer. Needed to find the spotter and kill him. Or her; watch your pronouns, Sergeant. He chuckled and then peered at the sky. Could one of the remaining jets have done it? Nah, they'd have heard the approach, even above the battle. A spotter, definitely a spotter.

And then the smoke suddenly cleared and Collier realized how wrong he was.

Because the tank was still there, looming and deadly, with a wreath of smoke curling from the end of its barrel.

"Fuck," he said, quietly.

The tank's barrel shivered a bit and then moved right and left, like it was shaking its head. The commander was, obviously, checking out the last hit and deciding whether to hit the same place again or pick another spot. Scorched and blackened, metal hung at odd angles at the front of the tank.

So, the AT had done some damage, but nothing vital. It had probably exploded at a tangent, driving the plasma charge through the armoring and not the interior. He wondered if this Abrams had reactive armor that helped deflect the charge. Whatever. Point was, the tank was very much alive and very pissed off.

"Swift," Collier said. "We've got a big problem."

He heard Swift scramble up and felt him settle there. "You all right?" he asked. Swift did not answer and Collier turned hard to see him. Swift was intent on the tank. Collier followed his gaze.

The tank was traversing its barrel, still searching for a target. Light winked from the middle of the turret and Collier realized they were firing the coaxial gun, trying to suppress any attack. The 7.62 rounds smacked around the ditch, widespread, but Collier ducked anyway. He didn't want to risk his one good eye with a flying piece of gravel. He looked again. The tank moved slowly, letting the machine gun clear a path. The AT had made them cautious but they would be here in moments, anyway.

Collier shaded his eyes from the debris and peered at the area beside the tank. He saw movement, what was left of the escort hugging the rear. Collier made out two or three helmets sneaking peeks around the tank and then snatching back quickly, but he couldn't tell how many there were.

"I think this is probably it, Swift," he said, quietly.

There was no reply and he turned to see. The corporal was at the bottom of the ditch, slinging two of the 72s around his shoulder and digging down to pull out his M4. Collier watched, surprised, as Swift stuffed a couple of clips in his pocket and then some of the 40s in his blouse.

"What do you think you're doing?" Collier asked.

Swift stood, the 72s clacking together to his front. He held up his bloodied hand while the other grasped his rifle. He regarded Collier for a moment. "Be seeing ya, Sarge," he said, then hauled himself up the ditch and rolled over it to the left.

"Fuck!" Collier cursed and dropped down, frantically scrambling for his own rifle and some grenades. What the hell … was Swift deserting? Collier came up on the lip, rifle ready and thrusting his one good eye out, the tank be damned, searching.

There. Swift scrambling along the bank. Collier watched him, puzzled, but then it came clear. "Sonofabitch," he whispered, admiration flooding his heart. Swift, that brave, stupid, suicidal bastard, wasn't deserting; he was after the tank.

Firing started from behind the Abrams and Collier

saw rounds fly around Swift and the corporal lurched as one nicked him. Collier cut loose a long stream to the right and left of the tank, trying to force the escort down. The tank turned to him, apparently having missed Swift's movement, and the co-ax zeroed on the ditch, blasting loose the dirt and stones and forcing Collier to roll right. The main gun fixed on him and Collier sprayed the tank wildly, emptying the clip. He slapped in another one as a bullet tore past his ear, stinging him. Keep on me, you metal bastard. Ignore the real danger.

Swift was in a decline against the bank about forty feet from the tank, which was almost parallel to him. He stood straight up and ripped off almost a full clip behind the tank, no doubt pushing the escort away. Maybe there weren't that many of them left, which explained Swift standing up like that, ordinarily a stupid act.

A surge of hope went through Collier, electric and soaring. Damn! They might actually pull this off!

He saw Reds scurrying around to the right of the tank, escaping Swift's fire and he turned the rifle on them, shooting through their center. He fired a 40 in the middle of them as close to the tank as he could, hoping to kill the remaining troops and de-tread the Abrams at the same time. The grenade exploded with a crack and bodies flew, some of them slamming into the tank and going under the treads.

The tank didn't like that and it lurched to a stop. The co-ax and the loader's gun now opened up on him and Collier watched as the hatch popped open and the commander emerged, tanker helmet askew as he grabbed his M2, joining the other two guns' assault on Collier's position. Collier stood his ground, ignoring the rounds marching towards him because he could see Swift, tall and powerful, the 72 up and opened and leveled at the bottom turret of the tank, right where it joined the chassis.

Collier watched.

Three things happened at once. The commander spotted Swift and frantically whipped the M2 in his direction. The main gun belched flame and smoke at Collier, while the rocket on Swift's shoulder belched smoke and flame at the tank.

Three more things happened simultaneously. Swift disappeared in two sequential blasts, one from the exploding rocket, and the subsequently exploding tank, which volcanoed red and yellow flame and debris up through the turret and out in a searing circle, dissolving the commander. And the tank's 120mm shell smacked the ground just behind the ditch.

All the air in the world disappeared, torn out of Collier's lungs and quickly coming back as a gigantic fiery fist, slamming into him with the force of a train wreck, smashing him into the ditch, trying to crush him into the earth, pounding and pounding and pounding. Rocks and shrapnel stitched him. His hearing disappeared while someone put his head in a vise and rolled it closed. He would have screamed but he had no air, only fire in his lungs, and his brain jelled by the vise so he didn't know how to scream anyway.

But just as suddenly as it started, the fire hammer stopped hitting him and the fist released him and he floated, just floated off the lip of the ditch, falling, sweetly falling, down, so far down into the soft, welcoming earth, a shower of dirt following him, blanket, comforter.

Mother Earth, I come to you, I seek my rest, give it to me, for I am too long a soldier and too long hurt.

Mom, I'm coming home, prepare me a meal under the trees, under the shade of the trees.

Dad. Dad. I am coming home, to the river, the wide, cool river ...

TU'AN

Blackness.

32

Kant held the pistol tight against the President's forehead. "Any last words?" he asked. And smiled. Such a ludicrous Hollywood moment: Kant ends the cliché of American democracy with a cliché of its decadence.

The President focused on Kant's finger wrapped around the trigger, which was about all he could see from his rather uncomfortable kneeling position, two M-16s jammed fiercely in his back by Kant's escort. The almost headless body of the Chief of Staff sat propped against the President's right side, its blood flowing down the President's arm and to the floor. Any moment now, the President would start blubbering and pleading for his measly, insignificant life.

But he didn't. Instead, the President, his milky eyes shining, strained past the barrel and looked at Kant, "You'll never get away with this," he said, quietly.

Kant burst out laughing. Cliché for cliché! "I already have," he said, expansively waving the pistol barrel around the smoke-filled command post, taking in the scattered bodies of the late, last American government. He paused for a moment to let that sink in, then slapped the barrel back against the President's skull, rocking it.

The President was strangely calm. "No, you haven't. You just *think* you have, you treacherous, back-stabbing Benedict—"

Rather than suffer any more abuse, Kant pulled the trigger.

The two guards let the President fall, ignoring the brains and blood that peppered their trousers. Just one more layer of executive offal to wash off. Kant nodded at them and they went to attention, blank-faced, hard-eyed, stone. His Praetorians.

Kant stepped back, keeping the look of triumph and optimism plastered across his face, but it was a mask: he actually seethed with rage and worry. The President was more right than he knew because this thing was not assured. Not at all. Communicating that would be disastrous, though, so maintain the pretense.

Kant turned towards the console, examining it with a look of satisfaction he did not feel. Colonel Brazos stood near the operator's seat eyeing him, her cold blue eyes flat and critical, as always. And there was much to criticize. Nothing had gone according to plan. On the contrary, all the things that he feared would go awry, had, jeopardizing his entire plot.

Kant shrugged. No plan survives first contact.

"Status?" he asked.

"The President's compound has surrendered. We are cleaning out the hot spots," Colonel Brazos's voice was husky and disapproving, so disapproving. She will require disciplining. Kant's smile became genuine. At least one good thing may result from this.

"Others?"

"The Navy and Air Force have declared neutrality, are awaiting negotiations. Our commanders have their units under control, some scattered fighting, but manageable. The Bear Division has deposed their commander and declared for us." She stopped. Kant was startled. That was quite unexpected, but quite good, news.

And he certainly needed some good news. The Ghosts' fierce resistance had proved his poodle was, indeed, a Doberman, and Kant had considered abandoning the coup and running for his life. But he decided to ride it out because everything else was in motion, so he personally launched the attack against the American leadership. Whether that proved a futile, isolated spasm of a still-born revolution, or an heroic decision salvaging the day, remained to be seen.

Caldwell. When I find you ...

Colonel Brazos remained silent and Kant knew her well enough, from all those years on the playas and in the dark, secret rooms of their childhood homes, to know when she was disturbed. She was most exciting when disturbed. "Problems?" he made his voice casual.

"The Mexicans have not moved."

He frowned. Damn. That was bad. He needed the Mexicans to fix the Western Army in place. If the Westerners got wind of the 1st's resistance, they might come storming north. Obviously, the Mexicans wanted additional concessions ... as if California and Texas weren't enough. Kant shook his head. For all their paeans to socialism, the Mexicans were as grasping as any norte.

They will hang for this. That is, if Kant didn't hang first. He smiled grimly at that and looked at her. "Anything else?"

"The Blue 4th is moving to help the 1st."

Double damn! Kant's teeth bared in sudden rage. That mealy-mouthed, spineless, double-talking 4th Commander, Colonel Owens, was actually showing some backbone? He held the rage for just a moment, then let it fall into an ironic smile. Men are variable.

"Destroy the 4th," he said quietly. Too bad. He could have used them for the coming suppression.

She regarded him coldly, "With what units? Sir." That last with such insolence. Oh, she was asking for it … but it was a good question. The 1st had tied up his main force; no one else was close enough. If the 4th reached the southern perimeter of the 1st's line, they could break through. Perhaps that was Caldwell's intent. "How many jets are left?" he asked.

"One."

One? "Have the Ghosts shot down another?" Were the pilots stupid or something?

"No. One can no longer fly." She paused, licking her lips at his discomfort. "Engine trouble."

Kant sighed. After taking power, one of his first priorities would be to restore some technical competence to these lands. But for now … "Have the remaining jet break off, rearm with nerve gas, and attack the 4th."

She arched an eyebrow but nodded. He nodded back. By any means necessary. A whiff or two of sarin should get Commander MealyMouth scurrying back to his little fiefdom in south Delaware. Kant could deal with him later.

If there was a later.

"Have we located Caldwell?" His expression was hopeful.

She looked at him with gloating eyes. "No."

He grimaced, hoping it expressed irritation rather than his true raging sense of humiliation. Caldwell had outfoxed him. Instead of a simple, one-day surrender of the Army and a smooth transition to the socialist state, Kant now faced a stand-up fight of months, maybe years. That is, if he lived through the evening.

So be it.

"I will give," he said quietly, coldly, "five gold coins

for Caldwell's head." He paused. "Ten, if he's brought to me alive." He savored a sudden image: Caldwell, trussed and bleeding, looking up in terror as Kant slowly sharpened a razor. He would make a lampshade out of Caldwell's skin. "And a gold coin for every Ghost tattoo." That he added more as an afterthought, but it would ensure the Ghosts' annihilation. Appeal to those vanities, Pai.

He turned, watching the bodies collected, command restored. He mused, extending timelines, making adjustments as he watched the activity. If the course of history was inevitable, as Pai believed, Kant should end up proving the recently deceased President wrong.

Should.

"Nothing's going according to plan, is it, Santos?" Colonel Brazos's contemptuous voice whispered in his ear and he felt a stir in his blood.

"I would be worried if it did," he replied simply, not bothering to look at her. "And you will report to me this evening, once you have fulfilled your duties." He felt her slight movement, her anticipation, then strode out. Oh yes, Carmela, this evening.

He almost whistled.

33

Burned. He was burned.

How'd that happen?

High-explosive tank shells don't burn, they obliterate. Heat was ancillary to their speed and detonation so, to feel burned like this, Collier had to be right next to the shell when it blew. But that's impossible; there wouldn't be enough of him left to *feel* burnt. Heck, wouldn't be enough to put in a sandwich baggie. So why was he still here? And feeling burned?

Collier lay quietly in the cool earth and mulled that over. Must have something to do with the ditch. The physics of angle and deflection had worked in his favor, sending the effects more up than out, thereby sparing him. Not that he could avoid *all* the consequences of a 120mm round exploding 10-20 yards away. This burnt feeling, for example.

He supposed he should get up and attend to it.

Collier tried to open his eyes, or eye, but no go. Now this just wouldn't do, so he spent the next twenty minutes or so carefully picking at the dried-over blood that had sealed his left eye, while brushing off the forty or fifty pounds of crap covering his right one. Hurt like hell, but kept him occupied while he came fully awake and mentally inventoried the rest of his pains. The worst part was the burnt feeling. He suspected, though, that he wasn't really burned: he was shrapneled. Lots of rock and gravel had stitched him from about the middle of his back to the top of his head. Which was good, because wounds were better than burns. Burns get infected. Wounds do, too, but not as quickly, and they allow greater freedom of movement. It's hell trying to walk with a burnt back. It ain't a picnic with a shrapneled one, but doable.

He finally freed both eyes enough to open them at least halfway and looked up. Blackness. What the heck? Was it midnight or something? Better be, or his retinas were detached. He closed his eyes again and carefully rubbed them. All right, let's try this again … yep, blackness. Great, I'm blind.

No, wait …

The blackness was moving. It went from Stygian to grey and back again and, hey, was that some kind of glow? Collier concentrated. Yeah, definitely a glow … ah, got it. Something was on fire off to the front, and the blackness was its resulting smoke. An eddy blew the smoke apart while he watched and suddenly there were stars, millions of diamonds winking through ebony cloth, so bright, so clear; he could even see the Milky Way. Collier caught his breath. My God, so beautiful.

God?

Collier breathed deeply to get hold of the pain, force it to the background, while wondering if he actually just said "God" as something other than emphasis. Well, yes, he just did. Dad would call that "praise," which was silly but, when stirred like this, and said spontaneously, what else was it?

Careful, Coll, you might get rapturous.

He smiled and watched the stars, hard bits of light

softened by the dark between. There were a lot of other things he should be doing about now, like getting the hell out of here, but c'mon, relax, take a moment. Such opportunities were fleeting.

In fact the last time was ... hmm. A while ago, certainly well before the Event, before even high school, probably when he was twelve or thirteen. Summer, yeah, in the backyard, in the hammock by the pool, drying off from a night swim and staring up at coaled skies, the diamonds in patterns that Dad named Cassiopeia, Cygnus, Castor and Pollux. Dad had said something else in the middle of his litany while Collier drowsed, not really catching it because, Jeez, Dad, would you stop with the stars already because Collier wanted to talk about movies instead ...

"When I consider the works of Your hands ..." Yeah. That was it.

A Bible verse, Collier knew that much. Which one, though, clueless. Hardly a Bible scholar, he. Dad had sent Collier to Sunday School for years before it became apparent Collier had no interest, and then it was quietly dropped. But Dad could quote Scripture and discuss the nuances therein with aplomb and authority, although he was as profane and earthy as any agnostic. Dad believed, but realistically, he always said.

How'd the rest of that go ...? "What is man that You regard him, or the son of man that You visiteth him?"

Something like that.

Dad had said it softly, in the dark while they both sprawled in hammocks and considered those works. The sense of it evaded Collier then, but the full force came to him now. Why bother with us, when You can do things like the universe? Why indeed?

What's the point?

Collier let out a breath and sadly shook his head.

Given the last five years or so, one could make a good case there was little bother and certainly no point. At any time during said five years, God could have thrown Coll a bone or two, but, nothing. Why not? Would have been good PR, help make Your case, Big Guy. But here I am burnt, or cut to pieces, whatever, and everyone I know is dead. Or gone. Hardly a rousing set of conditions for embracing Your Generous and Loving Self, is it?

Enough of this crap.

Cautiously, he stirred his limbs and flexed, testing arms and legs and hips and shoulders until he was satisfied they were in reasonable working order. Okay, okay, move.

He sat up, then lurched to his knees. Ow, my back. With a push, he got to a crouch, moving quietly because he had no idea who or what was about. Probably no one, given the silence, but you never knew. And because you never knew, it wasn't very wise to go about unequipped, either ("Naked came I from the womb" … another one of Dad's Bible quotes. From the Book of Job. Collier knew that one). Slowly, squinting in the dark with his one and half eyes, he felt around, sifting through the ditch to see what was there.

After about five minutes, his fingers brushed metal and he pulled at it. Bingo: his rifle, complete with an already loaded 203. He shook and brushed it until it was reasonably clean, although what it really needed was a complete breakdown and oiling. Later, about, say, twenty years from now. The clip was still in, half full, and he knew where to get three more so he scrambled over to where he had thrown up all over his good pants (dammit) earlier and started digging. Took about a minute before he felt the top, grasped it, and pulled his backpack out of the loose soil.

He sat, settling the pack lovingly onto his lap. Lost,

and found, twice in twenty-four hours. How 'bout that? Collier hugged it a bit, then inventoried. Yes, three frags on the outside pockets, several candy bars and beef jerky mixed in with them, three clips of .45 for the pistol (which, surprisingly, was still holstered to him), the three aforementioned M16 clips, a poncho, an emergency blanket, some underwear, another pair of pants (Post-Event, unfortunately), razor, toothbrush, matches, Sterno, spirit light (carried since Fishburne), compass, field hammock, but, most important … and his fingers caressed the book wrapped in oil cloth, and the leather-bound one beneath it.

There you are, Dad, there you are.

He let out a slow breath and rocked a bit, still hugging the pack. Inside a few square feet of Army canvas was the sum total of his life. He held great promise once, played football at a starter level, played guitar at a tolerable level, had lots of friends and heard his name called out several times a day. He was going somewhere, would leave a noticeable mark on the pages of his generation, be remembered. Now? He chuckled.

The nature of change. The individual was forgotten, evidence of his passing just a few scraps of crap left in a backpack flopped on the side of a road within reach of moldering bones. Whether it was this ditch, or one somewhere along the way to somewhere else, maybe the Valley, didn't matter. The world would go on in broad strides, not always forward, not always in progress, the direction based on the collective movement of all the other lost individuals. Right now, they were reversing, in the grips of a new Dark Age, so it would be gigantic steps backwards, guaranteeing his lonely death on some lonely road, his few possessions scattered, and his name forgotten.

You too, Dad. We're both forgotten, like we never

mattered, like we were never here. In the new Canterbury Tales arising from these new Dark Ages, we will be the cautionaries: the Soldier, the Father, Everyman, and no man. Mere allegory, in singsong and pentameter, a grim fireside lesson.

Gone. He will be all gone.

Okay. Fine. Now, can we *get* gone?

He pushed the pack to the side and got to his feet while keeping below the ditch lip. He swung the pack onto a shoulder because his back hurt too much, relocated the clips and grenades, gathered the rifle, and adjusted himself. Ready?

Let's go find Rosa.

She was somewhere in the dark; exhausted, numb, asleep on her feet but one foot followed the other in the silence of a night only broken by the creaks and clinks of an armed group moving. Urgency moved her: keep going, don't stop, the other side of the river awaits and rest under the shade of the tree, but you have to make the river first so march, death march, forty or fifty miles while the Dragon stirs and sniffs the air, aware of her but distracted by the fires and murder in the small town by the Creek so keep going, Rosa, keep going, while the scaly eyes look away from you.

And then, Rosa, stand on the banks of the grey river and look back at the Land of Death in the grey morning with your hair, your sacred cover, wind-whipped about your warrior face and call out, *mi corazon, mi alma, donde, donde, vengas a mi, ahora, ahora en las alba, encuentreme en las alba.*

I will.

He slowly raised his head above the ditch and peered towards the glow. The tank, of course, fire whipping from its rear and cascading over the top from time to time but mostly leaving it in silhouette, backlit by its own consumption, lighting the smoke but leaving dark the banks on either side, which made for an eerie scene. Odd how a thing of metal could burn so. Collier frowned. Not good; the tank was a beacon, a call for local Reds to come over here and see what happened. And, while you're at it, look in the ditch.

Best go.

Common sense told him to turn around, scramble up the ditch, head into the woods then line for the Creek, follow the track of his woman and then stand before her in the dawn, her hair whipping around his own face. But he hesitated, common sense be damned, and cautiously walked down the ditch to the other side, away from the Creek. Had to do something first: had to find Swift, or what remained of him. Owed him that much. Owed him a line in a bard's tale.

Collier got to the end of the ditch and about to climb out but his foot caught on something. Cursing silently, he reached down and ... well, whaddya know, an M72. He pulled it up and ran his hand over it and yes, it was undamaged. He shook his head. What else was in this ditch, Blackbeard's Treasure? Is this what You do, God, forgo the white horse and hordes of righteous angels for the small miracles of a found rifle and backpack and an undamaged rocket? Not bad. Would prefer the hordes, though.

He climbed out, crouching on the edge, rifle ready. He watched the sides of the road, the only movement the flickering of flames. He trod down the bank, coming on the bodies of the two Reds who'd gone to ground there, lying almost arm in arm. A function of Swift's well-placed 40, that, not dying declarations of love or camaraderie. He checked them quickly and found a few extra .223 rounds, which he pocketed. After wiping the blood and gore from his hands onto one of the Red's pants, he moved on.

Collier approached the tank gingerly, his path illuminated by the fire, then oriented himself. Yes, right about here, that's where Swift stood when he fired. Collier searched the immediate lip of the road and the angle of the bank but nothing, nothing at all. Not even a blood smear. Okay, Swift, where the hell did you go? Collier sat back on the decline, dropping to his elbows after a moment and, using the backpack as a prop, leaned back carefully, wincing from his wounds. Did the Law of Falling Objects apply to Flying Bodies, so that Swift was blown farther away than common sense would dictate? He looked at the banks and wondered at a force that could lift a guy Swift's size and hurl him out of sight. Need to go see but gimme a minute here: seems the back is protesting a bit.

He watched the stars and the flames and the sparks flying upward and left Swift alone for a moment. Maybe he should just leave him alone permanently. There would be more magic in that. Swift stands heroically and fires a bolt and then, in the pure light of vengeance, disappears, maybe carried away on angels' wings, maybe just turning and walking away, duty done, ready to answer a later call. We just don't know.

But the tale will be carried, Swifty. Like your pal, Tu'an, carried the tale of that guy Part Hard On, or whoever you said.

I'll be your Tu'an, Swifty.

Collier regarded the bank. Any blast strong enough to send a human body sailing 30-40 yards would also have turned Swift's insides to Jello, killing him instantly. So, why bother?

Because.

Because there was a very slim, outside, minuscule chance that Swift was still alive. After all, Collier survived the 120. And any slim minuscule chance in this lifestyle was sufficient to spur action. So. You bother.

Enough lollygagging.

Collier scrutinized the tank and the area around it and then sat up slowly, standing when he felt everything was clear. He turned and looked at the ground and the bank where Swift might be, searching for the easy climb. He put one boot up and was about to push off when spidey sense jangled and he froze.

A rumbling undertone, off towards the New Lisbon Road. He listened, holding his breath, not wanting to believe it ...

Oh, hell's bells, another damn tank.

"Sonofabitch" Collier muttered as he dropped low and crawled as rapidly along the bank as his protesting back allowed, parallel to the wrecked tank until the flame no longer illuminated him. He ignored the remains of the Red escort as he sloughed through them. There was a culvert pipe sticking almost intact from underneath the asphalt and Collier rolled up halfway inside its mouth.

Guess ya shoulda run when ya had the chance, huh, sport?

Yeah, maybe. But, spilled milk. And, there's an upside: sometime in the next ten minutes, I get to trade what-happened-to-you? stories with Swift in Valhalla.

The rumble of the tank grew. Well, now I know why the Lord gave me the 72. Collier eased it off his shoulder and quietly opened it to firing position. Okay, last time we saw this work, it seemed to do quite the job when striking the chassis joint from the side. Yes, but if you'll recall, Grasshopper, you softened up the behemoth with a nice shot from an AT beforehand.

Happen to have an AT, Sarge?

He shook his head. Nope, don't, and shut the hell up, will ya? Your crap will make me doubt, and the last thing

I need when going up against a tank is doubt.

Well then, let's remove all doubt. You are not going to survive this.

He rounded on that thought. Didn't have to be true. He could run, clear the bank and head pell-mell north, hiding and running for a couple of days until the Reds left or got sloppy, then go south, looking for Rosa.

But if he didn't fix the tank, then it would be on Rosa's trail within the hour.

So, as previously stated, you are not going to survive this.

The tank rumble grew and he knew he had only one chance, up and over the culvert's edge, aim, fire the rocket, then start spraying the escort while throwing grenades. Maybe he'd get about half of them before they got him.

Give Rosa another half hour.

He slowly moved out of the culvert's opening and leaned against the pipe's right side, bracing his foot against a rock to give him leverage for the quick shot. He tied the bottom strap of the backpack to his web belt to hold it tight against his shoulder. Ready ... wait a minute. He cocked his head.

There's something odd about that engine sound. Too whiny. And where's the tread squeak? It just isn't big enough. It's ...

... not a tank.

Collier rose to road level and sighted along the 72, his target clear and stark in the firelight down the road: a Hummer. I'll be damned. Where'd they get that? Better yet, where'd they get the fuel?

Remind me to ask any survivors. He pulled the trigger.

The rocket coughed smoke and fire out the back of the tube and streaked towards the Red emblem located on the

Hummer's grill. A white-hot explosion roared from the front of the vehicle, engulfing the cab and sending showers of metal and fire out and up and away into the dark. The concussion lifted the truck on its back wheels until gravity reasserted control and slammed it back down, the front axle collapsing and the flames roaring out from underneath. There was a secondary explosion as the fuel tank went. Collier heard screaming.

He leveled the rifle and ripped off three or four bursts into the cab then fired the 40 to the right side of it, throwing a frag to the left. Short, but, hey, grenade: horseshoes and ... Both explosions bracketed the wreckage in turn, and he fired off the rest of the clip to either side, hoping to get any riders who might have fallen out. He slapped in another clip and crouch-ran down the bank until he was directly opposite the Hummer. He pulled out a frag and held it ready.

The Humvee burned brighter than the tank, and Collier saw the driver and a few passengers inside, cooking. They shouldn't give him any more trouble. He watched the side and the area behind but there was no motion. He furrowed his brow. Did he get all of them? Where the hell's their backup?

Collier waited, but nothing. Weird. He put the grenade back on the strap and cautiously stepped out, rifle ready, then quickly ran to the rear of the Hummer while sweeping the road behind and to the sides. He crouched there, knowing he made a great target in the firelight and almost wishing someone would shoot just to break the silence. The cracking of the flames was the only sound.

Then someone coughed.

He dropped and wheeled, rifle up and searching for a target on the right side along the bank, where the cough came from. He ran around the Hummer, avoiding the flames and expecting a bullet to take him in the chest or stomach because it was just damned stupid to run backlit. He swept the area frantically, looking for the cougher, but there was no one standing.

A rustling and a groan from the ditch caught his attention and Collier jumped in, trigger half depressed, ready to light up whoever was there.

"Please don't hurt me," someone said at his feet.

Surprised, Collier brought the gun down and jammed it in the face of the Red lying there, smoke wafting from a few places on his uniform and blood oozing from several more. "Don't give me a reason to," Collier replied.

"I'm not armed," the Red put his hands up, showing them empty in the firelight. Collier stared at him. A kid, maybe seventeen or eighteen, real thin, like he hadn't eaten a full meal in a year or so.

"Wadja shoot us for?" the kid groaned, "We weren't doing nothing. We were just looking around. What, djou think we were, Blue or something?"

"No," Collier replied, "I knew you were Red. But I'm Blue."

The kids eyes widened and his jaw dropped in terror, "What? What? There ain't no more Blues here! They're all dead!"

"You've been misinformed."

"Please, Mister, please ... Sergeant," the boy, almost crying now, finally recognized Collier's stripes. "I'm not a soldier, I'm just a clerk. I ain't even been in a battle. Please don't kill me."

"Then what the hell are you doing out here?"

"We were bored, so we went out. We saw something burning so we came to look."

Collier pressed the barrel hard against his face, "Yeah? Just to look? Bunch of fuckin' tourists, huh? In the middle of a fuckin' battle?"

"But it was supposed to be over," the kid wailed.

"Well, it ain't. We're still here and we're pretty pissed, especially when faggot clerks show up to loot our homes."

The kid blanched and started trembling and Collier knew he had him. "Where's the rest of your fuckin' looter friends?" he snarled, pushing the barrel hard into a wound.

"They're gone!" the kid screamed, "Everybody went north. It was just us left."

North? "Where north?"

"I don't know! Someone said Trenton."

"What?" Collier blinked. Now why in the world would they go there?

"Mister, please," the boy moaned, terror glazing his eyes, "I don't know anything. The whole Group's gone to get some gold coins. They told us to stay here and watch the equipment and everyone left."

"What in the HELL are you talking about?"

"Mister, I told you, I don't know, I just worked in Supply! Some Red Colonel's paying coins out for heads and tattoos or something. I just don't know."

Tattoos?

Without moving the barrel, Collier yanked his sleeve up, keeping his own groan of pain suppressed, and tapped his upper arm. "You mean, like this one?"

The kid goggled at the Ghost snarling down at him, turning paler, if that was possible. Collier reached down, grabbing the kid's throat and pulling him halfway up and shaking him hard, "You better start making some sense," he said, fierce and murderous.

The kid gurgled and choked and flailed weakly at Collier's hands, "I don't know, I don't know! It was all supposed to stop today, you guys were going to surrender but you didn't and there was some big fight with a big group of you at that Hollytown place and then a big fight in the little town over there and they said they'd pay bounties for your heads or something so everybody ran up here and that Hollytown place and someone said you had all gone to Trenton and they all went up there to get coins! There wasn't supposed to be anyone left here and we just came to look, I swear!"

Collier threw him to the ground where the boy rolled into a ball and sobbed and begged for his life. None of that made a smidgen of sense, but it didn't matter, didn't matter. Relief buckled his knees, and he had to take a step to keep balance.

It worked. For some baffling reasons involving gold coins and Ghost tattoos, but worked, just the same. Rosa, you're going to make it. You will stand on the grey banks.

I will come for you. In the dawn.

Collier took in deep, deep breaths, suddenly overwhelmed. There was an end to it, an actual end. He would take her to a safe place, home, the Valley, where they would build a real life, like the one they all remembered, the one they'd all lost. The Valley would hide them, protect them. Rosa, I see you standing in a glade, sheltering a creek that winds slow and soft in eternal woods enveloped by mountains. And this God, Who had shown Himself these last few days, Dad's God, would be waiting for us. At home.

Home.

He whispered it to himself, mantra, ward. Dad, I am coming home.

But, first, back to reality.

The kid was openly crying, terrified, fat tears pouring out of his eyes and unable to talk. Collier actually felt a little bad. It was like beating a puppy.

"Get ahold of yourself," Collier ordered. "This Colonel. Wouldn't, by chance, be a chap named Kant?"

"I don't know!" he wailed.

"Bullshit. You know. You want to live through this?" and Collier put the rifle against the kid's head.

The kid's eyes were so wide Collier thought they would pop out. "I don't know anyone named Kant! But I heard some other things," he said between sobs, "I had a friend in HQ. He said there was a guy in Ohio pretending to be a Blue and killed your President and everyone and was going to get y'all to surrender. We were all going home by June." That last said with some hope.

Well, that certainly explained a lot. HQ had made some incredibly stupid decisions in the past year, things so incomprehensible some Blue officers had muttered "Treason." Like, abandoning the Ghosts when the Reds cut them off in the Piedmont and drove them north. Like sending so many resources down to Texas where they weren't really doing a lot of good, like failing to rein in the Navy and the Air Force. Made no sense, if you apply logic. Made sense, if the Reds had some guy at HQ pretending to be a Blue.

"So why Ohio?"

The boy stopped crying and stared at Collier, genuinely puzzled, "Don't you even know where your government is?"

Collier looked at him. "Son," he said, "I don't even know where I am." He was speaking metaphysically, of course, but the kid didn't need to know that. He prodded him with the rifle, "Roll over."

"Oh please, Sergeant, please."

"Jesus H. Christ, I'm not going to shoot you, so shut up already."

The boy stopped immediately, stiffened, and rolled to his stomach. Collier could see some deep cuts and burns showing here and there through his crappy uniform, but nothing serious. "You armed?"

"No, no sir."

"Don't call me, sir, dammit. If I find a weapon on you, I'm going to gut you right here. So, are you sure?"

"I got a pocket knife, but it's just for cleaning my nails."

Collier grunted and did a quick search, locating the knife and pitching it off. Some worthless old nickels and pennies, some worthless papers about supply transactions, a wallet with a cardboard ID that read, Wallace L. Fortune. "Fortune," Collier chuckled. "That you?"

"Yes, si ... I mean, Sergeant."

"You're ill-named, kid." Collier threw the wallet on top of him. "Don't move. You move, you die."

"Yes, Sergeant," came Fortune's ground-muffled response.

Collier stepped away, keeping his rifle ready and watching Fortune because even a noodle sometimes got brave. He backed towards the burning Humvee, splitting his attention between it and the kid until he was as close as the flames would allow. He looked inside. Three guys, all doing the hot seat shuffle, almost bone by now, juices cooking off their eyes and head. Obviously, the Humvee was a goner so he did a quick sweep around it but there was nothing he could use. He walked back to Fortune.

"How many more of you?" he asked, poking the prostrate kid in the back.

"There's six of us."

"Six? That include your three barbecued friends back there?"

"They're dead?"

"Yep. Wanna join them? Lie to me one more time."

"Oh shit," the boy started blubbering again. "They're dead, KC and John and Kerr. Oh, man, why'd you have to do that? They weren't hurting anyone ... we weren't hurting anyone!"

Savagely, Collier reached down and grabbed the kid's

shirt, lifting him with one movement and throwing him, frenzy-eyed, to his knees. Collier ignored his own screaming back and kicked Fortune viciously in the back, sending him flying down the bank with an "*Oof*!"

Collier strode over and drove the rifle hard into the kid's abdomen as Fortune struggled to sit up, preventing him from getting air.

"Want to know how many of my friends are dead, motherfucker?" Collier shrieked, pure fury engulfing him, "Huh? Wanna know? Wanna know about my family, you cock-sucking faggot piece of shit? You Red Commie butt-fucking socialist asshole? What the fuck? What the fuck did you all start this war for?" and he stabbed the kid hard with the rifle, pushing him over and pinning him to the ground. "The fuckin' enemy was the 'Slams. 'Slams! The towelheads, you asshole! Remember them? We were beating them until you shitheads showed up. What the fuck, man! Why'd you do this? Huh? Why? You fuckin' answer me!" and he kicked the prostrate kid one more time, the rage in full possession and urging him to open Fortune's guts with a stream of .223 rounds.

The kid looked at him, death imminent, tears and pain racking his face, and choked out one word: "Brotherhood."

Collier stopped short, completely surprised. "Brotherhood?"

Fortune nodded, eyes squeezed shut, trying to breathe, and convinced it was his last time to do so. Collier held the rifle against Fortune's chest but did not squeeze the trigger.

Brotherhood.

Slaughter each other by the thousands for a vision of brotherhood? Kill their brothers because they weren't brother enough? Absurd, absolutely absurd. Ignore the real enemy and make an enemy of your neighbor because of a concept. Incongruous, ridiculous, oxymoronic ... but made some brutal sense, actually, because if you end up killing everyone who disagrees with you, then you have brotherhood. Until someone else came along with a different concept of brotherhood and kills everyone who disagrees with *him*. Or her; watch your pronouns, Sergeant. On and on, on and on ... that old song started singing in Collier's head and he almost laughed. The rage evaporated. Incredulity took its place.

Collier shook his head, "Brotherhood. Holy shit, kid, how stupid are you? Been tried, you know. Remember Russia?"

"They didn't do it right," Fortune replied, opening his eyes.

"Is that what they told you, your commissars or whatever you call them? Ever think that they DID do it right?"

"Huh?"

"Try this, Fortune. What if the Russians did it exactly right, exactly the way it was supposed to be done, and it all fucked up and went to hell anyway? What does that say about your philosophy?"

The kid said nothing, just stared at the barrel still jammed in his chest. Collier backed off, keeping the rifle pointed at him. Fortune looked genuinely relieved, and Collier felt helplessness rise in his chest. He could shoot this kid and run, or not shoot him and run, shoot or not shoot some more kids as he ran, find or not find Rosa, shoot more and more people and run farther and farther, forever and a day.

Because it was never going to end. When the fight is about an idea, instead of land or plunder, it never ends.

Another kind of weariness rose through Collier's spine and settled on his head, different from the constant physical exhaustion of the past five years. It was the weariness of wasted effort, and the weariness of the waste to come. God, he was so tired of this.

He looked at Fortune, pulling the rifle up to his shoulder. The kid stared at him, puzzled, not sure what Collier intended. Collier didn't either. He looked off to the burning town.

"Go home, Fortune, just go home," eternal world-weariness suffused his voice. "This war is over. There'll be another one soon enough."

He strode past Fortune, who flinched and then stared at him in utter surprise. Collier did not look back. He mounted the bank and took in southern stars wheeling over the woods that marked the edges of the Creek. He looked back, once again, at Pemberton's inferno, then slapped the bottom of the pack, hearing Dad rustle there. He stepped off.

Find home. Find peace.

Find Rosa.

About the Author

D. Krauss resides in the Shenandoah Valley. He's been a cotton picker, a sodbuster, a librarian, a surgical orderly, the guy who paints the little white line down the middle of the road, a weatherman, a door-kickin' shove-gun-in-face lawman, an intel analyst, a school-bus driver, and a layabout. He has been married over 45 years to the same woman, and has a wildman bass guitarist for a son.

Website:
http://www.dustyskull.com

Goodreads:
https://bit.ly/3bkPDCm

YouTube: Old Guy Reviews Books
https://bit.ly/3y3KHLY

MeWe: dkrauss